The People's Bachelor

THE PEOPLE'S
BACHELOR

AUSTIN BUKENYA

MALLORY

Published by
Mallory Publishing,
Aylesbeare Common Business Park,
Exmouth Road,
Aylesbeare,
Devon,
EX5 2DG,
England

For a complete list of titles, visit
http://www.mallorypublishing.co.uk
e-mail: admin@mallorypublishing.co.uk

First published in this form 2006 by Mallory Publishing
Copyright © Austin Bukenya 2006

First published in 1972 by
the East African Publishing House, Nairobi, Kenya.

ISBN 1 85657 100 9

Cover design © Mallory International Limited 2006

Mallory Classic African Writing
An Introduction to the Series

Mallory International is one of the leading exporting booksellers in the United Kingdom, and works particularly in Africa, where our customers include many Ministries of Education, Universities, and other institutions.

We have found from experience that many classic works by African writers are out of print, or no longer available, and this series is intended to remedy that situation, making available for ongoing distribution a range of titles, both fiction and non-fiction, which might otherwise disappear.

I hope you enjoy this book. If you do, and you are aware of another important title which could usefully be reprinted, please contact us. E-mail addresses and contact details can be found on our web site.

Julian Hardinge,
Chairman,
Mallory International

Contents

1 Sexual broomsticks

'Note the symbolic sexual significance of the broomstick in this scene.'

There is something very peculiar about the way Britishers pronounce their *u*, especially in the word *Sexual*. Perhaps it was this peculiar sound in Senior Lecturer John O'Goat's utterance that brought Mutwe's mind back from Lisa's heaving breast, where it had followed his wandering eyes in a most unacademic, embittered sexual orgy.

Lisa was an absurdly beautiful girl. I mean, that kind of artistic perfection which makes you suspect that the gentleman who manufactures these goods is given to occasional fits of showing off his skill. Beneath her mass of gleaming, coal-black hair and her streaks of creeping brows, rolled a pair of perpetually bewildered eyes whose baby whiteness threatened to break into passionate tears at the slightest provocation. Her tremulous, lisping voice always breathed suggestions of a soft excitement under the touch of an amorous hand; and her breast and waist declaimed physical raptures with such innocent eloquence that they made one wish sex was as incessantly necessary as breathing. Mutwe and his two Academics Anonymous colleagues, Kale and Peso, had, in a flash of repressive genius, nicknamed her the 'Virgin', an entirely wrong label for what the mere sight of Lisa made you desire and imagine.

The trouble was that it was always when you were

sitting next to this highly inflammatory figure, or, as Mutwe was this morning, directly before her that the learned Senior Lecturer B.A. (Cantab.), M.A. (Lond.), Ph.D. (Inferno or whatever it might be) chose to expatiate upon sexual broomsticks, or to analyse the movement of a play scene in terms of an orgasm. And the seminar rooms at the People's University of Maalas, planned in such a way that the whole seminar group of students could link hands under the dust-coated conference tables, were one of the very few aspects of the university life where the barriers of sexual apartheid came reasonably close to breaking down.

It seems there was a deep-seated, liberal belief among the members of the Faculty of Arts and Social Chaos at Maalas that it was a mark of intellectual acumen to discuss everything - whether it be broomsticks, bread prices or bushfires - in terms of sex. Moreover, in this particular case, Mutwe was in a particularly slippery position. For he was desperately in love (for lack of a more meaningful word) with Virgin Lisa. Why should we hide this, the maddest, saddest and possibly only meaningful streak of the story we are going to tell?

For even now, at this late Thursday morning seminar in the February of the year Seven of *Uhuru*, as Mutwe turned his bitter eyes towards John O'Goat's face and looked at his thick but greying hair-line, his bony, sallow cheeks and his D-H-Lawrentian bush of a beard, he felt his heart contract with hatred and the passion for revenge. For Mutwe, this learned Doctor of Philosophy, once his mentor, had become nothing more than a goatish quadragenarian - the boy had slightly spoilt himself by the habitual use of such words and now his mind could hardly do without them - a goatish quadragenarian furiously competing with him for his own twenty-year old girl. And to think that this anaemic intruder had, on the very first night out with Lisa, crashed all the gates that to Mutwe seemed to be eternally sacred, and been farther inside that mock-paradise than he, Mutwe, had ever imagined himself even in his wildest dreams!

But then this goat… Well, he was white all right, and British on top of it all. But that was stuff to impress prostitutes and gatekeepers withal: though one might rightly wonder who among all the Africans in Maalas did not have the mind of a gatekeeper or a prostitute where the white man was concerned. This goat had money, had a car, had the experience of having undressed so many women that now he could do it as easily as if he were unwrapping a chocolate, and had, above all, examination marks to give.

2 Spoofs

'Shall I give you the "agenda" for the whole of the evening? Or should I let every item drop as a fresh surprise from up my sleeve?'

Virgin Lisa giggled. John O'Goat, B.A., M.A., Ph.D., was standing at the door to his bedroom, combing his hair carelessly. He was in shorts now, and his pale cream legs, despite the caterpillar-bristle that covered them, looked as thin as drumsticks.

'I won't have very much of a sleeve anyway,' he added after the Virgin's giggle. 'Do you mind national dress?'

The Virgin giggled again. Then, suddenly realizing that her opinion was required, she said, 'No, no. Please yourself.'

National dress in those days meant a collarless, sleeveless jacket in coarse but light and often elegantly-coloured material, worn over a mere vest or, better still, on the bare body, with matching pyjama-like trousers, and leather sandals. A very reasonable outfit in the Lake Basin, where temperatures were normally well above forty-two centigrade, even in the 'cool' of the evening. But O'Goat had learnt through a series of experiences that most educated(!) nationals, especially the females, hated it and preferred the good old *Engleesh* tie and dinner-suit.

The President and the ministers, even those who were thoroughly educated(!), wore national dress, it is true. But that was only because national dress, like black socialism, was party policy. And the moment they were off duty, making their rounds of private beaches and exclusive bitches, they reverted to *Engleesh*.

Engleesh of course meant imported, generally. For very few of those ardent advocates of *Engleesh* suits had ever seen an English suit. And if they had, they would have shuddered from it. There is no stronger basis for love than ignorance. But Senior Lecturer John O'Goat, who, when he arrived in Maalas, had nothing but English suits, was determined to cling to Tchwezan national dress as long as he remained under the sun of African freedom.

(Tchweza, by the way, was the people's new republic in the heart of Africa, of which Maalas was the capital and university city. The republic was divided into four regions: the three plateaux - southern, northwestern and northeastern - and the Lake Basin. The Basin was more or less in the centre of the country and it contained the gigantic Lake Tudor, on whose western shores Maalas, and several other old towns were situated. 'Montania' had been the name of the country as a colony. But after independence, and after a series of attempts to Africanize that name, attempts ignored by all the world and especially by the citizens of the new republic, that name was completely scrapped. 'Tchweza' a name from the legendary super-race that features so colourfully in Northern Bantu folklore, was substituted for it.)

So, O'Goat resorted this evening, as on so many other evenings when he had a girl who mattered (the ratio of girls who mattered to those who did not was one to nineteen), to that finest stroke of British colonial rhetoric:

'Do you mind…?'

What do you expect after winding a clock and setting the alarm at a certain hour? After nearly twenty years of drilling a child, with the help of examination, politeness and civilization threats, into saying 'of course not' every time she hears a 'Do you mind. . .' can you pretend you are giving her a chance when you ask her that question? and on her first night out with a Senior Lecturer B.A. (Cantab.), M.A. (Lond.), Ph. D. (Inferno etc. . .)? And that about national dress was only the first of a series of 'Do you minds' and 'May I' and 'How abouts' in the course of that evening, and night.

(Mutwe and his Academics Anonymous friends had, in a moment of anti-colonial enthusiasm, rehearsed and decided to use a number of unconventional replies to these mechanical questions. Kale, the 'reporter' of the Academics Anonymous, narrated how, at one those meaningless, aimless campus parties, he had made a visiting Professor of Social Psychology, a starched lad of about fifty, turn as dirty-purple as the tinned salmon sold in our fresh food supermarkets. Kale sat next to him on the long tribal mat. The intellectual world has long passed the use of chairs for informal gatherings. The Professor asked Kale whether he minded his smoking. Kale answered with slow, calculated emphasis that he did. But Prof. MacHeath - British of course: you could not hope to get a professorship, not even a visiting professorship, in Maalas unless you were, or pretended that you were, born in that corner of Paradise that survives as a tiny island off the bleak shores of northwestern Europe - Prof. MacHeath rapidly recovered from his shock. He told himself that the tiny young man beside him did not know enough English to realize the significance of what he had said. And he happily lit his 'Treble-Five' and puffed away in complete British indifference.)

Still, to return to our story, O'Goat was unusually flustered this evening. What sinner, however hardened, remains totally unrepentant in the face of beauty? His 'Do you mind ...' was more of a fortunate reflex than a calculated trap. For now, after a hurried 'thanks', he repeated, 'Well, closed or open programme?'

Virgin Lisa giggled again, and John O'Goat felt a little stupid. 'What programme?' she asked.

'Oh, come on!' O'Goat shammed an outburst. 'Come off that *Inch Allah* Tchwezism. You must work, or relax, according to plan. You don't go out for an evening expecting the lake breezes to blow you from one place to another!'

'But we aren't going any places, Dr. O'Goat,' the Virgin protested. 'I'd like to come home immediately after the film and finish *Middlemarch*. I haven't so much as even glanced at books seven, and eight...'

'And the finale? ... Anyway, not many of your colleagues have. In any case, these exam charades are set and marked by – human beings.'

There was a long pause through which came the clanking of a clumsily-played piano from the neighbouring block of fiats. O'Goat finished combing his hair; he was thinking, remorselessly, about the insinuation he had just made about examinations, and about Lisa's lisp. It was very pronounced. Yet it was not one of those tribal or denominational characteristics that told the whole story of every student's origin and educational background the moment he opened his mouth to speak. Lisa's lisp was a peculiar and very personal trait, lack of which, you thought, made other women so much less attractive.

'But you'll have something to eat before I bring you back to your *Middlemarch*, won't you?

'Well …' Lisa began.

'You aren't going to tell me you had supper before you came down. It's only seven-thirty now, and you couldn't have broken through the queue and eaten in five minutes!'

*

The queue! That is what meals meant in Maalas.

A smart self-service type of restaurant, seating about three hundred people at a time, had been set up among the first dazzling buildings that formed the core of the campus. The external appearance of this cafeteria, together with the punchy smell of onions frying in stale cooking-oil which floated out from its kitchen to the pricked noses of the starving cleaners and grass-cutters between eleven and one every day, helped to popularize the impression that every delicacy sucked out of Tchwezan land and loaded off the steamers in the ports of Lake Tudor came to feed the 'few privileged' students on University Hill.

Perhaps the labourers, in their own way, were right. For the Lake Basin was a region where every grain of rice and every bean sown announced its sure barrenness by turning dirty yellow the moment it shot out of the salty sand. In such a region, an onion was a rare luxury. Moreover, the petty labourer was a creature caught in the thickening urban wilderness of landlessness, soaring prices and stupidly low wages. To such a man, for whom the obtaining of a kilo of maize *unga* and a handful of bitter greens for his large family's only meal each day was always a miracle, cooking-oil, even if stale, was as undreamt-of as caviare.

But whether the socialist government leaders were right in using this popular misconception to whip up the envy and fury of the masses against university students, calling them suckers and ungrateful exploiters who 'feasted sumptuously every day and wallowed in feather-beds at the taxpayer's expense', is another matter. Perhaps the government leaders too, after their own fashion, were right. For they only made these accusations after the students' anti-government strike and demonstration, towards the end of Mutwe's career at Maalas. (But that is a story in its own right. A bloody, I mean blood-stained, story of tyranny, irrational cowardice and deep disillusionment on all sides. Perhaps the only thing which might be said to have happened during the void of human existence recounted in this narrative.)

Moreover, it was difficult, at least for an outsider, to

find any valid reason why four out of every five *debes* of cooking-oil were stale; why nine packets of butter out of ten were mouldy; why nineteen potatoes in every twenty were rotten; why there were two pebbles to every grain in a spoon of rice, or why of every two consignments of chicken one was invariably poisoned. Nor could a reason be easily found why half the dishes served at every meal were always burnt or half-cooked, saltless or oversalted; why there were mosquito carcasses in the vinegar, flies in the tomato sauce or moth hams in the sugar; or why the glasses were practically no longer transparent, because of the muck, and the cups were always coated with two centimetres of grease and the like. Kale had once made a very apt joke about the situation when he observed: 'In the true spirit of black socialism, we share all our meals with blue-bottles.'

But quite often, once a week on the average, you paid dearly for this socialist hospitality. You woke up, or rather crawled out of the toilet, one morning, and ran to the University Dispensary. There you found a writhing herd of fellow learned males and females, each clutching at his or her stomach with one hand while the other was held in readiness to thrust the treatment card into the face of the first nurse to appear on the scene. Sometimes the numbers of those affected were so large that you hung there most of the morning, and. as often as not, marched straight from the dispensary queue, not without some trepidation, into the cafeteria lunch queue.

Yes, it is that queue we were talking about. The

beautiful cafeteria, as we said, had been designed to accommodate three hundred students. But, in a situation where about double that number rushed up every year to the poisoned meals of the People's University of Maalas, it was not long before it had become absurdly small for the thousand-and-some-hundred knowledge-seekers there were. Many of these frequently had the good sense to keep away from lectures and tutorials, but never from those items of knowledge imparted at the cafeteria counter.

And, contrary to what had been laid down in the national five-year development plan, all building at the University had been arrested for a year. The official government explanation was that all funds allocated to university development had, in post-plan planning, been transferred to the development of Tchweza's Southern Plateau. This region, it was said, in spite of all its potential, lagged far behind the other regions of the country in every aspect.

But rumour had it that the publication by the Tchweza Socialist Union of a new manifesto, in which they had failed to condemn United States imperialism strongly enough, had led to the cooling of diplomatic relationships between Tchweza and a certain other socialist country - which had promised the loan for university development. The refusal by the TSU, the rumour ran, to 'tone up' the crucial clause in the manifesto, despite the protests of the 'comrade' state, had forced the latter to withdraw the promised loan. And in Tchweza, as in so many other places, one felt more inclined to trust rumour than official releases.

But whatever the reason was, no building had been undertaken on University Hill for over a year now to cope with the growing community. And, to put it mildly, overcrowding was rife. Hence the queue. The cafeteria was forced to seat five hundred at a time. But this still meant that another thousand and more students had to queue outside while the first arrivals served themselves and ate. And, instead of staggering sessions according to faculties, or halls or even years, the dynamic(!) university administration had left everything to Tchwezan chance, with the result that meal-time at the country's moat cultured institute became a classic instance of the survival of the roughest.

A group of boys from a certain tribe in Tchweza's northern neighbour had made themselves notorious for jumping or simply 'roughing the *chew*', as their colleagues put it. Tribalism was the strongest dividing factor after sex at the University. A gang of these thugs would plant themselves at the cafeteria gate about twenty minutes before opening time. And the moment the gatekeeper's head was seen through the window, they would start battering at the doors with such savage violence that the poor gatekeeper almost invariably had to jump out of the way the moment he unbolted the rattling doors. If some tribesmen happened to be late and thus find themselves some few hundred people away from the gate at opening time, they would start hurling shouts, over all those heads, at the gang in the vanguard, which in turn screamed back instructions or advice.

Then, before you knew what was happening, you would be writhing and staggering out of the way, with an elbow jab in your side, if you were stupid and resisted, or simply too faint to move fast enough, you were simply trampled over. It happened to many students who were affected in the queue by the mercilessly hammering rays of the Lake Basin sun. The tribe had to reunite at meal-times, at all costs. And you, as a *foreigner*, were no cost at all. A girl had her blouse torn on her back during one of these stampedes, and Mlambo, a fattish, stupid-looking fellow, was once rushed to the Dispensary as an emergency case after a lunch-time queue incident.

And if you expected such bleatings as 'excuse me' or 'may I' to warn you of the approaching storm, or 'sorry' to inform you it had affected you, you were gravely mistaken. Such expressions, along with all the other nonsenses of colonial politeness - 'please' and 'thank you', for example - either obstinately refused to enter the English vocabulary of our learned friends or dropped out of it the moment there was no neo-colonialist secondary school teacher to insist on their being used. The situation here, however, depended very much on the tribes from which people came. And, on the whole, the girls were more conscious of the lubricating power of these nonsense words to the machine of civilized existence.

*

Virgin Lisa had, understandably, not broken through

the queue and eaten in five minutes. So, she accepted John O'Goat's suggestion that they should dine out after the film.

'Good. We can go to the Canton and have some Chinese chop,' John O'Goat suggested almost jubilantly (disgustingly enthusiastic, as Mutwe would have put it). 'Ever tried Chinese food? I'm simply crazy about it.'

Snob is a word which has, fortunately, dropped out of intellectual parlance. But one cannot help wondering how many of those intellectuals(!) who say they are mad about Indian music, fascinated by African sculpture or crazy about Chinese food say so because they know or feel anything about these specialities, and how many say so simply because that is what everyone else is saying.

O'Goat was not aware he was doing all the talking, nor would he have acknowledged, had the Virgin pointed it out to him, that he was nervous.

'Or we may dine at the Ghala Toplife, and I'll show you those gorgeous specimens of your sex as we eat.'

'What ?'

John O'Goat stopped and turned abruptly. He was just disappearing into his bedroom to put on his national dress when the Virgin came out with that bark-like 'what'. It was characteristic of her when she was startled, and it was one of the very few unlikeable idiosyncrasies she had.

'Now, now!' Dr. O'Goat rushed to the sofa and sat beside the girl. 'Don't be so susceptibly Christian. I mention sex, and, like a good little mission girl, you hit the ceiling.'

The Virgin giggled and looked away. Suddenly, she felt her cheeks warm up and slightly itch. It was all right sitting beside O'Goat in a car, or at a desk with an unintelligible absurdist novel before you, or even on a sofa, provided there were some other... other girls around. But now... Moreover, O'Goat was right about that sex bit... She did not realize that her body communicated her quickened feeling to the man beside her. Her European teachers had taught her to believe that Africans do not blush visibly. But John O'Goat, Doctor of Philosophy, after three years and some months in Maalas, and after about a thousand African girls, knew better than Virgin Lisa, or most educated(!) Africans for that matter.

He felt an urge to plant a kiss on the young woman's flushed cheek. Instead, however, he buried his head in the hollow between her neck and her right shoulder. 'Aren't I right now?' he murmured.'

'Don't, please!' The Virgin raised her shoulder and bent her neck to the right. Her cheek touched O'Goat's crown just as her left hand reached his right breast to push him away. She could not have told which way she was helping things to move.

John O'Goat did, however, give in. For now he sat up like a good boy and said, 'Oh, don't worry, dear. There are no bed scenes on our programme tonight. I too have my monthly periods, you know.'

'What?'

'There we go again!' John O'Goat jumped up. He

had learnt not to regret the violence in his speech. The good 'chums' liked it; and, as for silly little girls like Lisa, was not his mission, so long as he lived some six thousand kilometres away from a prudish Christian mother and taught Literature, to shock them into some sort of realistic attitude to life? Wasn't that the purpose of all modern writing and art?

'*Mrs. Sparsit is quite shocked,*' Dr. O'Goat quoted a chapter sub-heading from a paperback edition of *Hard Times* as he snatched away Lisa's thin light-pink cardigan from over her shoulders.

'No, pl-' the Virgin was trying to protest.

But John O'Goat, in a very un-senior-lecturer-like dash, had dived into his bedroom.

3 Academics anonymous

'I'm going to hack away at this all night,' Mutwe said.

'More intelligent men are going to be hacking away at their women,' Kale suggested.

'I work all day,
Earning my pay,'
I work all night,
To keep you all right.'

The quietness and care with which Peso sung this verse would have made a newcomer to the group think that he was more concerned about musical perfection than about making a contribution to the conversation. But the other two boys understood perfectly, for now the trio roared with laughter.

'I couldn't dream of keeping any woman all right tonight; I'm too busy,' Mutwe returned to the 'argument'.

'Even if it were the Virgin?' Kale ventured and then felt suddenly embarrassed.

But Mutwe took it all lightly. After another laugh he quoted from Donne:

'He which hath business, and makes love, doth do such wrong, as when a married man doth woo.'

'Anyway,' Peso put in, 'Mary Ann isn't too bad to spend a night with.'

'Who?' Kale had missed the point.

'The *Middlemarch* woman. George Eliot.'

'I'm going to prove she was a moron,' Mutwe said with a tinge of curiously good-humoured fierceness in his voice. He brought his fist firmly down on to the open volume of *Middlemarch* on his desk as he said this.

'I don't think that's worth spending a waking night for.' Kale was the 'negative' side of the triangle.

'I'd give anything to prove she's useless and irrelevant reading for African students.' Peso, despite his natural calmness, was more political-minded than either of the other two boys.

'African students who want to read African instead of English,' said Kale. His sneer was intolerable to those who did not know him well. But to Mutwe and Peso it had become one of the traits which made his company even more pleasant.

'But if I establish that she was a ninny,' Mutwe reasoned, 'I'll have proved that, English, Chinese or African, she's not worth reading.'

'*Non sequitur.*' Kale had learnt this phrase from Mutwe, but he uttered it with a flat finality which brought out all its disappointing nuances.

'One might even wonder', Peso reflected, 'whether some books aren't read just because they were written by idiots...'

And on and on they whirled, from triviality to sublimity, from joke to philosophical argument, with a naturalness and smooth confidence that might have been the envy of any Professor or Senior Lecturer.

*

For this was the spirit, this was the spice that distinguished this small group, marked it out as a tiny rockhead in the shoreless sea of mental blankness that blanketed the university campus in Maalas. Other groups there were, hundreds and hundreds of them. In fact the university community-well} conglomeration - was a savage mosaic of all sorts of tiny cliques. This was especially noticeable in the famous cafeteria.

First, there were the large, and, to an experienced eye, easily discernible divisions. Sex, as we said, was the primary dividing factor. The women - or women students as the administration called them - seemed to be an impenetrably close-knit group. Though no 'reservations' were practised, or possible, in the restaurant, you sort of felt instinctively that this or that was a women's table; and you avoided it more carefully than you would avoid any other group table. It was not unusual to see a young man standing rock-still with his tray of victuals, waiting for some man to vacate a place at the 'permissible' tables rather than join a quarter-occupied female 'reserve'. In the lecture theatres, in the laboratories and in the seminar rooms, or even on the campus paths, it was the same story of the discriminating female group.

And a pitiable group they were! For one thing, if the female intellectuals of Maalas were a case to go by, there was a lot to be said for Kale's 'law'-expounded to the Academics Anonymous - that, in the human female, beauty varied in inverse proportion to intelligence. Remarkable exceptions of course there were, like Virgin Lisa, to prove the rule. But on the whole, the 'learned sisters' were a hideous lot. And the furiousness with which they spent their meagre allowance - the taxpayer's money - on cosmetics and dress, to counteract the sense of rushing years, made one wonder whether woman was intended to be 'universitied' at all.

Still, that was no reason why these women should have kept themselves starving in a wilderness of starving men. For, as a group, the girls were very chaste. At least they did not, contrary to popular belief, 'practise' with the men students. (That a large number of them were each 'run' by a doctor, a principal secretary or a minister downtown was a fact which one did not discover until one visited a beach club on a late Saturday night. Need we also add that every professor, senior lecturer, lecturer or simple tutor had a sort of divine - that is, examination - right to the 'goods' of any girl in his department? It was difficult to ascertain whether the female teachers claimed similar rights over their male students, though glowing stories were often heard.)

Perhaps this near-hostility between men and women students was due to the firm belief of the administration that men and women should not meet unless they were forced to do so. Nay, it was positively dangerous for men and women to meet at all on any personal basis. Old traditions die hard. But here it was difficult to tell which tradition perpetuated this instance of nonsensical prudence. Was it the tribal system of separate education and initiation for boys and girls? Or was it the tradition of church-founded, celibate-taught, all-male mediaeval British universities? Well, these universities came to accept women. But they still regarded them as pests which could be best controlled within the framework of university authority, but should, whenever possible, be scrupulously avoided by any student who took seriously his entrance oath 'to live circumspectly'.

Maalas was neither British nor mediaeval - or wasn't it? It had been founded as, and remained, until the year after Mutwe's entrance, a college of one of the mediaeval British universities. One of its unwritten laws still was that you had to have studied at a British university to be employed in any capacity on its campus. The grass-cutters, *askaris* and cooks too had had their vicarious British experience in the homes of colonial governors, district commissioners and agricultu1al officers, or from the boots of commanders in the King's African Rifles.

In any case, the oath 'to live circumspectly', among other things, was still taken by every entrant to Maalas. Whether it was to ensure circumspection in one particular respect, or just a surveyor's whim, the gorgons lived on their own side of Residential Hill, away from everyone else, in a kind of isolation ward. The ward was surrounded by a strong fence of concrete posts and three wreaths of barbed wire. There was only one gate through this fence, and the louts who guarded it were among the wildest of the whole insolent brood of campus 'extras'.

Any male student who tried to find his way into Margaret Plantagenet Hall, and several rebels did, to join their fellow rebels resident there, was bound to 'get it' one way or another from the *askaris* at the gate. Semi-lynchings, strippings and wild reports which led to automatic expulsion or 'rustication' were but a few of the instruments of torture used by these guardians of the gate to - heaven. The truth is that they knew, educationally speaking, that they were eunuchs as far as the university girls were concerned. Hence their murderous hostility to any man who seemed to have any prospects of sucking at the nectar that was eternally denied them. But one often wished they were physically castrated, in the best harem-keeper tradition, if the finality of their fate could have instilled some humility into their hearts.

As things were, Margaret Plantagenet remained a world all by herself. Her inhabitants never ventured out into 'enemy territory' without a genuine and serious reason, such as hunger and thirst, for food and water, or for knowledge, or for a minister's love on a Saturday night. They never came out for such trivialities as social evenings or dances.

For some such were occasionally organized or, more precisely, left to chance to bring about. For, besides announcing that on such and such a date there would be a Freshers' Ball, a Graduation Ball or a Fund-Raising Dance in aid of the liberation movements, the Students' Union Secretariat for Social and Cultural Affairs did very little else that could be called organization in the generally accepted sense of the word. There was a permanent bar attached to the students union premises. And, once word got around that there would be a campus dance, the wandering jazz bands would come of their own accord. For there was good money to be made from a performance up there. Every student paid a good thirty shillings subscription to the Union every year. Most of this went to dances and to student leaders' tours in the guise of Moscow and London conferences.

Perhaps another item of organization which the Secretariat never overlooked was to send the university bus to fetch the 'pixies' from the Nurses Hostel at the main hospital. This was in all fairness since the 'obtaining of women' for dances always ranked high on every general election manifesto. The nurses were girls whom the university male students genuinely liked. First, they were younger than their own *femmes savantes*. Secondly, their educational inferiority constituted no challenge to the men's jealously-guarded belief in the superiority of the male. And, above all, according to some experts, the pixies' familiarity with pills made them much safer than any other brands on the market.

Incidentally, the fierce animosity with which the women undergraduates regarded these 'pus-suckers', as the nurses were known in Margaret Plantagenet Hall, could not but set one wondering whether all that show of hostility between university men and women was not mere reaction-formation, encouraged by a malicious or simply blind administration.

Well, the pixies came to the balls. But what difference did that make? Even if the bus went twice, it could bring only a hundred and twenty of them. And, as it happened, those who were most eager to come were the already 'occupied territories', whose regular boys, if they brought them to the dance hall at all, would keep them there only until they had sufficiently warmed up to be taken to the halls and be shown their rooms. In any case, what are a hundred and twenty girls to a thousand five hundred men?

Hence the popularity of the 'Bull Dance'. Adaptability has many a time saved the human race from extinction. In Maalas, the adaptability to stagnation, that is, learning to do without what men normally regard as necessary or desirable, was the *sine qua non* of a peaceful(!) existence. So, when you marched into the Main Hall on a dance night, what greeted you on the whole was a monotony of shabby *Engleesh* suits out of which stuck flushed *mvule*-brown, normally thickly-bearded faces; hands holding in the right a glass and in the left a bottle of 'Lake Basin' *booze*; and heavy-shoed feet kicking away to the intriguing *merengue* rhythm - each suit wriggling and boozing away in its own ray of isolated obliviousness.

The few and scattered islands of British and American lecturers and senior lecturers torturing their puppy-haired wives and girls as well as themselves to a rhythm they could not understand in a light-year of lectures were discernible only to a very close observer. So were the few co-operative, probably unoccupied, pixies, gracefully sharing the floor with the lucky few that had plunged on time. The brightest islands of all were of the happy rebels, male and female, who had managed to lift the lid off the Margaret Plantagenet coffin.

The dances as such were never discussed. Any talk resulting from a dance night invariably turned to the 'munching' opportunities the evening had provided. *Munch* was the most popular four - no, five - letter word in Maalas vocabulary. Perhaps it was the most popular word all round. *Goods* was another. They used to be thrown about carelessly during everyday conversation: which woman was likely to be generous with her goods, which was the most munchable, or people simply stating that they were dying for a munch and they would pay anything for the first batch of goods to come into sight.

For, contrary to what the strict separation of the sexes suggested, nine conversations out of ten, in either camp, were somehow about members, of the other camp or, more precisely, about their sexuals. The girls, being entirely exempt from social activities, spent all their leisure time, and what little of their money remained after the dresses and the extra-strong bleaches, on the punchiest, latest publications from the American and Italian sex markets, making themselves exquisite, theoretical, connoisseurs. And among the girls, there was none of that 'munch' and 'goods' euphemism. They went straight to the point: how they would never let that bearded so-and-so approach from the front; what wager they would lay on the bet that so-and-so had drunk himself impotent; what professor couldn't hold a safari for three minutes; such, and much more, too Kinseyish for amateurs like you and me.

But the boys holding on to the good ancient doctrine that men need no instruction on sex, remained largely raw about it. *Munch* and *goods* were their words. So, the day after the dance, the men's halls, and their cafeteria tables, were full of rumours, and true reports: how Juma had been heard munching a screeching pixy; how Masusa had missed both dance and goods, having tried to solicit from a new and close-fisted (the women would have said tight-arsed) pixy. Sometimes the participants themselves in these sensational dramas told of their own exploits, to their tribesmen.

*

For tribe, as you remember, was the second major factor determining campus relationships at Maalas. But interpretations differed here. Many culprits escaped untouched, while several innocent souls were mercilessly victimized. Take the tribal instinct that brought together the American and the British Anglo-Saxon students, for example. Maalas had about two hundred of these on her student rolls, a surprisingly small number in view of the fact that Britain was only six thousand kilometres away and the U.S. not much farther. This group, instead of being taken for the tribal grouping it was, was vehemently denounced by the African students as an imperialist, neo-colonialist clique.

Particularly, there was the Asian tribe. Hardly a day passed in Maalas without a students union official attacking the 'separatist, uncooperative Asian students', or an anonymous poster going up, declaring that the socialist revolutionaries would bundle up all the 'lousy *Mongols* and dump them in Bombay' or, better still, 'drown them in their own *peppered* coffee'. The *Maalas Daily* - this was the suggestion book in the Junior Common Room at the Students' Union building - carried several pages of attack on the 'hideous frigid crones' who inhabited the 'Plantagenet dungeon'. It contained strongly-expressed opinions about the suitability of cafeteria meals for pigs, and about a thousand other topics.

But no topic was as widely, and as nastily, covered as 'these Baboos and Patels, these inveterate exploiters who have over all these ages refused to integrate with the majority African population'. A writer who loves his paper would not blotch it with the mildest remarks made about Asians in the *Maalas Daily*. Every African fresher in Maalas, like every African baby in the country, was suckled on the breast of hatred for the Asians, the Indians or the *Mongols*, to use the kindest names for them. This perhaps was the only issue on which the African students, male and female, were united; and the extent to which it was exploited was alarming.

'Asians will be staging civil rights demonstrations down the streets of Nimela in ten years' time,' Peso, the politician, once remarked, talking about Tchweza's eastern neighbour. Peso was always loose with numbers, and in this case anyone could see that, at the rate at which victims were being made and confirmed in places like the People's University of Maalas, matters could not possibly wait ten years.

Meanwhile the African intellectuals in Maalas went on holier-than-thou-ing against their pink- and yellow-skinned colleagues, knowing all the time, but never caring or daring to acknowledge, that the only point of unity among them, besides their *anti-Mongolism*, was their dark brown skin and pale, kinky hair.

In the cafeteria, for example, if you missed your clique and wandered to the nearest or to the furthest black-occupied table, you were sure to get one or more of the million and one nightmare flavours to your meal. (Clique! well, there was no negative suggestion about this fact of Maalas life, or, if there was, everyone had long come to take it for granted.) After you were greeted by wordless glares, which obviously meant 'how dare you?', you felt your neighbour(!) shrink away from you, the way one would shrink from a leper, into the tribe. Then the Luo, Chagga, Ganda, Luba, Tsusu, Bemba or Kakwa palaver resumed. Sometimes it mercifully ignored you entirely, when it was about women. Sometimes it was aggressively and most undisguisedly about you.

If two or three more members of the tribe happened to be received at the table - the usual practice when you found your tribal table full was to pull a chair from the nearest table rather than be separated from the tribe - you, the stranger would find yourself with friends(!) on left and right as well as before you. Then the whole shouted conversation, saliva, food particles and knife gestures *withal* flowed forth and back across your face and even behind you.

Sometimes a request was barked at you. Before you had time to show you did not understand, a long hand had shot over your plate - shoving your nose out of the way if you did not remove it fast enough - and picked up the salt-cellar, vinegar bottle or whatever had been asked for in a language which you did not understand. Meanwhile a wave of idiotic laughter would be warming you up into a cold sweat of angry embarrassment. As for your asking for anything yourself, it was the wildest dream you could conceive.

In moments of fraternal elation, these people forgot, literally forgot, things like English or Kiswahili, or the existence of anything beyond their tribe. Yet somehow you felt that the whole thing was calculated to discourage you from such mad pursuits as integration or African Unity!

The halls of residence themselves were patterned into tribal blocks. Not by the administration this time, for on their official lists they scattered numbers and names as blindly as any Son of Justice would have. (We have mentioned overcrowding. But, frankly, such things as three people sharing a room originally designed for one, the use of double-decker beds and the queues outside bathrooms and toilets, especially on those 'cafeteria' nights, such things are slightly below the standards of decency of this story. Moreover, they had long come to be accepted as inevitable facts of life. And, fortunately, the student characters on whom our attention is focused in this death struggle had entered Maalas in the happy days when the numbers of those applying made it possible for those admitting them to reason that they should take only as many as had been planned for. And now, being at the end of their career, they were spared most of the socialist sacrifices that the younger generations knew and were to know for years to come.)

But Residential Hill was always repatterned only a week after term began. Rooms were swopped, trans-hall and trans-floor emigrations and immigrations were effected, all with a rapidity and smoothness that made one admire men's ability to co-operate on destructive undertakings. You could tell with absolute certainty which hall was predominantly Rundi, which floor was Nyanja, and so on. The halls were towering sky-scraper jobs which left you in no doubt that ugliness in design was as necessary for winning an architect's contract as was a British name.

*

Smaller groupings, however, existed, though on an almost negligible scale in comparison with the major two. Normally, the minor groups were formed within the framework of the sex or of the tribe, but occasionally beyond it. Extra-sexual or extra-tribal relationships of course meant automatic ostracism so long as such relationships lasted.

40

That such fraternities as the Academics Anonymous, or those of religious enthusiasts and, especially, of the 'rebel' lovers, which transcended sex and tribe alike, existed, despite the thorough ruthlessness of the excommunication, was a touching sign of the irrepressibility of the human mind. Or perhaps it was because of this being shut out that the victims stuck together, sometimes in spite of themselves.

For, imagine a young man going downtown on a Saturday evening. He finds himself a customer at the same bar, or the same brothel, as a fellow student from a different tribal grouping at the University. For lack of better company, and perhaps because of the absence of tribal censure out here, these two boys would drift together, possibly booze away until they had missed the last bus back to the campus, or simply spent their last cent. Then they would decide to march, in support of the socialist manifesto as they put it, the ten or so kilometres back to the University.

If by some chance this fellowship was noticed by a telltale tribesman, the next morning the offenders would get an oppressively silent reprimand. And if, through some misfortune, one 'seducer' came to the other, to try and recall their adventure, the axe would irrevocably fall. The two islands, now forced together by tribal earthquakes, would be jammed into a close relationship. They would be forced to 'explore' each other. And, understandably, in most cases so many more similarities than differences were discovered that genuine friendship ensued from these unfortunate beginnings.

The disturbing fact, however, was that very few, if any, of these 'transcendental' groups, which were rarely more than three persons in size and never more than five, could claim to have had their origins from an intellectual or even barely academic pursuit. This fact made the observer wonder whether, in spite of all the lofty declarations heard on the university lawns from time to time, and especially during the great *Strike Week*, this lost generation knew or seriously accepted their primary purpose, their *raison d'être*, in this hotch-potch of colonial butt ends.

Take the Academics Anonymous, for example. As we have said, intellectual inexhaustibility had become its distinguishing feature. Indeed, it was far more committed, intellectually, than the University's own Academic Board. But where and how had it begun?

Not in a brothel, admittedly. But the instincts that brought Mutwe, Kale and Peso together were basically the same as those that led such large numbers of Maalas scholars(!) down the road to the brothel. These were the yearning for the assurance of some form of human contact, some real existence outside oneself which would give one some sense of order and shape in this welter of sweet dreams and nightmares that we call life.

The question is, why did the majority of these enlightened young men and women seek their sense of reality in such illusions as brothels, tribal herds and *anti-mongolism*? Why did they refuse to recognize and take advantage of the very object that they had come to contribute to and to share from, the intellectual tradition? Was it due to the mounting conflict resulting from the romantic *uhuru* dreams blared out from political loudspeakers and the nightmare reality of this academic world where the African had, or was presented as having, made *no* contribution whatsoever? But this should have only spurred the right minds on to a vigorous and obstinate assault on this rock of reality or myth.

Or perhaps it was the dimness of any possibility of expecting, after sowing so many purely European seeds in one's mind, a harvest that was African or even tolerably half-caste. (And, but for Peso's healthy and untiring pull towards the 'African bush', the Academics Anonymous, for all their intellectual acumen, stood perilously close to the edge of the cliff over the tempting seas of aged and sickly European intellectualism.)

Or, equally, it might have been that fossilized tribal fear of standing apart 'like a wizard', it might have been this fear of the isolation necessitated by intellectual commitment that kept the Maalas group from it. This fear indeed became such a haunting reality the moment you moved into a boarding school that you wondered whether it was not the promptings of evil spirits that pushed you further on.

What perhaps the Maalas students did not realize was that it was too late for them to turn back and expect acceptance anywhere. Understandably, it is maddening to know that, because of your birth you remain a nigger and a Jim Crow to those who have educated(!) you, and, because of your education(!), you become a *Mzungu*, a vagabond and white-hearted leper, to those who bore you.

But should that be any reason why these wretched '*Wazungu*' should shirk the intellectual effort required to establish them as a 'tribe' apart? For now Circumstance had effectively isolated them. But it was expecting too much of Circumstance if they thought she would give them the tenets that would shape the formless jelly they were into recognizable individuals and a recognizable society - unfortunate but confident walkers on the thin edge between the lion-haunted bushes and the whale-infested seas.

*

'But, whatever her faults might be,' Peso said, 'she never compromises philosophical depth for narrative thrill.'

'But isn't that an instance of underrating the reader's intelligence' Kale asked.

'And who would give ten cents for George Eliot's philosophy today?'

'*You* are going to give your night's sleep,' Peso reminded Mutwe, and they all laughed.

They had been doggedly analysing *Middlemarch* for over two hours now: two hours and forty-seven minutes, to be exact. Mutwe in particular was radiantly elated. For several weeks now, since the strike in fact, the Academics Anonymous had been only 'half-living' as a 'clique'. So many things had wedged themselves between the three boys. The most important of these were first two girls and, most recently, perhaps more as a consequence than as a cause of the split, a third girl, Virgin Lisa, out on her first date with Senior Lecturer John O'Goat that very evening. But that is a story that goes more with the strike than with the Academics Anonymous or their state of mind this particular night.

They had been forced back together by the self-preservation instinct before the bleak prospects of the final examinations. They had become so used to working together that each of them knew deep within that, in spite of all the disputes, near-quarrels and quarrels that had cooled their personal relationships over the past month or so, he could not hope to work more perseveringly or more profitably by himself or with any other partner than with the other two. So, they had cautiously glided together again and finally resumed their evening 'bouts'. But tonight, in Mutwe's room, called the 'godown' because of the air of elegant negligence that prevailed about it, was the first night in the new phase that their spirits had risen appreciably close to their original pitch in the heyday of their youthful intellectual discoveries.

Hence Mutwe's bubbling joy. For, by some sort of tacit consent among the three, he had come to be regarded as undisputed leader of the group. Perhaps it was because of his obvious intellectual superiority, or because of his steady and imposing personality. For, as far as the founding of the group went, he and Kale had certainly met half-way.

Both must have sensed at a very early date in Maalas the social and intellectual barrenness of the isolation camp to which they had come to earn paper degrees.

It must have been a shattering experience for those sensitive young natures, after all the overblown 'maturity' of the secondary school fifth and sixth forms and the promises of a 'lively exchange of ideas at university', promises held out by teachers some of whom had never seen the inside of a university lecture hall. As Kale put it once, comparing school with university: 'There the struggle is for growing up; here it is for remaining immature.' Mutwe summed up his experiences in a proverb from his coffee country: *'The berry that makes your mouth water will have no beans in it.'*

*

They first met after a literature seminar at which Mutwe, who had had a faultless if blinkered classical secondary education, had violently attacked Professor Hogg for a remark which the latter had made, linking Rousseau's 'noble savages' with the ancient Greeks and Tchweza's tribesmen.

Professor Hogg, the Head of the English Literature Department, was a stocky fifty-year old bachelor whose humble and unassuming manners made you think more readily of a plumber than of a British professor of English Literature. He never put 'letters' after his name, not even in the university prospectus. In public he would let himself be addressed as 'Professor'. But he always took the

46

earliest opportunity to beseech his interlocutor: 'Just call me David, please!'

Often, indeed, his manners looked embarrassingly obliging, not to say cringing. If, for example, you went to his office, or to his house, and asked him to lend you a book, he would jump up in a state of intense nervousness, saying, 'Oh yes! I think I have a copy of that.' (He had a copy of *everything*). 'I had it somewhere...' and he would go rummaging about among his walls of shelves, muttering, 'It must be somewhere... Now, I hope I haven't lost it... Novels, novels, novels...' and then, turning to you, 'What's the title again?'

'*The Wound and the Bow,* Professor Hogg.'

'Oh, just say David, please...The Wound and the Bow, that's Edmund Wilson, isn't it? ... Ah, now I think I know where it is.' And he made straight for a particular shelf, reciting, 'Criticism, criticism, Ward, Williams, Willoughby, Wilson, here we are! *The Wound and the Bow.*'

Before you had time to say 'thank you' - if you were the thanking type - the Professor would be continuing for your benefit, 'If you're interested in this line of approach, you might also look *at (et cetera, et cetera, et cetera - et cetera).*' Ten or more authors and titles - of which you were lucky if you heard one - rattled off for your bibliographical reference.

Sometimes you got more: 'And I think there's something in French...You don't read French? No? Well, you might consult ...'

And there you were, caught between a strong

urge to run away from this battery of erudition and a sincere and respectful sympathy for this ageing man who, unlike ninety-nine point nine-nine of his tribesmen and academic colleagues, knew nothing of that classic bored-tourist attitude that was as much a feature of the lecturing profession in Maalas as were the lines of letters after people's names. David Hogg lived for, nay, lived his literature.

But the connoisseurs of Margaret Plantagenet gave an interpretation of their own to Prof. Hogg's behaviour. They insisted that he was a 'toothless bulldog', suffering from chronic impotence. And the reason why he behaved as he did when a girl went to his house was that he did not want her to settle down to any personal conversation, in case she 'challenged him to it'. They assumed that he only behaved in the way we have described when he was visited by girls. Was there any truth in this? Perhaps that is immaterial. What is interesting is the philosophy at which this kind of reasoning points. Did the girls expect to be personally engaged every time they went to a tutor's house? And did they 'challenge the tutors to it' if the tutors showed signs of 'toothlessness'? And for what purposes?

But, to return to Professor Hogg: again, unlike most of his colleagues, he seemed to respect, or at least to be willing to listen to, everybody's opinion. It was in this spirit that he had let Mutwe engage him in that discussion on noble savages at a late afternoon seminar in the August of the boy's first year at Maalas. Mutwe was perhaps more violent than the situation warranted. And he sounded even more so because no other student in the whole group of twenty contributed a word to the ten-minute argument. Perhaps they genuinely knew nothing of what was being discussed. Or perhaps they still clung to the old school practice where they let the teacher do all the talking; after all, they were only 'freshers' then.

But this was a tricky problem. When you attended a second-year seminar, you were tempted to think that the students there said nothing because they were not preparing for any examination and therefore they had read nothing about what was being discussed. Someone attending a finalists' session like the one at which we caught John O'Goat pointing at sexual broomsticks, might assume that it turned into a tutor's monologue because the students had become so keenly aware of the intricacies of literary criticism that none of them dared come up with anything that was not thoroughly considered.

And all the while, for humanity's sake, you might be by-passing the only universal and valid reason for this intellectual calm: that these creatures were dumb beasts who refused to have anything to do with thinking and would at best be happy with swallowing as much nonsense, and sense occasionally, as the learned lecturers chose to spit out, and regurgitating it in more or less deformed chunks when the need arose. Their more depressing fault was the sheer surprised contempt with which they regarded any of their colleagues who dared to think and to express his thoughts.

One could not help the distressing suspicion that,

apart from the exciting overseas tour it was and the absurdly colossal allowances one received for the cardinal virtue of being an expatriate, a lectureship appointment at Maalas was particularly attractive because of the lack of intellectual challenge that it meant: the sheer assurance that whatever one said from the rostrum or from the tutor's chair at the dust-coated conference tables was swallowed with the low-minded readiness of a cultivator's fowl swallowing worms in the wake of its master's work.

'That was great,' Kale said to Mutwe after that his first refusal to swallow the worms. 'Pity no one supported you.'

'I think we too often let them get away with utter nonsense,' Mutwe said, still so deeply absorbed in his own feelings that he did not look at the yellow-brown, round-cheeked and snub-nosed face of the short, thin boy talking to him.

'I was just going to say something when... Oh, poor you!'

Mutwe had stumbled on one of those steps that led from Academic Hill to Residential Hill. It was tea-time and the boys were hurrying to get to the cafeteria before all the reasonably clean(!) cups were taken. Mutwe did not fall but his books and pens were scattered on the steps. Kale helped him to collect them, and, as Mutwe said 'Thank you' and took a book from Kale, their eyes met for the first time. Mutwe was what you might call an 'eye-fetishist'. He sometimes gazed at a dog, a cat or even a goat for minutes on end, studying its eyes. Back home on the eastern highlands, in the crowded city where he was born, it had become his favourite pastime during the six months he spent at home between school and university to stroll down the streets 'arresting' every oncoming girl with his eyes. Like the newly-found self he was, he enjoyed guessing how lascivious the daily-victimized girls in his part of town thought him.

That particular August afternoon, as Mutwe discovered Kale's eyes, tiny, close-set eyes that shone with the reflected rays of the four-o'clock sun into which they were walking, he felt a wave of excitement grip him. It was the kind of exaggerated thrill that comes over you just before you catch a fever. But perhaps in a world where people jump so readily on to *queer* rocking-horses of interpretations, the less said about such relationships the better.

The two boys walked on, first down, then up those stupidly irregular steps that joined the two hills. Perhaps these steps too were designed to promote circumspection. But, as things were, their immediate result was to provide a little extra work to the dressers at the university dispensary, who were already busy enough with the campus 'extras' - labourers, houseboys, sweepers, *askaris*, cooks - and their families.

'Didn't hurt yourself?' Kale asked as they reached the narrow bridge over the dry gorge between the two hills.

'No, I'm all right, thank you,' Mutwe answered, rather urgently, as he dragged his right hand over the railing protecting the bridge.

They did not speak for the rest of the way to the cafeteria. Yet both their minds were a turmoil of rather similar emotions, and fears. *He must be angry with me*, Kale thought; *I distracted him from his thoughts, and made him stumble. That deep voice has a peculiar kind of confidence in it- almost authority. He doesn't sound like a mere student at all... I wish he would say something, now. Now he will think I'm hanging on to him... I should say something... But it should be something intelligent. He mentioned the Spartans, and the Laconians. I wish I knew something about them...*

Mutwe's thoughts were more selfish, but no less flustered. *I wish I had had another look at those eyes! ... There's something unusually sharp in them ...Why doesn't he say something? He was saying something when I stumbled. I should say something. He will think I'm sulking. And what if I should lose him in the crowd? ... now we are just about there ...*

Yes, they were at the cafeteria, but neither lost the other. The queue was not very thick, because numbers had not yet swollen to frightening proportions by then. Moreover, some instinct told many students that, however faultlessly *Engleesh* they wanted or were wanted to be, it was a bit of self-torture to swallow a steaming 'cup that cheers' in the hot bath that the Lake Basin, and in particular Maalas, always was at four o'clock. One only took tea because one had missed lunch and was starving, because one had promised to meet someone at the cafeteria, or, like Mutwe and Kale that afternoon, because one was passing by and drifted in for lack of a better thing to do.

So, our 'newly-discovered' friends were able to line

up one behind the other. When they came to the tray of cups, Mutwe, who was in front, picked up two and gave one to Kale, saying, 'This isn't too bad.'

Kale started a little as he took the cup, and his heart thumped with something like joy. *Ah, so he hasn't forgotten me! That voice! How sure in its disinterestedness!*

They filled their cups with clay-coloured tea from the huge chromium electric brewer. Then they went to the counter and collected a couple of sugarcoated biscuits each, from the bare and sweaty hands of a stocky, khaki-clad Lake Basin *mwananchi*. He was the waiter on duty.

This time it was Kale who spoke. 'Let's go and sit down there.' He pointed at the very last table at the back of the hall.

'O.K.!' Mutwe said, raising his voice rather curiously at the *Kay*.

They walked down the aisle of the hall. Both felt intensely nervous. Were they simply conscious of each other, or did they somehow perceive the censorious gazes of the tribes?

Half-way down the aisle, Mutwe turned to the left and talked to Kale, more because he wanted to counteract the shyness than because he really wanted to say anything.

'By the way, what's your name?'

'Kale; Moses Kale.'

'I see. They call me Mutwe.'

'Yes, the Professor asked you at the Seminar, and I heard you tell him.'

'And you still remembered that?'

They both laughed heartily. That had helped. They were now only a few paces away from their table, and they rushed and sat down as hastily as a bare-breasted woman would grab any throw when she hears a knock at her door. Kale sat against the wall, facing the aisle down which they had come. Mutwe faced Kale. He sat squarely before him and started scrutinizing him with his dark, serious and often impatient eyes. But now Kale felt a sort of warm elation, like someone who has just won a boxing bout, and, although he did not gaze at Mutwe, he looked him straight in the eye when he talked to him. Nothing could have pleased Mutwe more.

The table was empty when they sat at it. For several minutes there was an undercurrent of fear in the boys' hearts, fear of an invasion by whatever tribe normally occupied the table. Fortunately, it did not belong to any one tribe. It was shared in twos and threes by three or four of the poorly represented tribes. Kale belonged to the largest Tchwezan tribe on the campus, and Mutwe, who came from Tchweza's eastern neighbour, belonged to the largest from his country. But, for quite some time after they met, the two friends did not consider it of any relevance to ask about each other's tribe. It was only in the course of their conversation that they discovered that they came from different countries.

They talked for four hours on end that first afternoon. After tea, they went to Mutwe's room, 'the godown', which was on the second floor of the oldest hall of residence on the campus, bearing the beautiful name of

Windsor Castle. It would have been much quicker for them to ascend by the wide flight of steps; but they were still excited about the discovery of so many modern amenities at the University, and eager to get the most out of them. So, they waited for the lift. Kale wanted to go to the fourth floor where he lived, surrounded by his noisy tribesmen. But Mutwe invited him to his room on the second floor, which too, in the best Maalas tradition, was a colony of his tribesmen.

'Oh, you play the guitar?' Kale asked as they entered Mutwe's room and he caught sight of the gleaming amber-brown instrument leaning against the door to the balcony.

'Well, more of a decoration than anything else. I like music.' Mutwe had yet to see a boy who did not get excited about the guitar. And he sincerely wished he could learn how to play it, as that was one sure way of influencing people.

'I like music too,' Kale said, 'though I'm afraid my tastes have been forced into only one direction. I had a teacher at school who made me listen to so much classical music that I think music has come to mean only that to me.'

'Nothing bad about that.'

'After school, when I got a teaching job, he persuaded me to spend nearly half my salary every month on London Philharmonic Orchestra recordings of Beethoven and Handel.'

'You have your discs?'

'Yes, my records of arrant nonsense. I could have built my parents a new cottage with all that money. And now I don't even have a record-player.'

'You can buy a small one when you get your bursary.'

'I wonder! The bursaries this year will be hardly enough to keep us alive. The sophomores tell me all Tchwezan bursaries have been cut this year; and part of the bursary is in the form of a loan for which you have to submit a special application giving details of how you're going to spend every cent. Then there are my brothers and sisters at school.'

They talked about how you became automatic head of the clan the moment you got your first job, head in the sense of money-producing machine than in any other sense of the word. Mutwe told of how his clan had cursed him for quitting his radio announcer's post to come to university. Kale told him there were rumours all over Tchweza that university students were paid monthly salaries far bigger than those of any officials below the rank of Principal Secretary. They talked of how selfish, unco-operative and often downright discouraging relatives were while you were still at school; how unreasonably rapacious they became the moment you got any employment.

*

That is how it began: desperate, disappointed man discovering disappointed, desperate man. What with the two young men's intellectual keenness and, as they discovered that very afternoon, their being in exactly the same academic departments, no grain of powder was lacking for blasting Maalas' traditional barriers between man and man. At supper that evening, and on a few subsequent days, some severe judges marked down Kale and Mutwe for punishment as they saw them by-pass their respective tribal reserves and join each other at their now favourite table at the back of the hall.

But the judges soon gave up the case for lost. And it was not long before confusion mercifully stepped in to wipe out any chances of further censure. For those who knew Kale assumed automatically that his new friend belonged to his tribe; and Mutwe's acquaintances assumed the same about Kale. As very few 'outsiders' ever stayed with them long enough to discover whether they used any language besides English and Kiswahili, this impression was established by incomplete evidence.

For, we must acknowledge this: breaking down barriers means but setting up new barriers. The important question is, which set of barriers does more justice to human feeling and reason? which set demonstrates better man's power of choice?

Before long, Mutwe and Kale were being taken, or rather mistaken, for brothers. And, as for Peso, after he joined the group, people swore he was Mutwe's twin brother. For, although the intellectual relationship between Mutwe and Kale was the closest that could be imagined, the stronger personal bond was certainly between Mutwe and Peso. There was nothing of the classic queer physical activity between them. But the emotional relationship between them became so deeply intimate that a frank and unflinching examination of it, as we shall see, was to drench Mutwe's mind with embarrassment and sorrow, at a stage when he could neither save nor mend anything that had been.

Neither Mutwe nor Kale could remember exactly where and when Peso had moved in. It must have been very early in the second term of their first year. Peso did English Literature with the other two. But, instead of taking Linguistics as they did, he read Government Arts. (That *Government Arts* was interesting. It had been started as *Political Science*. But it was later decreed by the powers-that-be that *Political Science* was bourgeois and reactionary, and obscene, in a newly-independent country, and it did not reflect the African Image - with a capital I.)

So, Peso met the other two less frequently than they met each other, at least during lecture and seminar time. In any case, the most remarkable thing about Peso was the smoothness and unobtrusiveness with which he went about everything. Even when he was in the thick of the fight, as he certainly was during the great days of the strike, he was always the most uncontroversial character of whatever group he found himself in. And in this many factors contributed to his success.

In the Academics Anonymous, for example, his natural quietness made him the ever-willing listener to the two greedy and tireless talkers that Mutwe and Kale were.

In fact one wonders whether the unreserved affection that both boys lavished on Peso was not, in part at least, due to the flattering service he rendered to their impetuous *egos* by listening to both when either was too concerned with expressing his opinion to listen to the other.

A buffer-state, perhaps that is how a student of government arts would have described Peso's position between Mutwe and Kale. And indeed many were the times that the quiet young man had averted a clash between his uncompromising friends.

'If Peso were here!' That was the nostalgic refrain that to both Mutwe and Kale summed up all the tragic consequences of the strike that slew the ghost of the dead life at Maalas and all but pushed the boys' little group over the precipice. Heaps of things certainly happened during and after the strike. But to Kale and Mutwe, who got back to the University some two or three weeks earlier than Peso, the strongest and most palpable symbol of the rupture was their young friend's absence. But that is anticipating our own story.

Another thing that won Peso the deep personal liking of the other two was that he was younger than they. In fact he looked much younger than he really was. For Mutwe was only two months older than he, while Kale was a full year older than Mutwe. Yet these two regarded themselves as age-mates; often indeed Mutwe assumed that he was older than Kale. But to both, Peso remained the image of the 'younger brother', and his apparent simplicity did everything to confirm the impression.

For, although he was a very bright boy himself, and was perhaps more deeply sensitive than either Kale or Mutwe, he was absolutely fascinated by the intellectual resourcefulness of these two. He nearly always assumed the role of pupil and questioner. But even in purely social dealings, Peso had a kind of childlike directness and sincerity that was the envy of his friends. He would, for example, walk into one of his friends' rooms any morning and ask to be lent a tooth-brush.

'I must have mislaid mine,' he would say, 'and if I insist on digging up the whole place this late, I'm going to miss breakfast.'

'But I've got only one tooth-brush, Peso,' Kale or Mutwe would say.

'Yes, but I can use it after you've finished with it.'

Who could have devised a cleaner *coup de grâce* to all that old muck of a hygiene that does not care for the mind?

This then was the stuff of which the Academics Anonymous was made. As we have already said, when we first meet them in the course of this story, they are a leaking craft whose two sides and bottom have been battered and cracked by the bitter waves of experience and stupidity. Or perhaps wisdom. For, in the absence of the intellectual spring that these three boys had, amongst themselves, tapped to quench their thirst, was it not wisdom to turn to the next and only purposeful(!) pursuit that was left: the preservation of the species or, briefly, women?

Whether those who choked this spring acted out

of folly or wisdom, whether the seeds of destruction were inherent in the boys' own little group, and whether theirs was the only fashion of combating the personal formlessness and often indeed deformation in which the Maalas campus was steeped - that is not the burden of this story. Its hope, for even in Maalas they hoped, is either that this little band eventually recovered from the blows and shocks of time or that, if it did not, each of its warriors had drawn enough marrow from its breast to keep his bones sturdy and straight through the lonely watch that life is ultimately bound to be.

Whatever the end, the A.A. had certainly had their day. Quite early in their career, it was before Peso came in in fact, Mutwe and Kale were, for sugar or for quinine, noted as *particular* by their colleagues and, above all, by their teachers. Among these was John O'Goat B.A. (Cantab.), M.A. (Lond.), Ph.D. (Inferno etc...). It was the vow that Kale and Mutwe had made to 'let no tutor get away with those shallow remarks' that drew O'Goat's attention to the boys.

The first time that they came to grips with him looked very very much like a *coup d'état* to his surprised mind. Not that the boys' contribution to that particular discussion was exceptionally deep or original. They were talking about Forster's *A Passage to India*, and Mutwe and Kale had been amassing background information about the novel. In their 'research', they had come across an exciting though perhaps overblown magazine article, by an obscure Pakistani scholar, called 'The Colonies of Devi'. The article discussed the colonial influence on relationships between the characters in the novel. So the boys came up with the 'colonial' theme at the discussion.

O'Goat was surprised. Normally, he did not expect any student to say anything at these discussions(!). And he had been attacked from an angle to which he had not given a single thought. You never really gave anything any thought when you knew you were assured of infallibility. He made a few half-hearted attempts to give his views. (Between you and me, he did not have any views.) But Mutwe and Kale simply ignored him and the rest of his dumb class. and went on and on talking away between themselves.

O'Goat felt challenged but not insulted. For he was quite a keen-minded man. He let that seminar pass off as smoothly as possible, and he decided he would always come 'better armed'. For the first time since his arrival in Maalas, he realized that teaching in Africa perhaps required some intelligence and preparation after all. And, as 'discussion' assumed a new meaning, at least in that particular group in which the boys were, he became increasingly aware of what that easy-won infallibility had hitherto made him miss. He learnt to like the two boys more and more for the frequent though admittedly immature intellectual tickle that they gave him.

One day he invited them to a party at his house: one of those informal occasions where you put on the funniest and shabbiest thing you had in your wardrobe, sat on the carpet or, better still, on the bare floor, and you kept answering the ever-flowing question, 'What are you reading?' in both American and English. You pretended to listen to all sorts of squeaks and squeals about how all sorts of lecturers and their women liked your country - 'weren't the lake beaches splendid?' 'a kinda climate we never get back *howme*' and so on. All you were doing in fact was to down 'boozes' until you were drunk or there was nothing more to drink. But it was a very infectious kind of function. Once you were drawn into the party-going club, you were bound to stay there. For you never left one party without an invitation to another.

It was at that first party at O'Goat's that Mutwe saw O'Goat's then wife, Vivienne. A particularly striking figure of a woman. She was so busy with her guests that evening that the young man could not take in all the details about her. But later, as his visits to the house became more frequent, he got to know her quite well, and to admire her unreservedly.

She was quite young and her two children, both girls, were only a year and a half and seven months old. Yet already there was something about her which to Mutwe inspired an unusual kind of confidence - something motherly, nay, grandmotherly. She did not indulge in any of those cheap antics popularly used by the teaching (equals *expatriate*) staff at Maalas to advertise their liberal-mindedness. Yet her gracefulness managed to remove all inhibitions and shyness and make one feel at home in her presence. Hence Mutwe's great shock at the story that brought her stay in Maalas, and with John O'Goat, to an abrupt end. But to the human mind, many things are unknown, and many that are had better remain unnamed.

But as for the Academics Anonymous, its remaining 'anon' was a sheer joke among the three boys. It was after they had started their evening 'bouts', comprehensive chats that moved pool-ripple-like for hours on end as we have seen, that the idea came to them.

'We're a secret society', Peso observed.

'What's there so secret about us?' Mutwe asked, spreading out his hands.

'Well, we must admit we're very exclusive,' Kale said.

They were in Mutwe's room, their favourite rendezvous, not only because it was the nearest from the cafeteria and the Academic Hill but also because it had the widest variety of books. Kale was sitting on the bed, thumbing a heavy old volume of *War and Peace*. Peso was sitting on one of the bookcases, near the head of the bed, and Mutwe standing in front of his wardrobe.

'Exclusive? So are the tribes,' said Mutwe as he shuffled towards his desk.

'Yes,' Kale agreed, 'but they are large enough to stand on their feet.'

'Quality, old man, is a better alternative to quantity. I'd rather have one strong and sound foot to stand on than a thousand jiggered, spliced, formless ones. Let's talk something academic.' Mutwe planted himself at his desk with an exaggerated gesture of seriousness.

'That's what I was going to say,' Peso always gave one the impression of 'venturing' in everything he did; he must have had very censorious parents or teachers back home. 'You two are too academic about things.'

'*You* are being very academic about us two,' Kale said, drilling a finger into Peso's left leg, which Peso, having kicked off his shoe, had planted on the bed to help him secure his place on the bookcase.

'The three Great Academics of Maalas!' Mutwe intoned, imitating the academic voices he had heard announcing, *'Mr. Chancellor, Sir!'* during the Graduation ceremony.

'We'd better remain anonymous,' Kale said with a sharply contrasting lack of enthusiasm.

As if to prolong the drama of the contrast, Mutwe continued in the same tone as before, 'The three Great Academics Anonymous of Maalas!' and a name was born.

Academics Anonymous. A.A. What had inspired that? Where had Mutwe heard something like this before? He could not tell. It is surprising how fast our minds record impressions and how tenaciously they retain them, even in spite of ourselves sometimes. You might come across that A.A. tag at the next street corner - not particularly interesting, something to do with alcohol - but to the three boys, who either did not know or could not remember where it had originally entered their minds, A.A. stood simply for Academics Anonymous, their happy, serious selves.

*

Kale was just leaving after the discussion on *Middlemarch* when the 'Bishop' tapped at the door and opened without waiting for anyone to invite him in.

'Hullo lunatics!' he hailed the boys as he came in, 'where did your madness wander tonight?'

The Bishop did not believe in literature, and he always called it 'madness.'

'We're doing nine hundred pages of pagan nonsense tonight,' Mutwe said.

'*Nine* hundred?' The Bishop took off his spectacles and frowned at Mutwe. 'Remember you need eight hours' sleep a night, according to Dr. Neurosis.'

Dr. Neurosis was the practitioner in charge of the University Dispensary. *Neurosis* was not quite his name. But he was so immovably convinced that people in such a sophisticated community were bound to have nervous breakdowns that his first diagnosis of any student case was always *neurosis*. And he would be hysterically disappointed when further facts proved to him that the cause of the complaint was a socialist lunch with the cafeteria flies or, almost equally often, a Saturday visit to the 'people's goods' in one of those *closed-houses*, as the French call them, which abounded in some parts of town.

Though Mutwe laughed with the others at the Bishop's observation, he was slightly disappointed at his reaction. For he had used the word *pagan* with the express intention of provoking the Bishop's Christian sense of values. The Bishop was an extremely serious Christian - hence his nickname.

He was a post-graduate student of - would you believe it? - Zoology. He was a very lonely man. This was not only because of the special nature of his pursuits and the inevitable isolation in a society where a post-graduate student was as rare as a stone's roots. His natural elegance simply refused to get acclimatized to the welter of vulgarity that life meant at Maalas. He had done his first degree at an old British university, an experience which, among other things, had helped to deepen his appreciation of Christian brotherhood. For, throughout his three years of exile on that Isle of Kings, the only niche in which he had found acceptance and security was the narrow but warm fraternity of the Christian Union.

He had taken to frequenting the Academics Anonymous first because he knew Peso. He had been his prefect at the old protestant school to which they had gone in their capital, in Tchweza's eastern neighbour. Peso had been only a little boy then, but the Bishop, his real name was Moses Sazangu, had noticed what a good child he was. And he was gratified to find when he got to Maalas, that Peso was still a practising Christian.

For all the three boys in the A.A. were practising Christians. Perhaps that was another link among them, though it could equally easily have been the apple of discord. For they belonged to different denominations. Peso was low-church Anglican, Kale was Lutheran. an Mutwe was, well, that most famous and feared brand of Christianity, Catholic.

And they did not spare one another any of the

traditional mutual denunciations when their 'bouts' turned to religion. Thus Mutwe had several times had to produce his tattered Bible, with a Catholic bishop's *imprimatur* on its fly-leaf, and scream, rather than read from it to his colleagues. This was to prove to them that Catholics did not only have a Bible but were also obliged to read and study it. But then he would only find himself badgered with questions about his Bible's containing 'unauthorized', 'uninspired' books, and about terms like *Canticle of Canticles*, *Apocalypse* and the like.

Or he would have to explain all that adulation for his girl-friend, the Virgin Mary. Mutwe had in fact stacked up a set of ready-made psychological and biblical explanations for this sexiest of all the points of controversy. But it was a less pleasant chore to defend papal infallibility, or such downright nasty historical incidents as the Spanish Inquisition.

But it was no easier for Peso, when his turn came, to account for Tyburn, or to consecrate good old Harry and his 'gospel-light-eyed' Anne Boleyn. And the gusto with which Mutwe asked whether the 'dissolution of the monasteries' was a 'symptom of nascent nationalization or downright robbery' fell only millimetres short of the malicious. Perhaps it was only matched by his own remark to Kale that poor Kale would have been a wild animist but for the dismal failure of a German catholic priest called Martin to stick to his calling.

'But he failed only because he didn't want to buy, or even sell your expensive indulgences,' Kale would hit back, and, as if to finish off his opponent before he responded, he would hastily add: 'By the way, has the situation been affected by rising prices?'

But they were all so good-humoured about these sneers that no one ever took offence. And, as time passed, the boys came to realize that these playful exchanges had not only given them a deeper insight into one another's beliefs but also thrown out a challenge to them to re-examine their own. Above all, they discovered from their smooth exchanges about this most inflammable of all topics that men remain men, whatever they might believe, or believe they believe. When the Bishop got to know them better and realized, among other things, the easy seriousness with which they held their beliefs, he got to like the three boys intimately, and he developed a kind of fatherly anxiety and concern over the future of their faith.

'The trouble with you men of letters, you see,' he said to them one day, 'is that you're so loud-mouthed that you sort of snatch the embryos of our scientific thoughts from our brains and start exhibiting their disfigured corpses as the world to justify your shallow unbelief.'

Perhaps he was right. You know how it happens. When you are a baby, your mother gives you a cloth frock to cover your physical nakedness, and a religious frock to cover your spiritual nakedness. As you get bigger, you visibly outgrow your cloth frock, and new clothes are, or have to be, made for you.

But as for things invisible... Well, for some reason or other-the urgency of teaching you English, the unwieldy size of the family, including mother's co-wives and, to borrow foreign terms, half-brothers and half-sisters; your mother's urge to have a man, sexually, I mean, all to herself - for some reason people might forget to change the invisible frock they gave you in the cradle; until one day you find it absolutely necessary to throw it off and saunter stark naked down the aisles of life. Not because of any exhibitionist or 'night-dancing' urge, but for the simple hygienic reason that that frock has become too mucky and too small for your adult mind to wear without squeezing itself to death.

But it is not easy to say bluntly, *'I'm going naked: no one thought of giving me fitting clothes at the right time.'* You have to find a more *refined* way of saying it. *'Those missionaries were liars and agents of colonial exploitation,'* for example. Or, *'As a good socialist you must know that religion is the opium of the people.'* Or, more popularly, and closer to the Bishop's point: *'Freud has proved that religion is merely sexual sublimation.'* Are we getting our names right? Was it Freud who coined that currency of 'defence mechanisms'? things like *rationalization*?

This evening the Bishop had come to talk to Mutwe alone. But, seeing the three boys happy together again, he was so deeply touched that he dared not intrude on their island in this shoreless sea of misery. For, just as the Biafran matrons who stayed at home heard more loudly than their warrior husbands the crack of Gowon's guns through their hearts, Moses the Bishop had for several weeks now, since the return from 'exile', borne the excruciating pain of being the helpless observer of the rapid and irreparable disintegration of that little group that he had come to know, respect and love so unreservedly. He had prayed over it and talked to the boys together and individually. But Mutwe's finally taking to Virgin Lisa, and the explosion of cattish rumours that followed it, had shaken his hopes almost beyond repair. Yet he was still praying, trying and hoping.

Shortly after the Bishop left, Kale too excused himself. He had to catch the late night bus and return to his wife in town. (Yes, that was the word - *wife*). And, after what had passed between them as we shall see, Peso and Mutwe could not stay alone together for any length of time without feeling that maddeningly intense strain of embarrassment that so often rotten friendship breeds. So, Peso left too and went to - Margaret Plantagenet.

When Mutwe was a little boy, he used to go to the lush green country on the western banks of a large river to visit his paternal grandparents. While there he would watch goats being slaughtered. When the goat was cut open, the little boys swarmed impatiently around, till the animal's urinary bladder was plucked out and thrown to them. They squeezed the urine out of it and inflated it with their breath. Tying its tube up with a soft bit of banana fibre, they would kick the bladder around like a ball till one of them accidentally stepped on it and it burst, or rather split, without even a soft 'pop', and shrivelled up into a wretched bit of dust-coated flesh abandoned to the self-reliant village dogs.

That is how Mutwe felt when Peso closed the door behind him, just like that bladder waiting for the unfed dogs. He looked at the thick open paperback on the desk.

(' *I fear the part played by the vultures on that occasion would be too painful for art to represent, those birds being disadvantageously naked about the gullet, and apparently without rites and ceremonies.*') (*Middlemarch*, Ch. 35.)

The words jumped from the page and slapped him thickly in the face. He clapped the book shut and threw it, literally, into the waste-paper basket. He went and threw himself prostrate on the bed. He turned his head violently from left to right, breathing thickly. He would have loved to cry, but he could not. He slapped his pillow repeatedly, he tugged at the ends of his blanket and sheets and kicked his mattress violently. Finally, the dogs of fatigue came for him. He lay quite still, with his hands spread out and hanging over the edges of the bed.

But this awkward sprawl was bound to tell on him quite soon. After only a few minutes, he felt his chest cruelly compressed, and he became uncomfortably aware of his male organ. He got up wearily, changed into his pyjamas and, as the routine carries on by itself once you set it going, he opened the shelves part of his wardrobe and squeezed a generous dose of toothpaste on to his toothbrush. His mind numbly conjured up Peso, who had borrowed this toothbrush so often.

The campus was unusually quiet for that time of night - it was only after eleven - and the water's inanimate gurgle sounded strangely loud as it bubbled down the basin. True, it was Saturday and those who were not broke or sleepy, and did not have essay 'crises', had gone downtown to try their luck at one thing or another. Still, a few radios should have been blaring. Maalas students' radios were always played at full volume, and if you wished to record a veritable pandemonium, you had only to come to the University between twelve noon and twelve midnight on any weekend day.

Or those who had 'imported' goods from town should have been spinning their 'tranquillizing' discs. You know students sometimes imported girls. The university rule was that guests, meaning women in the case of boys halls and men in the case of Margaret Plantagenet, should be out of students' rooms before 9 p.m. - as if anything tasted any different after that magic hour. But the normal practice was to import your goods on Saturday evening and retain them till late on Sunday, provided you did not show yourself, and them, to the diabolic custodians.

When Mutwe returned to his room, he switched off the reading lamp at his desk and he crept into bed with a weary sigh. For several minutes he lay on his back, thinking nothing, gazing at the ceiling. Then he ran his hand over the top shelf of his bedside bookcase. It was lined with volumes of verse by African poets. Without looking he pulled out Senghor's *Ethiopiques*. The billowing French sounded almost annoyingly complacent, but Mutwe buried himself in the verse, murmuring quietly to himself as he always did when he read French, and by the time the amber light of the bedside lamp began to tell on his eyes, he had soothed his nerves sufficiently for him to feel sleepy.

We all have little personal habits that are unknown even to those closest to us. Not even Peso and Kale knew that Mutwe used verse as a narcotic, and Mutwe always wondered what their comments would be if they knew. He slowly closed the *Ethiopiques* and placed it carefully on the floor beside the bed. Then he switched off the light, turned on his left side and closed his eyes.

Before he dropped off to sleep, he remembered, without any particular feeling, that he had not said his evening prayers. *'The devil might come red-eyed during the night,'* his mother used to say to him when he was a little boy. And even now, twenty years later, that remained her only warning to him when, on the rare occasions he went home, he forgot his prayers. But his father complained more irritably, though certainly less eloquently …

The figures of his family in the poor suburbs of his home capital floated across his mind. The tiny sitting-room with its rough sturdy table, its three wooden chairs, its multi-coloured palm carpets neatly covering the floor and its litter of crucifixes and pictures of saints and popes covering the walls. Two hours after nightfall and the air so tense with a myriad barely-perceptible sounds that it seemed to sing in its stillness.

Buxom Mamma, her wood-brown, full-moon face bent over the new coil of mat she was weaving. Tall, lean Papa, a builder and lay preacher, sitting on the chair by the table, holding the tattered old Bible close to the hurricane

74

lamp and reading aloud monotonously from it, or simply reciting, folk-tale-like, its stories. This was a more exciting performance for the kids - there were thirteen in all, and nine of them had not yet left home for boarding school. The youngest whirl restlessly round their mother, waiting for dinner. Then Uncle Pantaleo swaggering in from the *pombe* shop, his drunken chanty tearing the air with the reek of his 'booze'. Papa administering his never-forgotten, and never-heeded, reprimand to his younger brother. *Living*, Mutwe thought, or *failing to live*.

He remembered how, in his early teens, he had travelled with another paternal uncle ('younger father' is the more accurate term), who was a priest to a men's monastery in the dark green hills to the east of Lake Victoria. They went for one of those catholic spiritual exercises called retreats. Mutwe remembered seeing the monks, the most miserable Europeans he had ever seen, working in the fields for five hours on end in the blazing sun, and feeding on sliced cassava and boiled beans despite the astounding harvests from their gardens and their livestock sheds. He remembered hearing them wake up in the small hours of every morning and chant eerie prayers which floated out on the misty air.

He had thought everything very strange then. It was only over the years that he had come to appreciate the significance of this concentrated example of men struggling to get hold of something that would give meaning to their life, and, especially, to their death...

...A spear, a Rwandese spear! One of those refined

murderous jobs with thorn-sharp hooks on the neck so that they would slice through the flesh if pulled out of a victim's body ... sticking out of the ceiling, and descending slowly but steadily and menacingly towards the helpless boy's breast, its murderous blade gleaming in the flood-light brightness that surrounded it. Mutwe's eyes dilated with terror as the weapon closed in on him. He tried to grab its shaft and push it back, but his arms lay limp and numb by his sides. He tried to scream, but not even the faintest squeak emerged from his throat. And the spear was descending, centimetre by centimetre. ...

4 The 'munch'

When Senior Lecturer John O'Goat emerged from his bedroom only four and a half minutes after he had dived into it, Virgin Lisa was trying to contrive a frown.

'Shall we be going?' he asked as he drew in his left hand to consult his watch. 'Actually we ought to have started a few minutes earl-'

'My cardigan, please.' The Virgin wanted this to sound very blunt, but, to John O'Goat, it only managed to sound so curiously personal that he was reminded this was not just another girl: you know, not the ready-made kind of mushroom or chicken soup that you buy from a supermarket and requires only five minutes' heating. A long and perhaps difficult preparation lay ahead of him if he was going to taste this particular dish. But blessed are the cynical, for the kingdom of patience is theirs.

'Oh look! You don't need a cardigan at all,' he said, planting himself straight in front of Virgin Lisa. She was examining her nails slowly and swinging her left foot slightly. 'Moreover, you look magnificent with bare arms.'

A senior lecturer can neither deceive nor be deceived. So, the Virgin Lisa who said, 'But I'm feeling cold' was only an enthralled little girl reeling with the thrill of triumph - or perhaps defeat. John O'Goat had certainly not deceived himself in the belief that the most effective compliment you can pay to a woman is one directed at her body. Nor had he had any intention of deceiving when he said that the Virgin looked 'magnificent'. For indeed she did, though perhaps more deeply than in the 'ultra-munchable' sense of the word intended by John O'Goat.

Her light-pink silk dress, with a narrow, frill-bordered neck, came to just about fifteen centimetres above the knee when she was sitting, revealing the light-blue and yellow flowers embroidered on the lace of her petticoat, and just enough of her brown thighs to set any normal man's eyes gleaming. The cut of the dress, so tight about the bust that the breasts were emphasized to a point where they made the observer wonder whether they were not a milligram too heavy for the poor girl, but so loose and round about the rest of her figure that it boldly spelt out 'MOTHER', left nothing unexploited in woman's sex. The bare, spotless arms breathed intact youth; and the total effect, completed when the Virgin threw her head back slowly to look at O'Goat - the thick black tresses piled up behind a pink ribbon, the full round cheeks, pale brown under a thin film of powder, the perfect, groundnut-red lipline, and, above all, those eyes that refused ever to leave the cradle - all seemed to be calculated to set any sufficiently detached observer wondering at the nature of a Justice that pitted such innocence against the buffets of the world.

'Come on, let's go.' O'Goat had been gazing at Lisa's face for some moments, and now he was sort of forcing himself angrily to return to the original business of the evening. Men want power, especially in matters of sex. The feeling that he is falling for, or being taken by a woman, instead of his taking her, is unbearable to an ordinary man. To many ghosts of manhood, in fact, for whom the sexual act has lost every trace of physical pleasure or spiritual meaning, its only attraction and value remain that sense of power, the sense of winning and possessing something, even if for only a few moments - and of course its illusive protection against death. Hence those angry outbursts whenever a man discovers (the truth in most cases) that he is in fact the one surrendering everything in the bargain.

O'Goat took Virgin Lisa by the wrist and raised her to her feet, and, almost in spite of himself, he pulled her so close to him that his manhood, now stiff as a wooden stick, touched her thigh. A slight shiver passed over the Virgin's body. O'Goat could not, in a century of leap-years, have devised a more effective compliment than this body's communication to the body. Another of those curious facts about sex. To attract, that is, arouse men, is one of every woman's main concerns in life. How then can we account for that invariable wave of flattered surprise that accompanies every woman's realization that she has aroused a particular man?

John and Lisa walked hand in hand to the door, in complete silence. They were so quiet that Lisa's shoes all but startled them as they tapped on the narrow strip of bare cement between the carpet and the door. O'Goat let Lisa step out first and he followed and locked the door. They did not hold hands again as they walked down into the basement where the cars were kept. O'Goat tried to take Lisa's hand, but she drew it away and clutched her handbag with both hands. Perhaps she did not feel secure any more, now that they were out in the open. O'Goat realized he was being stupid again and he was annoyed with himself.

John O'Goat's dirty and tattered Volkswagen estate groaned out of the basement and up on to Hekima Road. It backfired once before he changed to second gear and, without even removing his hand from the lever, to third. Contempt for respectable or well- maintained cars was one of the classic marks of intellectual enlightenment. Anyway, you could always be sure of selling your ramshackle car, provided you put the magic formula, *'European owned. Ring: (Anglo-Saxon name), University 2251,* on the small ads page of the local paper. As Peso once remarked, one could not help wondering what happened to African-, Asian- or American-owned cars when their owners wanted to sell them.

The evening was beginning to dissolve some of the heat lumps in the air. But it was still very dry, and the gentle breeze that wafted a faint scent of fish from the bay towards the campus rustled audibly through the thick foliage of the dark cashew trees which lined the road. There was no moon, yet the glimmer of Lake Tudor could be discerned across the four or five kilometre stretch of shrub between it and University Hill. And, if O'Goat had had the time, he would have thought about the glittering sands bordering the water, and about the scores of women he had driven there on moonlit nights. But already they were coming down on to the main road and turning sharply right towards the city.

They overtook a huge petrol tanker and. about three hundred metres ahead, they turned a sharp corner and got out of its lights. O'Goat slowly lowered his left hand from the steering-wheel and clapped it on Virgin Lisa's knee.

'Hey, what's all this sacred silence about?' he asked recklessly. The evening air had cleared his mind, and he was happy to know that he could now make things move at his own chosen pace.

The girl started and giggled. 'I've nothing to talk about,' she said.

'Talk about Dickens,' O'Goat said and squeezed her knee.

'I'm fed up with Dick … ah no, please, don't!

O'Goat's hand was moving up the Virgin's thigh, and she grabbed it suddenly. The car swayed a little, and just about that time an oncoming car shot its undipped lights through their windscreen.

'Blast!' prayed O'Goat, and he gripped the wheel and hastily dipped his own lights. The other driver did not reciprocate this gesture of considerateness. O'Goat braked sharply, if not frantically, and swerved his vehicle to the left as he passed the lazy driver's car. Lisa did not know much about cars. Despite the violent jostle, she was not aware how close they had been to an accident until John O'Goat, after several moments of swearing and cursing, said, 'We wouldn't like a bloody *Mzungu* bringing out a beautiful daughter of the land and sacrificing her to his road.' They were silent for some moments and O'Goat continued, half-musing to himself, 'Surprising how often drivers here

81

risk people's lives out of sheer laziness. Sometimes you feel another car was the last thing they expected to meet on the road. Half-asleep at the wheel like that!'

'Maybe the heat affects them.' Virgin Lisa had been taught, back home, that it is very bad manners to let a man talk to himself like a lunatic. This is why she felt she had to say something. She was not interested in the subject.

'And all these bloody Indians working out their colossal sums of money in the middle of the road!' O'Goat suggested another reason.

He knew, or at least believed, that every African hated the Asians and, like all his tribesmen, he took every opportunity to curse the race before any African audience, and to make them believe that the Asians were responsible for all the money which disappeared out of the country - to Britain.

The Virgin laughed quietly, and John O'Goat lowered his hand on to her thigh again. 'You all right after the jolt?' he asked.

'Oh yes, thank you. I barely felt it.' The Virgin did not try to push his hand back this time.

They were now driving through the *European*, I mean the smartest and most exclusive, residential part of the city. It had originally been built for whites only. The only black people who lived there before independence were night *askaris*, houseboys and ayahs. The guards lived in greater comfort, out in the open cool air under the street lights. But the ayahs and houseboys were obliged to shut themselves up in their circular grass-thatched huts behind the *Mabwana*'s palace-like bungalows. The heat and darkness inside those windowless huts were suffocating. But the white experts on ethnic shelter swore from their airy, air-conditioned offices, sitting-rooms and bedrooms that the Africans who lived in those huts were happy. For that was their natural environment.

Things had changed with the coming of independence. Not for the guards or the ayahs and houseboys. The *askaris* still walked the length of the hedges under the amber lights, from dusk to dawn. The houseboys and ayahs still curled inside the grass-thatched, windowless huts to sleep or bake. But several *Wazungu* families had now left the bungalows, bequeathed them to lucky and successful political black families. And these of course drew in their brothers, and uncles, and cousins, and second cousins, and quarter cousins and - as many members of the endless clan as could be found a vacant bungalow for.

Of course, what with overseas advisers and technicians and volunteers, and all sorts of overseas something-or-other, the whites still outnumbered the blacks in the area. But change there was, and perhaps it was more striking because it was a move from what had previously looked like sheer impossibility to a natural and accepted order of things, the taking over of some bungalows by black families.

Perhaps in some subtle way this meant a change for the ayahs and houseboys as well, if we may go back on what we said. For, unlike the white experts, the black experts in their airy, air-conditioned offices, sitting-rooms and bedrooms did not bother about any justification for the shape of the servants' huts. They were too busy forging the African revolution. And the huts were not as hot as they had formerly been. For now the walls were full of cracks, and the thatch was rotten, so that the roofs leaked for weeks after a shower of rain, keeping the inside relatively cool if a little damp.

*

The film was being shown at one of those foreign cultural centres which formed a chain of indoctrination across the Tchwezan capital. This particular one was on the fourth floor of a huge block of shops and offices. O'Goat and the Virgin could have gone up by lift. But already there were a large number of people waiting for the lift, and perhaps O'Goat felt instinctively that a walk with Lisa might advance his cause. So, he took Lisa's hand and said, 'Let's go up the steps.'

The Virgin responded readily to his gentle tug and they started up the wide, gently-slanting staircase. The ease with which the Virgin let O'Goat take her hand did not remind him that he could have made a fool of himself again, this time in public, if the scene on the steps to the basement had been repeated. But perhaps he too was instinctively feeling free from the oppressive atmosphere of the campus.

The film itself was the usual *avant-garde*, experimental 'success' that every academician went to see because a certain so-and-so had said it was worth seeing and, though, or perhaps *because*, absolutely unintelligible, never received any negative comment from anyone. For any negative commentator would be labelled old-fashioned and conservative, or downright insensitive.

Apart from the so-called academicians, the audience consisted of the citizens of the country which owned the cultural centre, old maids (mainly British) who took every opportunity to run away from the frightening silence of their houses, and a handful of Government agents who came to make sure that there was nothing neo-colonialist or anti-revolutionary in the picture. These last-mentioned slept through more than three-quarters of the film. Lastly, just about as duty-bound as the government agents, were housewives, secretaries and students who had been dragged there by their husbands, bosses or lecturers, because it was more decent to appear with a lady than alone in public, or for some other motives.

Virgin Lisa, like ninety-nine per cent of the audience, did not like the film at all. After straining her eyes and mind for a few minutes, trying to make out who was who in the whole litter of blonde harlots and grizzled murderers, and to read the English subtitles, she gave up the whole wretched business and sat back in her chair, thinking about the good films she had seen. She remembered she liked films which told a story, preferably a love story, and with a happy ending. Films like *Loving you is my Destiny*, or *The Hell with Heroes*, though there was too much killing in that, She thought she had not quite liked *My Fair Lady*, because Rex

Harrison forgot to give Audrey Hepburn that 'necessary' hearty kiss at the end. Titles and names raced through her mind as fast as the images of the film were racing across the screen before her. *The Sandpiper*, Liz Taylor, and the stupid pastor, Richard Burton. *A Faith of Blue*, Sydney Poitier …

Meanwhile, Senior Lecturer John O'Goat was trying, genuinely trying, to understand the *avant-garde* picture. He tried to apply every theory in his head to it: *the ravages of the Second World War, the existentialist norm, the drive of the subconscious, the inevitability of the absurd…* But he too finally gave up, after about twenty-five minutes of sweaty toil, and he sat back in his chair. He raised his left hand slowly and put it round the Virgin's shoulders. It so happened that she was at that very moment thinking about a very sexy scene in Cleopatra and, although she shivered a little at the actual moment of physical contact, she did not show any negative reaction to this instance of dream flowing into reality.

'Do you like it?' O'Goat asked, putting his bushy mouth so close to Lisa's cheek that she felt his warm breath.

'I don't know. Do you?'

'I'm still trying to figure it out,' said O'Goat, and he squeezed the Virgin's left shoulder. After some moments he said, 'I wish we could get out of here. I'm terribly hungry.'

'This thing should be just about ending now,' the Virgin said.

A bulky figure in front of them turned a starched, sickly face and a bead-loaded neck towards them. She did not say anything, and Lisa just had time to notice her six-centimetre-diameter white or light-blue ear-rings before she turned back to the screen.

Apparently they were disturbing. O'Goat now proceeded with his move, interrupted by the woman's turning to them. He had managed to slip his hand under the Virgin's arm, and now he touched her left breast. The Virgin started and she grabbed John O'Goat's hand, because she was tickled. She was not thinking anything, and she was so bored that, instinctively, she found this alternative to the film particularly entertaining. Moreover, the old vixen's censorious eye had whipped up some vicious spirit in the young woman's breast. She had wanted to spit at her and tell her she was free to bloody well do what she wanted.

You know how it happens when something or someone scratches that festering wound of our undefined *uhuru* turmoil: whether we are really ever going to get our own back on that whole brood of colourless humans who have inflicted so much suffering and humiliation on our race. Virgin Lisa held O'Goat's hand in her cotton- wool soft one and squeezed it till the end of the film.

*

The most interesting part of such evenings was looking at the people around after the show. The men exchanged empty politenesses and introduced their wives or girls, and the women smiled bored smiles at everyone while they took in all the details about every couple. Not such things as fashion - there was very little to show in that line. It was particularly to see who was going with whom.

Expatriate wives, especially, were anxious to note which of their males had picked up African girls, and why: whether they had divorced their wives or were simply leaving them at home, or whether a bachelor's resolution was finally breaking - in the wrong geographical region. As for the white girls who were going with African boys, no one really cared. After all, most of them were university researchists or career girls and did not belong to that class of average European woman in Maalas, and were, by the very nature of their professions, harlots.

The trouble was that, deep within, that business of blackman-whitewoman or, worse still, blackwoman-whiteman was bitterly resented, especially by the poor expatriate wives who in their faithfulness had followed their husbands even into the African wilderness, only to find themselves sunk in the boiling misery of stiff and maddeningly unfavourable competition with bloody wogs. One secretly longed for a Rand-style immorality act. The Asian I community had in fact achieved something very close to this in the thoroughness with which they censured any of their erring girls, through the Jamat Khanas, Goan Institutes and other such exclusive clubs. But among the promiscuous Africans and Europeans, there were apparently so many people involved in the dirty business that no form of control seemed possible.

As for John O'Goat, his story was so well-known that no one was surprised to see him with any woman now. In fact he attracted a surprising amount of sympathy from the good women of his tribe. (He had slept with a surprisingly large number of them: on those frequent evenings when, husbands away on upcountry safaris, boredom drowned all traces of resolution and faithfulness, but not the racial pride or the telephone instinct to dial University 2347 and ask the 'poor lonely man' if he would like to come to dinner.) 'He's such a nice person' was the general verdict regarding John O'Goat among his (non-academic) tribesmen and, especially, tribeswomen. And they were convinced that he was not responsible for his misfortunes or even his degeneration to wog-hunting. If there was any strong feeling for him this particular evening, it was perhaps that his new find was so captivating that he might drift out beyond any hope of recovery.

'Let's go and get something to eat,' O'Goat said, taking Lisa's hand after he had dished out hurried *hullos* to those few people he could not avoid.

Some strange spirit seemed to be whipping up a curious sense of urgency in his mind. Perhaps he was only desperately hungry as he had said during the film. Or perhaps he did not want to meet his colleagues from University Hill, for they would immediately have started discussing the film with him. Or perhaps there was a woman so recent in his life that he did not want her to see him with another woman.

This particular thought flitted through Virgin Lisa's mind as they walked towards the car, and it helped to sever more of those threads of reserve which had begun breaking in the film hall, or perhaps in the car, or even farther back, in O'Goat's flat. Now there was a sort of aggressive possessiveness in the readiness with which she let the Senior Lecturer take her hand, and in the intimate closeness in which she walked with him to the car. *My man*, some instinct seemed to be saying within her, *if only for tonight, and that whole race may say or think what they like.*

They drove down to the main street, and if you know the layout of most African capitals, you can make an intelligent guess of its name: something to do with *uhuru* or freedom or liberation, some reminder that we have only recently been slaves, followed by one or other of the hundred-and-something English words meaning *road*. They came to a set of traffic lights and O'Goat drove past without even slowing down.

'The light was red,' the Virgin told him.

'Oh yes, I noticed,' said O'Goat, his voice rough with impatience. 'But ours was the only car at the junction. We can't have robots living our lives for us,' he added as they turned into the car park of the Hotel Ghala.

This was the most expensive hotel in Maalas, and only very rich American tourists, and Tchwezan M.P.s, could afford to live here. Its small dining-hall was practically reserved for Europeans who clung to home apparel. Not even Tchwezan national dress was allowed here. You had to have on a tie and a jacket to be let in at all. Some aggressive young men had written screaming letter after screaming letter to the press, and to several ministries, condemning and deploring this practice. But the ministries were apparently too busy forging the African revolution to bother about such trivialities. And, as for the Management of the Ghala, their motto had always been, still was, and will perhaps always be: *to hell with black apes*.

But, as if to compensate for the fossilized conservatism of the dining hall, they had established the Ghala Toplife on the roof of their skyscraper. This was an informal restaurant and bar where you could eat and drink in perfect freedom, whether you were dressed in Masai skins or in British royal robes. This freedom of dress, a necessity in the Lake Basin climate, together with the purity of the lake breezes that played constantly round the topless Toplife, and the sense of power it gave one to see the whole city, State House included, prostrate below one's eyes, ended up by turning the last prospective guest away from the doors of the colonial dining-hall, towards the Toplife.

And there were other attractions too. 'Those gorgeous specimens of her sex', for example, which O'Goat had promised to show Virgin Lisa. These were the 'high-class' self-vendors. Their whole life consisted in going round the best department stores during the day, buying dresses and cosmetics, dressing up and perfuming themselves in the evenings and going to the Toplife, where, sure that moneyed public opinion was unwaveringly on their side, they boldly planted themselves at the tables of bored Italian technicians, bored British lecturers and excited American tourists and shared their bananas and beer glasses while they waited to be taken to bed.

Senior Lecturer John O'Goat and his student Virgin

Lisa selected a table in a corner away from the main street and they sat, facing each other. Almost at once, they were surrounded by about eight waiters, all eager to do their bidding. All those who served in the Ghala, as in most other places in Maalas, were very sensitive to the customer's skin colour. If you happened to be a *makaa* customer as the designation went, you had to be prepared to wait some fifteen or twenty minutes at least before anyone, including the street girls, took any notice of you. Often you wondered indeed if you would be noticed at all under the dim blue, green and red lights.

Not that the waiters were race-minded. All of them were black after all. They were simply so used to serving whites, and to receiving huge tips from them (even after the Tchwezan Government's official order that tips should be abolished as they did not reflect the African Image and were in fact a form of bourgeois and capitalist blackmail), the waiters were so used to this order of things that they could not help regarding a black customer as a useless intruder. Moreover, these waiters knew, and the rough insolence with which they did you the favour of listening to your order at all made no secret of it, that but for the grace of God, you would be squatting on the hard earthen floor of a tiny round, grass hut in the heart of the bush, chewing bitter cassava or swallowing dirty-brown millet cake with slimy vegetables - even if you were a minister or an M.P. now.

When the squadron of waiters was finally gone, one with the order for food, another fetching drinks, a third full of 'natural' thoughts about Lisa's breasts and lips, and the rest bitterly disappointed that the *Mzungu* did not seem to even notice them, the Virgin sighed lightly and looked around at the people on the roof. Nearly all the men were white, and they were horribly dressed, she thought. Say what you will about your freedom of dress, you could not expect a girl with Lisa's colonial upbringing to approve of that melee of sandals, super-mini shorts and unbuttoned *kitenge* shirts in a public place. The girls(!) fascinated her with the boldness and originality of their fashions, and she thought them very good-looking. If the lights had been brighter, she would have been shocked by the emptiness and boredom in their eyes, and by the startling gullies of cosmetic erosion on their faces.

Then there came someone the Virgin knew. It was a lady radiant in a gorgeous *kitenge* robe with light yellow, brown and coffee-flower white patterns against a deep blue background, with a foot-or-so high matching turban. She was Bibi Chanze, the only woman M.P. in Tchweza. The Virgin did not know the man who came in with her. But it was obvious from the elegance of his cream national suit and from his general personality, i.e. bloated cheeks and pot-belly, that he too was an M.P.

Bibi Chanze had a name among the girls in Margaret Plantagenet Hall. There were some girls whose contempt for her was beyond measure. They argued that even her membership of the House was only the limelight of shame. For everyone in Tchweza knew that she had abandoned her children and her husband and now slept with any man at hand, nay, even went out of her way to pay for any young man she thought exciting. But to the majority of university girls, Bibi Chanze was the very body and spirit of feminine emancipation.

The Virgin remembered an evening before the strike - no self-respecting M.P. or Party man could have anything to do with the 'ivory tower lepers' after - when the girls invited Bibi Chanze to address them in their Common Room. It was one of the very few things that Lisa could remember the girls ever doing together as a group. They expected Bibi Chanze to address them in Kiswahili. She had only been to primary school and then trained for two years to become a vernacular teacher. But she insisted on making her speech in English - such peculiar and uncommunicative English that no one, not even the most enthusiastic of her supporters, understood a word of what she said. Virgin Lisa wondered what she thought when, at the end of her speech(!), Asha, a lovely Lake Basin type and the only African Muslim girl at the University then, who had chaired the meeting, invited questions and everyone remained silent... But the Virgin was to hear Bibi Chanze speak again, during the strike.

One of the waiters brought the French aperitives which John and Lisa had ordered some ten minutes earlier. You never went to a restaurant in Maalas when you were in a hurry, not even if you were white. For the length of time between your being noticed and your being served always bordered on centuries. And especially once you had committed yourself by tasting anything: the intervals between each two items became longer and longer until you ended up wondering whether you wouldn't one day be discovered at that small table by some diligent archaeologist of the post-nuclear age.

Mutwe had once encountered a very interesting case when he dined out with Kale and his wife. Having exhausted all the usual excuses for delay, the waiter decided to fill in the 'remaining minutes' with the very polite question, 'Shall I bring you the bill now - Sir?' (The 'Sir' was always an afterthought in the case of *makaa* customers.) 'No, thank you,' Mutwe answered readily, and he and his friends roared with laughter. The confused waiter walked away in blind fury, more than ever before convinced that it was a bloody hell to serve Africans.

'Cheers!' said O'Goat as he raised his wine-glass towards Virgin Lisa.

The Virgin raised her glass slightly and returned a 'cheers' whose huskiness was smoothed over by a dimpled smile, and they sipped at their drinks. John O'Goat raised his eyes over the brim of his glass and watched the Virgin's lips touch the brim of her glass. He did not think or feel anything particular, and the muffled voices in the Toplife did not encourage speech, especially for a man as sharp-voiced as O'Goat.

The minutes which the Virgin had spent studying the characters around and musing about Bibi Chanze had been filled in for him by a clumsy youth who brought in a set of those bastard items of beadwork fabricated in the Maalas slums and sold to tourists as genuine tribal art.

As the boy dangled the bangles and necklaces before his nose, John O'Goat stretched out his hand and inspected them - knowing very well what they were. He asked about the price, laughed and bargained for minutes and finally dismissed the boy.

Now he was watching a group of Americans who came in just as the waiter served John and Lisa with drinks. The new arrivals sat at a large table behind Lisa but a little to her right. There were six of them, probably two families: two men, two women, and two little boys. One of the women, apparently the mother of the boys, was a short, tiny blonde with indifferent yellow-brown locks hanging long and heavy over her cheeks. She was very talkative, and she appeared to be one of those common restaurant characters who know everything about everything on the menu, and on a thousand other menus in Nooyork, London, Paree, Naples, Noodelhi, Nayrobi etc., etc., and would miss no chance of giving a lecture on them. O'Goat hated her vulgarity. Yet he could not take his eyes off her. Something in her appearance rang a bell somewhere in his mind ...

At last he remembered, and his heart shrank with the memory. It had been another American girl, much younger than this one, and a lot more elegant. Out on the northwestern coffee plateau.

O'Goat had learnt that John Horley, an American friend from his Cambridge days, had come out with some American volunteers and was teaching at a secondary school upcountry. John Horley arranged for O'Goat to spend a short vacation with him and meet his wife Lynne. *'The climate here will be a real revelation after your baking years in the Lake Basin,'* Horley wrote, *'and we have a whole palace of a house.'* O'Goat accepted the invitation readily, and whether to ensure that he used as much of the palace-house as possible or that he did not cuckold good old Horley, he asked whether he could bring his African girl with him. *'A very nice and cultured young woman,'* he explained rather apologetically, *'I'm sure you and Missus will like her.'*

(O'Goat had had a regular girl, one who stuck to him longest, despite his erratic affairs, since he divorced his wife. Some people 'on the outside' indeed whispered that this Miriam had been the cause of the breach. She was a short and fleshy dark-brown creature whose thick chocolate thighs were always dangerously straining at her *kuliko-uchi* mini-skirts, as the city *wazee* called that particular symbol of emancipation. She was a rebel of her own brand, a reckless history honours undergraduate who, although she let everyone know that O'Goat was her first 'principle', dispensed her goods with a disturbing generosity to any applicant.

And that is how misfortune had overtaken her. Some three weeks before this Lisa – O'Goat evening, she had been caught, so it was reported, coming out of one of the boy's halls at about five-thirty in the morning. The punishment for first offenders in this respect was a month's 'rustication'. She insisted that she had not been to any boy's room. That she had been suddenly taken sick and that she had been going to the cafeteria to get some drinking water when the custodian who reported her had tried to rape her.

The administration, however, did not believe her story, probably because, as some students observed, the reporting custodian was some sort of cousin to the Vice-Chancellor, and believing the girl's story would have meant his losing his job. So, down Miriam went, only a few weeks before the final examinations. An extensive search for the boy from whose room Miriam was coming mercifully proved fruitless.)

Two days after O'Goat and Miriam arrived at the Horleys', on a bright Saturday afternoon, the Americans took their guests to see the Kachomero Falls, a beautiful sight on a stream about three miles away from the school. Lynne had asked them to bring their swimming gear and, after they had been admiring the dancing rainbow above the water which leapt and roared with a miraculously sustained regularity over the darkened slab of rock on to the lower bed ten metres below, she led them downstream to a broad, pebble-bordered pool of still water in the middle of the stream. This was her private swimming-pool.

'I can't do without water,' Lynne explained as she emerged in her green bikini from behind a shrub. 'John and I have been working on this ever since we got here.'

'No snakes?' asked O'Goat. He and John Horley were in their swimming trunks too. But O'Goat secretly wished he could somehow avoid stepping into the water without offending his hosts. He deeply envied Miriam, who claimed she could not swim.

'I haven't seen one around,' Lynne said with a mixture of horror and annoyance in her voice.

'You see we've cleared the place, and snakes wouldn't easily come over open space like that,' John Horley said, pointing at the narrow strip of well-mown grass surrounding the pool, bordered with thin bougainvillaea bushes and dahlias.

John Horley was a very shy man, with tiny bat-like eyes and a pathetic mumble in his voice. Miriam thought she fancied his shabby blond beard.

'Is it deep?' John O'Goat had detected the displeasure in Lynne's voice and he now decided to ask a neutral question.

'Yes, rather,' she answered, 'about ten feet at the centre. We've more or less cleared the bottom; we can drain out all the water downstream, and John chlorinates the water up there when we're going for a dip.'

John Horley had decided to set the ball rolling by plunging into the pool. John O'Goat observed that Lynne regarded this pool as her only significant achievement in Africa. Of course she taught at the school. She did not have any qualifications, but, as the Headmaster, an ex-colonial district commissioner, had put it, 'after all, she spoke English and she would help out with the lower forms.' But there she neither saw nor cared for any results from her pupils, whom she secretly dreaded and regarded as either inveterate idiots or highly potential psychopaths. All Negroes were: hadn't her mother said so? Now as she stood pointing at John Horley's ingenious chlorine tank some seven or eight metres upstream, O'Goat noticed that she had a very shapely and 'well-proportioned figure. And the gleam of sunlight in her ripe-corn hair hanging thickly over her cheeks and neck had something romantic about it. But O'Goat's two years in and with Africa had taught him to dislike thin women.

'It's beautifully warm in here,' John Horley said, as his head emerged from the water.

'Oh, is it?' O'Goat feigned a kind of eagerness, but before he did the duty of jumping into the pool, he remembered his watch, whose 'waterproof' label he knew but did not trust. As he handed it to Miriam who squeezed his fingers, Lynne Horley made a sharp, head-first dive into the pool. John Horley had gone under again, and O'Goat thought he might take the opportunity to defer his plunge if only for a few moments before his hosts noticed him. When John Horley came up again, he swam towards the opposite bank; then he did a competitor's breaststroke race toward O'Goat's bank, beating up so much water that he did not notice O'Goat until he was resting only a few paces away from under his feet.

'Hey, come on in' Horley said to O'Goat after he had spurted out a short jet of water.

'Yes,' said O'Goat, feeling uncomfortable. 'I was taking off my watch. But Lynne -'

'Well, what about her?'

'She's staying too long down there.'

John Horley went under again, just as John O'Goat jumped clumsily into the pool, feet first, near where Lynne had dived. As soon as O'Goat could open his eyes under the water, he noticed a tonic-coloured streak rising towards him, and, following it, he came upon Lynne, sprawled out on the pebbly bottom of the pool. He looked at her for some seconds, then touched her arm, shuddering as he did so. Lynne did not respond. John O'Goat tried to raise her by the top of her bikini as John Horley approached too. But the cloth snapped off Lynne's breast and John O'Goat rose to the surface with an absurd rapidity, the green bit of cloth in his left hand. Seconds later, John Horley emerged, struggling under Lynne's bleeding body which they dragged to the bank and laid on the mat from which Miriam had jumped and fled, screaming hysterically.

'She must've hit a stone,' John Horley said, and he bent down to try a kiss-of-life. But he stopped short. Lynne was bleeding from the mouth as well ...

While John O'Goat was chewing this cud of recollections, sparked off by the talkative American woman, Virgin Lisa was studying the city below her. To her left, only a few hundred metres away, were the tall flood-lights of the pier, and the dark, gaunt cranes. She remembered a late Saturday afternoon when she had walked there with Mutwe after a film; how the men who worked there had used shockingly filthy language and how ashamed she felt when she discovered that she had been madly angry with Mutwe, as if he had used the naked words. A large steamer had just arrived, but it was waiting for the morning to come on to the quays. With its funnel and hundreds of bright lights, it was now a mini island-town in the dark waters of the Lake.

Before Lisa, over John O'Goat's shoulder, lines and lines of amber and green street lights stretched out into the distance until they stopped abruptly at what seemed to be the borders of wilderness. Lisa knew that it was not quite a wilderness. That dark patch was the workers' residential area.

Beneath the blanket of darkness were scores of sandy streets lined with hundreds of thatched and *debe*-roofed shanties with crumbling mud and wattle walls, housing thousands of near-destitute families. There, too, were the few amenities available to their thorn-bordered lives: fly-littered vegetable and *unga* shops, stinking *pombe* bars and, here and there, beneath a palm or a flamboyant tree, a sandy clearing for the stubbornly unkillable *ngoma*. Here too were whole streets of 'special houses' inhabited by the people's black-mantled, yellow-brown common women. These streets, the Virgin had heard, were popular with the university boys.

To her right, out near the dark horizon, rose University Hill, separated by some nine or ten kilometres of darkness from the city. It looked so bright, immense and imposing that even that superficial night contrast seemed to provide sufficient explanation for the savage glee with which town persecuted gown during the insane hours of the strike. The Virgin wondered what the girls in Margaret Plantagenet were doing. Mutwe's haughty, serious face flitted across her mind as she looked at the sharp outline of Windsor Castle. She quickly let her eyes stray away from the Hill down to the 'European-brow' housing estate through which she and John O'Goat had driven earlier in the evening. Then she looked at State House, only six or seven hundred metres away.

Her only image of the man who lived there was of a skin-clad savage haranguing a massive savage mob - one of the fruits of the strike. But Lisa remembered how motherly the President's wife looked. She remembered a magazine photo of her surrounded by her children...

Virgin Lisa thought of her own mother, out in the location near the Blue Crater Lake: a plump but tough wife and mother, squatting by the fire in the evening, stirring a huge pot of porridge. Last Baby, her ninth, and only five months when Lisa was there last, sitting on her knee, squeezing her sweet-potato shaped breast, envied by the three or four older imps whose cheeks are gourd-red in the firelight. *Most of life*, the Virgin thought, *is just living, not making sensational movie or novel tales*.

She remembered how little her mother talked to her now, when she went home. How she had her meals alone, at the tiny table in the sitting-room, served by her mother, who kept chasing away her little sons and daughters when they intruded. This reminded her of that boy who turns into a gigantic cockroach and loses touch with his family, in Franz Kafka's *Meta-*

'Hey, *where are you roaming, mistress mine?*' John O'Goat clapped his hand over Virgin Lisa's on the wine-glass, and she started so violently that a little wine splashed over and was sprinkled on both their hands. O'Goat said 'sorry' but did not remove his hand from Lisa's, The Virgin thought the Senior Lecturer's hand was beautifully warm and soft. 'You haven't been drinking any of this wine, apparently,' O'Goat said as he put out his other hand across the table and arrested Lisa's other hand as she tried to mop up the wine on their hands with her tiny, cream handkerchief.

'Yes, I have,' said the Virgin, unable to conceal the agitation she felt at being so suddenly awakened out of her reverie, and being so boldly courted, she thought, in public. 'Let me put away my hanky, please.'

O'Goat ignored her request and went on holding both her hands between his, round the tiny stem of the wine-glass, and gazing at her face with wide open, unwinking eyes. He hated thinking of death, and he loathed himself whenever he caught himself at it. Hence the violence with which he had wrenched himself away from the memory of Lynne Horley and hastened to clutch at the first warm and solid object of life before him. Now he wanted to talk and to be talked to, to make sure that he was still living *here on earth*. He was an atheist, you see, and, as he had said to Mutwe and Kale once, 'even if he saw a thousand legions of angels in the sky twing-twanging on their blasted harps, he would still prefer to live here, on the solid earth.'

'Do people ever tell you how beautiful you are?' he asked Virgin Lisa in a deep demi-whisper.

'No,' the Virgin said, smiling.

'Now, now, don't lie.'

Yes, the Virgin was lying, and O'Goat had learnt that Africans did not object to being told this to their faces. But there were two complications here. First, you had to know what was an African. Secondly, you had to ascertain how African any African was before deciding how to approach him. In this case, for example, the Virgin was bitterly offended, and O'Goat could not miss the angry flash in her eyes. Yet he did not want to say 'sorry', for that would have shown that he was aware he had given offence.

Very conveniently, the waiter arrived at just about that moment and started serving them. They ate in silence for some minutes, until John O'Goat, who could not help a certain sense of guilt over his 'Africanized' tongue, felt he should try and wash away words with words.

'You seem to be thinking very distant thoughts tonight,' he said.

'Yes. I'm thinking about my mother.'

'Is she as pretty as you are?'

'*I* am not pretty. *She* is beautiful.'

'Does she share your father with other wives?' O'Goat asked, genuinely meaning no harm. Then, almost immediately, he regretted the question. It is so difficult to know what to say.

'My father is a Catholic,' Lisa said, and O'Goat was greatly relieved to note from the calmness of her voice that she had not taken offence.

'Well,' he said. 'there are lots of catholic polygamists around this place.'

'Those are not good Catholics,' said the Virgin with the aggressive certainty with which a little girl of six will declare you a fool if you happen to be ignorant of something which she knows. It is rare that a Catholic will fail to pick up a religion-laced gauntlet.

'Are you Catholic too?' asked O'Goat, and he added as playfully as he could sound. 'I mean a good Catholic.' The Virgin laughed and wiped her lips. 'Are you a church-goer?'

'Oh, yes!' the Virgin said, 'even tomorrow, I'm going.'

'I think I should go to church one of these days,' said O'Goat, happy that he had at last found something to make Lisa talk. Somewhere in the remote comers of his mind, a decision was being born. If he slept alone that night, he would think of Lynne Horley ...

The Virgin was thinking about her Catholicism. How she had gone to a girls' secondary school run by nuns; but, there being no fifth and sixth forms, she had been forced to go to a government co-educational school after her School Certificate. The anguish with which her father had accepted the necessity, and the joy with which he noticed that his daughter was still 'practising' when she completed her course at the government school. Practising... yes, doing one's Christian duties... but what else? The Virgin caught herself wondering whether she knew any more what exactly she was practising.

'Would you like to go dancing?' O'Goat asked the Virgin as they stepped out of the lift on the Ghala's ground floor.

'No, thank you,' the Virgin said, feeling her feet rather light after the unaccustomed draughts of aperitif and dinner wine. 'It's getting rather late, and I think we should be getting home.'

To O'Goat, the phrases were nostalgically reminiscent of Vivienne, his ex-wife. For some moments in fact he expected Lisa to add something about the children. But when she did not, he put his arm round her and said, 'Of course, darling, you've got to sleep early and be on time for mass tomorrow.'

The Virgin was grateful for the arm round her, for she was not sure she could make it alone to the car. She did not notice the '*darling*', nor did its author. At the entrance to the Ghala, a girl - well, a prostitute at the hag-end of middle age - was exchanging sharp words with a bulky, bald-headed Italian (all stout, shabbily dressed, copper-skinned Europeans passed for Italian in Maalas). Perhaps they were discussing business, but, apparently, the discussion had taken an unpleasant turn. Anyway, both of them were dead drunk.

*

Out in the cool air of the car park, O'Goat pressed Virgin Lisa closer to him. She felt warm and soft and, what O'Goat did not notice or feel surprised at since he was dreaming of his first few days with Vivienne in London, she was compliant and all but snuggled against him. Lisa was not thinking anything. She just felt wanted, and she liked it and responded to it. As they came apart at the car, the Vivienne image suddenly dissolved in the thin late evening mist. But other things remained.

Warm, soft, solid, living, here on earth. No! no thoughts of death tonight. Must have a tangible symbol of life in the dark. A particular girl, this one. Will she stay? Too late to look for another. Catholic. Yes, headaches sometimes. Lynne Horley. No, no, no ... at all costs. Must be fun 'dethroning' a good Catholic.

'Ah, here we are!' Senior Lecturer John O'Goat switched off the engine and pulled in the handbrake. They were in the basement beneath his flat.

Virgin Lisa was not in the least aware of what was happening. She wondered in fact, when they pulled up, whether she had not been sleeping most of the way. A young woman's mind is easy to drain of activity: a rich meal, a sprinkle of wine, an arm round the waist, a late hour, the hum of a car engine ... Lisa stirred numbly in her seat as John O'Goat quickly turned up his window, jumped out of the car and locked the door. He came round and opened the other door for Lisa.

'Feeling tired?' he asked.

'Yes, rather,' answered the Virgin, and she felt a cool stream of air flow past her legs as she stepped out of the car. John flipped the handle of the car-door and slammed it shut.

'Come in for a nightcap,' said O'Goat, 'and I'll run you up to M.P.' *M.P.* was short for *Margaret Plantagenet*, but the girls did not like it. For to them, the abbreviation meant '*monthly period*', and they did not consider that a phenomenon to be reminded of every now and then.

'Thank you, I think I'll stroll up,' said the Virgin,

her brain now slightly cleared by the cool breeze and the unusual stillness of the campus.

'O.K.' Dr. O'Goat had been told by other girls that they did not want to be seen with any man on the campus unless and until they had committed themselves to him.

They went up the steps from the basement, O'Goat's hand round the Virgin, naturally now. At the top of the stairs, he was just wheeling her towards the flat when the Virgin offered a slight resistance and said, 'Well, goodnight; and thank you very much for the ev -'

'Aren't you coming in for a drink?'

'No, thank you; I really must go to bed.'

'How about your cardigan then?' A very casual question.

The Virgin started as if out of a dream. She had not remembered the cardigan at all. 'Oh, yes! I'd forgotten,' she said, as she pulled herself away from O'Goat and trotted to the door of the flat.

For novice girls, you see, the most dangerous, or, depending on how you look at it, the most profitable times are not when they have deliberately decided to be naughty. That rarely ever happens. It is when they are simply not thinking.

Dr. O'Goat walked with a slow, deliberate step to the door, where Lisa was uselessly turning the handle. He unlocked it and gestured her in with an 'After you.'

It was during the two or three seconds between John's closing the door and his switching on the light in the sitting-room - it was during that brief moment of darkness - that the Virgin first suspected that there might be … might be something … calculated about the situation. But there was simply no time between that realization and the moment she did or said or heard the next thing - there was no time for her to make a decision.

'Sit down, please,' O'Goat said as he switched on the light. He sounded senior-lecturer-like, almost as if he was in his office on Academic Hill.

'No, thank you. I'm feeling so tired I'm afraid I might not get up at all if I sit down.' Lisa noticed that she was slightly breathless.

'Well, you can sleep here if you fear you're going to collapse on the way,' said O'Goat; the Virgin laughed a short dry laugh, and O'Goat added quickly, 'I have two beds here, and some feminine night things… the advantage of being divorced.' Dr. O'Goat fixed the girl against the door with his eye. Good Catholics were supposed to frown when you mentioned *divorce*. Lisa did not frown or show any kind of reaction. *The paralysis that strikes a spider's victim*, O'Goat was thinking, but he found his thought suddenly interrupted by a pang of paternal pity for the Virgin.

'I'll bring you your cardigan,' he said, and he sauntered into his bedroom, in a turmoil of emotion. *I'm being unfair to this poor innocent girl. I must let her go home at once.* Even you, John, he thought as he picked the cardigan up from the bed, even you must set a limit somewhere. He remembered the tiny, talkative American woman, and Lynne Horl - Oh no! and he dashed out of the bedroom.

'Here we are!' he said, stretching out his hand to

Lisa. The Virgin took two steps towards O'Goat, ready to take the cardigan. *Now she is … I really must make up to her. But how? You're becoming too wretchedly insensitive, John.* As the Virgin took the cardigan from him, O'Goat put an arm round her shoulders, drew her close to him and asked, flatly and barely audibly, 'How about a goodnight kiss?'

'What?' asked the Virgin. 'No, no, not tonight,' she said hastily and tried to duck and slip free under O'Goat's arm. But O'Goat put his other arm round her waist and squeezed her. His fear of failure was now taking over.

'Please!' he said looking down at the girl's hair and feeling his eyes slightly misty.

The Virgin's mind was now a glow-worm flashing dimly at a thousand-and-one screens. *Lord, he means it! Well, there's no one looking. It's a sin. Yes,* 'thou shalt not …' *But I haven't been any company to him …* drawn closer and closer to him. … *No, I shouldn't let myself … But how shall I face him again in the seminar-room if I refuse?* A hand under her chin, slowly raising her face towards the light. *A sin, a mortal sin;* her face tilted towards his face; 'Please, Lisa' again. *Inevitable.* And lips touch lips, and the Virgin feels the slight bristle of O'Goat's beard, but already her tongue is straining at his mouth.

Kissing for its own sake is such a rare practice in this part of the world that some people go even to the extent of generalizing that Africans do not kiss except in bed. Perhaps what we might venture to suggest is that to many girls here kissing is a very serious gesture. For them, there is no middle way-the peck sort of thing-with it. You either keep your hands off altogether or go all the way. Certainly Lisa's and O'Goat's two-minute lick-squeeze-and-wriggle had stretched a centimetre beyond the standard first-date goodnight kiss when they parted. Lisa laid her head on Dr. O'Goat's shoulder, her eyes moist with tears. Dr. O'Goat kept rubbing his hands over her back and squeezing her until he had regained his breath. He raised her mouth to his again. He pulled her handbag and her cardigan away from her hand and threw them down on to a stool beside them.

When their lips parted again, John O'Goat led the Virgin to the sofa and said, 'Let's sit down.'

That is just what Virgin Lisa needed. Her legs were weak, she was breathing heavily and there was a curious kind of hollowness in her chest. They sat perfectly still for some moments, and Lisa felt so calm that she could study the spines of the books on the shelves before her and, against the wall behind the shelves, the grand array of tribal spears from all over Africa, dominated by a huge Rwandese spear standing in the centre.

The glow-worm seemed to have disappeared under some thick shrub. But it started all over again, though dimmer and dimmer, as O'Goat pulled the Virgin to him and started all over again. *What will it feel like? 'Do not do it with any man,'* Mamma's voice, *'not even once, before you are married.' But how long should a girl keep her hands off life?* A hand removing her shoes and forcing her flat in the sofa. *I wonder what it will feel like.* Fingertips trotting up her thigh. *Oh, no! Pregnancy;* tugging at her panties. *My dress;*

a squeeze on her breast. *Oooh! just like a lift beginning to descend.* A turgid manhood straining against her thighs; heavy warm breath on her neck. *V.D.* The panties rolling down her legs. ...

But Senior Lecturer John O'Goat B.A. (Cantab.), M.A. (Lond.), Ph.D. (Inferno etc...) promised us no bed scenes. Moreover, there was nothing very spectacular about that time on the sofa, once it had got under way. For even the Virgin... well, you see, she was not quite a *virgin*. One of those teenage frolics common in co-educational schools: another brief moment when she had not been thinking. Only, that first time had been so unpleasant that she had kept her hands off for over four years now, till this evening.

They later left the sofa and went to bed, O'Goat triumphant and happy that death would not come that night, the Virgin disturbingly aware that she did not have a hand towel to 'touch the man' with. '*As important as the hoe,*' she had heard her tribeswomen say about that piece of cloth that every woman should wipe her partner and herself with after every *safari*. She found it difficult to convince herself that other tribes and peoples do quite happily without it.

*

But where had it begun? *Middlemarch*. The Virgin got quite puzzled about a point made by an F. R. Leavis regarding George Eliot. She wanted to ask Mutwe, but his explanations were always too complicated. She decided to 'dare' approach O'Goat. Everyone of course knew the stories about John O'Goat; but this was an absolute necessity. The examinations were only a few weeks away, and O'Goat was the authority on the English novel. She went to his office on Thursday morning, after the seminar, and O'Goat gave her such a good explanation(!) that she felt she knew everything about George Eliot.

O'Goat himself was very pleasantly surprised by Lisa's visit. For she was a girl he had not had the chance to speak to for any length of time. He had been marking her essays and noting that she worked hard though perhaps she was not very intelligent. And of course everyone knew and said that she was very beautiful. But O'Goat wondered whether, at his age and with his experience in women, beauty really touched him any more.

The call from the Cultural Centre came while the Virgin was still in the office. When O'Goat put down the receiver after a series of 'Yes... yes, yes, certainly, O.K. Thank you', he looked up at the girl and said, 'I wonder whoever gives these people our names!'

'Who are they?'

And he told her. He explained that they were showing a film with a rather exciting title. He said it in the original and then he translated for Lisa. Then, without either knowing what the words exactly meant, O'Goat asked her, 'Would you like to come?'

You know those moments when someone has been so good and kind to you that you are dying to find a solid gesture to express to him how really grateful you are...

When O'Goat awoke next morning, the Virgin was sleeping peacefully on her back beside him. Her lips were firmly closed, though, O'Goat thought, still half-smiling. Her breath was regular and very quiet. O'Goat rose slightly on his elbow and planted a light kiss on the sleeping lips. It was something almost entirely aesthetic, but when the girl stirred, O'Goat's animal passions rose. He pulled the Virgin to him and they had sex again. Lisa grabbed O'Goat's beard as they reached the crisis, and it was just about that moment that the tip of the Rwandese spear touched Mutwe's breast and he awoke, bathed in a cold pool of frightened sweat.

5 Ghosts

For about three minutes he lay quite still, his eyes fixed at the ceiling, grateful that this terror had been only a dream, as he thought, and yet paralysed by the sharp vividness with which it had struck him. Then he slowly raised his hand and looked at his watch. It was approaching seven-thirty. He turned over on his right side and switched on the small wireless set by the bed. The *Voice of Tchweza* was broadcasting *Sunday Morning Serenade* and the announcer had done the rare and curious thing of including a French tune among his choices. Mutwe joined his hands on the pillow under his head and looked at the ceiling as he listened to *La Génération Perdue*. He wondered how the announcer had come to choose the tune.

He had mispronounced its title and the name of the singer, and he did not seem to know what it meant. Well, *Voice of Tchweza* announcers mispronounced everything, and did not seem to know anything either. It had been largely due to their laziness that efforts to africanize 'Montania', Tchweza's colonial name, had failed. Perhaps the only thing that they knew how to pronounce was the President's name, for each of them found himself obliged to utter this so many times during the course of his duties that somehow it got stuck in his head.

But beyond that, nothing was pronounceable, or, more accurately, had to be pronounced correctly. Not even the name of the Party, the Tchweza Socialist Union.

When the announcers said it in full, they invariably forgot the initial *T* in *Tchweza*, a cause of profound annoyance to His Excellency the Head of the Executive, since in his own tribal language, *chweza* meant only the rather unpolitic act of *love-play*. And they came up with so many versions of *Socialist* that, unless you were exceptionally lucky and your version happened to be uttered, you were bound to miss the word. And when they tried to abbreviate it to *T.S.U.* six times out of ten they called it *T.C.U.*, causing confusion between the Party and the Town Cleaners' Union, a remnant of the colonial trade union movement; and the other four times they read it backwards or starting from the middle. Perhaps there was some valid excuse for these slips over political terms. For the announcers were civil servants and were, therefore, according to the constitution, supposed to keep their hands off politics.

But they talked about *parliah-ment*, and *mini-stars* (radio version of ministers), and they sometimes came up with such ingenious things as *Brightons* (radio version of *Britons*). And, in the news bulletins, for example, for every ten times the reader mentioned Tchweza or Tchwezan, there were ninety *Britaynes*, *Breeshes* or *Brightons*. For, apart from Tchwezan news, which simply meant what the President had said, the rest of the bulletin was invariably London news. So, things reached a stage where the radio distortions forced many people, especially the *Brightons* at the University, to suggest to the *Mini-Star* of Information and Broadcasting that he should get some (colonial-voiced expatriate) volunteers to act as announcers until such time as ...

But that would not have solved all the problems. One of the necessary conditions for being an expatriate volunteer was that you had to mispronounce every African name, when you had to pronounce one. One expatriate guest commentator on the *Voice of Tchweza*, for example, discussing the affairs of a neighbouring state, kept pronouncing the name of the President there in such a way that to most Tchwezan listeners, especially those in the north, he seemed to be saying 'President Flying-Fox' all the time. How then would volunteers have managed with that name that made Tchwezan daily news?

Then there were the Swahili announcers. These spoke the people's lingua franca with such an exquisite *ki-settlah* accent that if any expatriate announcer was recruited it should have been to replace *them*. And they did not translate the news bulletins into Kiswahili at all. The so-called Swahili bulletins were a mad mixture of Kiswahili, English and Anglo-Swahili words, *ki-settlered* off with the most thorough indifference: a bastard no-man's-language apparently calculated to uncommunicate. The belief, surviving from colonial times, was that a radio announcer did not have to be well-trained, or even educated at all. Any third-grade 'O Level' thing would do.

Such a good title wasted on trivial words, Mutwe was thinking as the music of *Lost Generation* died away when the announcer exclaimed 'Wonderful! Wonderful!', mentioned Franco and the African Fiesta and returned to the daily bread of the *Voice of Tchweza*, a Congolese guitar melee. For African music meant post-colonial Congolese guitar rhapsodies. The sweat had dried on his body now, and he felt sticky under his pyjamas. Then he remembered he had to get up at once if he was going to get breakfast and get to Holy Mass on time, at eight-thirty.

*

There were many things one did in Maalas for lack of better things to do. For many students, and quite a handful of lecturers, church-going was one of these. But the Catholics, who flocked to their chapel in surprisingly encouraging numbers every Sunday had a better reason for their devotion - habit. It just didn't feel like Sunday without Mass: one simply had to go there to make things look real somehow. This is not, however, to deny or minimize the importance of a small but concentrated group of those who attended out of genuine conviction, and people like Mutwe among the Catholics, or Kale, Peso, and especially the Bishop among the Protestants, are a case in point.

The services themselves were, well, very average - which is not saying very much for a church service anywhere in the world. In the Catholic chapel, for example, this came something very close to the chaotic. Some two or three years before this story, a huge group of bishops had sat in Rome with the intention of modernizing the church: reviewing such topics as birth-control and the marriage of priests (both of which they tossed back to the Pope without making any favourable decision on them), and the streamlining of public worship.

This streamlining they handled with brusque and brutal efficiency as was demonstrated, for example, by the abolition of the use of Latin in church services. Generally, this meant, as the old people in Mutwe's home parish put it, that 'the faith was spoilt'. For with the vernaculars came intelligibility, and with that, all the magic flew out of the faith. Who cares to go to a witch-doctor who speaks ordinary every-day language? In Maalas in particular, the vernacularization, meaning in fact the Anglicizing, of worship meant buying hurriedly-printed 'standard texts' which kept changing as rapidly as the issues of a newspaper. And no one wanted to spend dear money on religious texts instead of a bottle of 'booze'.

So, those who had Latin mass books with English translations, translations as different from one another as *Das Kapital* is from the Bible, insisted on using them, while those who bad depended on their memories for the Latin responses, and did not have an inkling of what they sounded like in English, simply chimed in in Latin, across the five hundred or so different English versions: creating a veritable pan - well, *panangelium*. For it was all aimed at Heaven.

Secondly, the vernacularization meant that even the little singing that there had been in the Mass was taken out. No one had experimented with any serious singing in English before, and attempts to chant, say, the *Credo* in this savage language sounded too uproariously funny to suit any form of church decorum. In a word, the confusion reached such proportions at one time that a group of militant Catholics drew up huge posters demanding a Latin High ~lass and posted them on the door of their Chaplain, who ignored them.

The Chaplain was an ancient American who always began his sermons by losing his temper. or rather by cracking excellent jokes, in English, and then losing his temper because no one laughed. Old crank of a priest! To imagine that people went to church to be amused! or, worse, that English was a language for cracking jokes in! One learnt English in order to earn one's living. To say, if one was, say, a lawyer, 'Eat ease my hamboh sabmishen, your hannah …' (It is my humble submission, your Honour, in colonial British), or, 'I which to catchegolicary refuche the allegation…' (I wish to categorically refute the allegation), if one was a politician - that is, a government artist.

For Mutwe, however, there was now added spice to church-going, as indeed to so many other things, since his presenting his credentials to Virgin Lisa, as the Maalas saying went. For she was always there at Mass, radiant in her Sunday best, and, after the sermon, she and her room-mate Immaculate, a girl as charming as she was plain, would take up the collection. Whether it was the American Chaplain or some other mind that had decided to have girls, and especially Virgin Lisa, make the Sunday collection, it was a very ingenious plan. Especially in the case of the boys, who were an overwhelming majority, it was felt quite a shame to be approached by a girl and drop nothing on the plate or, worse, drop there a mere piece of copper.

As he went up the chapel steps this Sunday morning, Mutwe was in a curiously flustered mood. He felt a kind of anxious eagerness to see Virgin Lisa, who, for about a month now, had come to be the only link between him and reality - the reality of fear, the reality of joy, the reality of hope, the reality of sorrow, the inexhaustible reality of the imagination. They had parted after lunch on Saturday, at the august gates of Margaret Plantagenet, under the gorgon eyes of its inmates. Lisa had said she would be going to visit her uncle, the Director of a huge Ideological College some eight kilometres south of the city, and she would not be coming back till late in the evening. Mutwe had asked if he could come with her, but the Virgin answered 'No', adding that her uncle did not expect or wish her to have any boy yet, let alone a boy from another tribe, and another country. For Lisa was Tchwezan.

This kind of talk always crushed Mutwe. It was like the air suddenly turning solid, rocky and thorny in your face just as you started to run. Why couldn't people, for once, forget tribes, or at least forget to talk about them? After all, they forgot so many important and meaningful things. Ministers got detained, and people forgot them. Government artists on the wrong side of government got hanged or 'eliminated somehow', and people forgot them. Workers' children were born and reared in rotting hovels, in stinking, undrained, unlit, unmentioned slums, which they inherited if Fate was cruel enough to let them live to maturity - and no one remembered them.

Mutwe shrugged such a painful 'Well' that Lisa found it necessary to add, 'Well, we meet at breakfast tomorrow, or at Mass.'

That was sincere enough. But a lie, a necessary lie, had already been told. No university girl, except the now-rusticated Miriam, could have had the courage to tell anyone that she was going to John O'Goat's house or that she was *going out* with John O'Goat - certainly not after his divorce.

For the inhabitants of Maalas Campus, with the exception of the 'rebels', were very *decent* people, very careful to show only that side of things which the society wanted to see. Things like kissing or holding hands in public, or even smiling at a member of the opposite sex, were considered intolerably obscene, and no one, not even the rebels, dared do them. Perhaps nobody cared for these empty demonstrations when deep inside they knew that the first thing any couple did once there was no one looking was to strip and have a 'munch'.

As he entered the chapel, Mutwe was contemplating doing something utterly unprecedented: braving the girls' pews and sitting next to Virgin Lisa. For not even before God, not even in the chapel, did sexual apartheid break down. Not that it was imposed on anyone, as was and still is the case in many 'bush' churches. It was simply the natural thing to do. And perhaps here it had the sanctification of time and psychology. For no matter how civilized man may become, so long as he remains religious, he will not relinquish the belief that 'commerce with women', to quote St. Paul, is incompatible with divine worship.

This, incidentally, was one of the theological arguments against women being ordained priests. For, with that meeting in Rome, a gang of emancipated women had raised a din about their ambition to become priests, even in the Holy Catholic Church. The catholic common man's, and common woman's objection, however, was simple: 'I wouldn't tell a woman my sins; I can't have a woman hearing my confession.'

But I think the first reason is more basic, and in a way the source of all the other arguments. Are we not all, especially the men, a little embarrassed at the thought that we were once injected formless into a woman's womb? that for quite a significant fraction of our lives we camped there, determined but helpless colonists and exploiters, until time and woman decided to throw us, and all our acquisitions in there, out? We may even venture the suggestion that the verve with which some men, in the name of love or free love or living naturally or having a good time, set against women's receptacles is in some way a compensation for the chagrin that this thought breeds. But there begins the vicious circle.

*

Mutwe did not join the girls' benches. For one thing, there were already enough females on them to frighten off even the bravest freedom fighter. For another, even as Mutwe paced up the aisle, his heart pounding more and more heavily, his legs feeling lighter and lighter with excitement, he could see that the Virgin was not there. She would be a little late. It was now only a minute to eight-thirty. And that old American was one of the few, very few whites in Maalas who kept time.

After all, everyone (meaning every Anglo-Saxon man and woman who had heard of the Empire and Commonwealth), everyone knew that Africans did not mind anything starting forty-five minutes late. (Between you and me, I am very African on that point: I wouldn't mind my death starting some forty-five years late.)

But it was curious. The Virgin was never a second late for anything. She was not in the cafeteria when Mutwe left. He had assumed that she was already in the chapel. He now scrutinized the rows of girls again as he knelt only a pew behind them and absent-mindedly crossed himself. There was no doubt - Virgin Lisa was not there.

Needless to say, Mutwe did not pray, or rather, said only one prayer, and that to no known god in heaven or hell: that Virgin Lisa should come; that this longest of all the long masses he had attended during all the long twenty-five years of his life should not end before she came. But, from the *'I will go unto the altar of God'* to the *'Go forth, the Mass is ended'*, Virgin Lisa was not there. Not even in spirit. For she was sleeping peacefully in the bedroom of Flat No.5, Hekima Road, in John O'Goat's arms.

After Mass, Mutwe braved a gang of women on the chapel steps and somehow managed to get out Immaculate, the Virgin's room-mate. 'What happened to your friend?'

he asked, and, as if to offset any suggestions of personal interest, quickly added, 'Why did she leave you to make the collection alone today?'

'Lisa didn't come back last night,' Immaculate said with a touch of genuine care in her voice, though Mutwe could not tell whether it was care for him or for Lisa, or for both. 'You know she went to see her uncle at the Ideological College. They might have kept her till very late.'

'Yes, I guess so.' Mutwe had felt a pang of - something like pain - on learning that the Virgin had slept out. But Immaculate's explanation was a straw you could cling to.

And she was continuing: 'You know, she hadn't been to see them for quite a long time. I remember the last time she was there - we went together - was a week before the strike.'

'Didn't she go there during the "exile"?' Mutwe asked.

'Oh no I she wouldn't dare, and no one in their right senses would.'

Immaculate told Mutwe about the Ideological College and about its Director, Virgin Lisa's uncle. Well, if you followed rigid foreign classifications, you would only call him close clansman. (Mutwe had never been, and probably never would go to the Ideological College. Apart from a dozen or so Chinese, Russian and East German tutors, and one Ghanaian socialist who was the Bursar, no non-nationals were permitted to enter the grounds of the College, under any pretext.)

Lisa's 'uncle' was a founding member of the T.S.U., started by the now President of the Republic as the MAO, the Montania African Organisation. Some years before Independence, he had received one of the few 'MAO scholarships' and gone to America where he read Public Administration and Political Science. The Americans, you know, are so mechanical-minded that they do not have any *Government Arts*. Some people whispered that Mr. Kabachi, Lisa's uncle, had failed in everything in America. Some members of the Opposition, before it was made illegal to oppose, used to shout it out from public platforms in fact. But if it was true that he had failed, everyone knew that the Americans were racists and segregationists. In any case, America is so far away.

Moreover, Mr. Kabachi was such a staunch Party supporter that, regardless of any academic contribution he could make, he was the ideal choice for an ideal Ideological College. And perhaps his failure in America would only endear him all the more to any thinking socialist: it simply meant that he had successfully refused to absorb and accept that country's capitalist, imperialist and neo-colonialist ideals, in spite of all the vigorous indoctrination and frequent threats of failure made by CIA men masquerading as state university lecturers. (These were not Immaculate's comments: but the author has heard them made by another American-failed socialist and thinks that they help to explain Bwana Kabachi's success and popularity.)

Certainly Bwana Kabachi, after several trips to Cuba, East Germany, Russia and China, was a thorough and unshakeable revolutionary socialist. Immaculate told Mutwe that when she and Lisa visited him, he spoke so violently against the University - even before the strike - calling it a bourgeois, colonial, anti-revolution, reactionary ivory tower, that, Immaculate thought, if he had had the power, he would have turned it into a pigsty.

'I've even told the President: I'm ashamed that it should be called the People's University at all,' Bwana Kabachi had told the girls, 'but he says we've got to start somewhere, and changing its name wasn't a bad start,'

How much better it is, Mutwe was thinking, *to be colonial, to be bourgeois, to be anti-revolution, to be reactionary and to be an ivory tower than to be what the People' University of Maalas is: a stagnant cesspool of rolling nothingness. For how can you be anything before you ever even begin to think of what you are?*

'So you understand why no university student would have dared meet Mr. Kabachi before the dust of the strike had settled, certainly not his niece.'

'Yes,' Mutwe said unenthusiastically as they came upon Hekima Road and started going up Residential Hill. Religion was of such purely academic interest that the chapels, and the mosque, were sited on Academic Hill. 'Even now, I only hope she hasn't been crucified for all our ivory tower sins.'

But Immaculate had just realized that she had carried on the Conversation too long. 'I'm going this way,' she said, and she turned up Hekima Road towards a path which went round the boys' halls to Margaret Plantagenet.

'O.K. Mutwe said, He knew she did not want to be seen walking alone with him, and the reason was floating in the very air they breathed. 'I might come over in the afternoon, if I don't meet you at lunch,' and he went up the irregular steps to Windsor Castle.

*

Julius Kabachi, the Director of the Ideological College, was a colourful, indeed a dazzling man. And, what with his relationship to Virgin Lisa and her room-mate's acquaintance with him, the Virgin's choice of his name and his house to cover up her date with Senior Lecturer John O'Goat had been quite ingenious. About ten-thirty that Sunday morning, Virgin Lisa was back at the maidens' hall, Margaret Plantagenet, and she was all kindness and sweetness to her room-mate.

'Weren't you afraid, alone in the room, my dear Imma?'

'I was more worried about you, Liz,' said Immaculate, looking up from the cyclostyled hand-out she was reading. 'Shall I mix you a drink? We've got some orange squash in there,' she added as she pointed at the dwarf locker between their bookshelves.

'No, thanks, I'm all right, Imma,' said the Virgin, rubbing her eyes, I had breakfast before I came up.'

This was not a lie. She had had breakfast with John O'Goat before coming up: coffee, toast and bacon and eggs. Lisa fried the eggs while O'Goat boiled the water

129

for the coffee, and they ate in the kitchen, in silence. John O'Goat felt a sort of dull emptiness as he watched the Virgin's breast gently heave under his divorced wife's light-blue negligee. Lisa liked the bacon and tried to remember when she had last tasted it. For no pig products were served in the university cafeteria, owing to the strong muslim element in the population, though this was more true of the cooks than of the students.

There was a large pool of Ismaili students, it is true. But the muslim element in the African student population was negligible. And the Ismailis did not really matter where diet was concerned. They were always on special diet. The Islamic missions to Africa, you see, built only Koranic schools, which did not teach English. The few African muslim children who wanted to learn English had until only recently often found themselves turned away from the Christian schools, and from the Ismaili schools. The first few Muslims to get into the schools in any significant numbers, after *uhuru*, had barely completed their '0 Level' and would not be at the People's University for another few years.

'Excellent!' O'Goat said, jumping down from a comer of the ledge that went round the kitchen. He put his arms round Lisa from behind as she rose from her chair and put her cup in the sink. He kissed her on both cheeks, murmuring, 'Sweet little thing..

It did not feel bad, but Lisa did not want to start all over again. 'I must be getting home,' she said.

'Home?' O'Goat asked, 'to M.P.?'

'Yes. I don't know what Imma's thinking, and I've missed Mass.'

'Missed what?'

'The Sunday service,' Lisa simplified as O'Goat let go of her and she collected the used plates and put them in the sink. 'Today is Sunday.'

'Oh, so it is' said O'Goat, putting a cigarette in his mouth. 'Is it a sin to miss Mass on Sunday?'

A keen observer, which O'Goat was not at this moment, fortunately, would have noticed Virgin Lisa's violent start. She had not expected anyone, least of all this Adam with whom she had just munched the fruit, to call things by what were, in catholic terminology, their right names.

'Mind if I smoke?' O'Goat asked, striking a match and inadvertently averting what to Lisa would have been an awkward silence. For she was not going to answer O'Goat's other question.

'You're sure you don't want a lift to your hall?' O'Goat asked her, after she had washed and dressed.

'I'll be all right, thank you,' Lisa said, seized now by a strong desire she could not explain to get away. O'Goat kissed her lightly on the lips, opened the door for her and stood there watching her walk up to the road...

'Ah!' sighed the Virgin as she sat down on her bed and kicked off her shoes. She smiled sweetly as she noticed that Immaculate had turned in her chair and was looking at her. Immaculate's eyes were always adoring, and every woman, even the vainest, regards it as a special achievement or

131

blessing to be admired by another woman. 'What are you reading?' Lisa asked Immaculate.

'Today's sermon,' answered the other girl, and Lisa felt a pang of remorse go through her heart. For three years she had not once missed Sunday Mass. And now there was going to be a gap in her collection of the ancient American's sermons, which he always cyclostyled and handed out after the service. Or perhaps there would be no gap...?

'Did you remember to bring me a copy, Imma? You know, just I couldn't make it back on - '

'Yes, I did,' said Imma, pulling another copy of the sermon from under her own, 'though you didn't deserve one after leaving me to make the collection alone.'

'Oh, dear, dear sweet Imma!' The Virgin was at Immaculate's desk now, and she hugged her fondly. Then, suddenly, the Virgin noticed that she was more keenly aware of the touch of human flesh than she ever remembered being before. She had hugged Immaculate heaps of times before, but she had never felt like this. She let go of Immaculate, picked up the hand-out and walked back to her bed, looking at the title of the sermon and asking quietly:

'What was Mass like today?'

'Well, the usual sort of thing,' answered Immaculate, 'the girls dumb as usual, and the boys simply chaotic. Hardly ten people went to Communion.'

The Virgin felt something rush up her frame again. When it got to her brain, it was interpreted as the realization that she would not, could not be going to

Communion again until she had confessed, told a priest, that she had slept with a man, a divorced, which to the priest would mean married, man; that they had done it so many times, *et cetera*. You know, when you have been at this sort of thing time and again, and telling priests about it, it becomes quite easy and natural. But the first few times... it also depends on the kind of priest you tell.

'Were there any announcements?' the Virgin asked, trying to push that confession thought under.

'Nothing particular,' Immaculate said. Then she remembered suddenly, 'Oh yes! Father Schmoll said he wouldn't be around on Saturday, and he has put confessions on Wednesday afternoon.'

Wednesday afternoon was free at the People's University of Maalas, a practice inherited from... from some colonial country. 'I wanted to put in an announcement that you didn't come back last night.'

'What?'

'Well' Immaculate oiled her voice, 'I'm only joking.' Then she continued with a fair amount of seriousness, 'But I was quite worried last night. You know you hadn't told me you'd be staying out overnight.'

'I hadn't told anyone, Imma: I didn't know I wouldn't be coming back.' The Virgin wished she could make her confession to Imma.

'That actually was one of my worries. I feared you might get into trouble with the gate dogs if you came in late.' Immaculate meant the *askaris* and custodians. "You remember O'Goat's Miriam?'

The Virgin's eyes flashed up from the sermon papers in her lap, and, lest Imma should notice the bewilderment in them, back to the papers. But now she was not reading at all. Every word that Immaculate said seemed to be calculated to accuse her.

'Excuse me,' she said and went out of the room and into the wash-room. Not particularly because she needed it, but because she wanted to be alone, even if for only a few moments. But when she was inside, she thought she might as well go through the ritual. She made what was in fact a short call. But she did not rise immediately. She remained sitting there on the toilet seat for over two minutes, her elbows on her thighs, just about where a moderately crazy mini-skirt would stop, and her face between her hands, thinking nothing, but subconsciously deciding that she had to be thick-skinned, now that 'things had happened'.

When she rose, she looked into the closet-basin, at her urine, before she pressed the Bush-handle. She had read about the causes and symptoms of venereal diseases and, since getting up that morning, she had been watching herself carefully. But nothing unusual had happened. She might get away with it … At one of the basins, she washed her hands and, for a reason that she could not stop to find out, her face. She did not wipe her hands on the roll of towel in the comer, but simply shook them dry, dotting the cement floor with irregular lines of tiny water drops. Fortunately, she did not meet anyone in the corridor on her way to and back from the toilet.

*

'At one time I even wondered whether you might have fallen into the hands of the City Cleaning Squad,' Immaculate resumed as the Virgin threw herself on her bed with a deep sigh.

The idea of the C.C.S. had been sparked off by a militant group of Party youth wingers who had sworn to make sure that every trace of bourgeois, reactionary and anti-socialist practices was stamped out of Tchweza, starting with the capital. They did quite a good job in Maalas, for they knew their city well and easily concentrated on the most notorious pools of depravity. They helped to report rogues to the police. They paraded in the market-places, with five-shilling notes peeping out of their pockets, so that they caught pick-pockets red-handed. They pretended to respond to prostitutes' solicitations and then, taking them to quiet places, they gave them such thorough and sound beatings that, even if they remained unrepentant, they would be 'out of use' for at least a fortnight. In short, they struck such general terror into the whole of Maalas that any would-he bourgeois, reactionary and anti-socialist liver would think twice before he embarked on that dangerous course.

But the campaign gradually reached an alarming degree of intensity and zeal. As, for example, when the youth wingers stormed the shop of an old Pakistani trader, broke his shelves and scattered his tubes of perfumes, bleaches and other cosmetics: for they considered these bourgeois and anti-socialist. This interfered with the traffic, for all the women and girls nearby rushed on to the street to try and stuff their handbags, shopping bags, or even their dresses and cloaks with as many of these tubes of bourgeois beauty as they could grab before the youth wingers chased them away. The Pakistani shopkeeper filed a suit against the Party, and quite a few hundred thousand shillings had to go to make good the damages.

Time and again they undressed girls on the streets for wearing mini-skirts or glad necks. Quite a number of people were beginning to ask in whispers of course, which was more black-socialist: walking down the street in a mini-skirt, or running to your house in, sometimes torn, knickers and a brassiere only. This latter was certainly more revolutionary than reactionary, for not many girls had dared do it before the glorious days of this movement.

Once the youth caught three young ladies who they thought had made up their faces to a bourgeois degree. They seized them, dragged them to the beach and washed their faces in the lake-water, scrubbing the lipstick off their brown-purple lips with the sand. The group which carried out this particular operation was quite large. While a few wingers were performing the purificatory rites, the others were chanting Party songs and reciting quotations from the writings of the 'Father of the Nation', the President of the T.S.U., and of Tchweza.

But the blacks could suffer by the million and no one would say a word for them. Things only came to a head when the youth wingers caught a fat old American tourist staggering drunk down the main street at about one in the morning. They dragged him to a quiet, deserted back street and bound him tight to a lamp-post, where he kept struggling and shouting until, totally exhausted, he closed his eyes and went to sleep in his posture of modified crucifixion. An Indian who lived some metres away from the spot - all the permanent residents of the city centre were Asian - saw him when he opened his window at about seven in the morning. But he was too frightened to approach him, especially as the American woke up at just about that time and started howling again.

Gradually, a crowd, including pressmen, gathered round him and stood making comments about the American or laughing but completely ignoring his barklike prayers to them to set him free. At exactly eight-thirty, the youth wingers arrived, chanting Party slogans and quoting from the 'Father's works'. They released their victim with an unnecessary and horribly-phrased warning to him to behave better the next time.

The following day, the Tchwezan Mail reported the incident and carried what by any standards would be described as a scathing editorial on it and all previous similar incidents, and against the youth wingers. The Editor called on the Government to act and asked the police to let no one, whoever he be, take the law into his own hands. *'These savages and gangsters'* wrote the Mail, *'terrorizing innocent citizens and violating the sacred laws of hospitality by torturing visitors to this country, all in the name of black socialism and revolution, will bring nothing but shame and ruin upon Tchweza, damaging the good image that her leaders are struggling to give her both here and abroad ...'* The *Tchwezan Mail* was the only independent English daily in Tchweza. It was owned by a London-based firm, one of the two which controlled all the independent papers, English and vernacular, in all these countries, including Rhodesia. It was quite popular and it had a fairly long history. It first appeared somewhere in the late thirties as the *Colonial Mail*, and it had actually retained that name until six months *after* Uhuru. One of those feats of courage which the British accomplish because they set about them so unobtrusively.

Even now, its headlines were never significantly different from those of any London paper, and it always carried front-page photos of London, Liverpool or some other gigantic British village. It was the The *Colonial*, or rather the *Tchwezan Mail* which carried that small ads pages with the '*European - owned*' nonsense tag accompanying every ramshackle second-hand car advertisement.

The other English daily was a Party paper, an illegibly-printed, depressingly badly-written and clumsily-edited excuse-for-having-no- paper that was as full of the President of the Republic - not pictures, for those were never visible even on the rare occasions when they were printed (!)-as the *Voice of Tchweza* was.

That very day that the editorial appeared, six youth wingers went to the house of Mr. Todd, the Editor of the Mail. It was about twelve- thirty, and the cook told the callers that *Bwana* had not yet come home. They waited for him. As soon as the tall, elegant bachelor parked his car at the foot of the steps to his door, the youth wingers pulled him out and set on him, shouting: 'Bloody imperialist... stinking racist... go to South Africa! This is not Rhodesia!' *et cetera*. His cook-cum-houseboy, who had run to open the door for his master, noticed what was happening and, banging the door shut, he ran to the telephone, dialled 999 and screamed.

The police came, and, for once in many months if not years, they came immediately. If the police had moved at their normal pace, the youth wingers would probably have lynched Mr. Todd. Perhaps the cook's screams on the phone had helped. The police ordered the youths to stop their operation, and the youths refused. After a short pitched battle, the six boys were captured and bundled on to a police Land-Rover. Later, at a court hearing, they were each given three years in jail for assault. But they served only a month of that. By some process of law which it would be very difficult to explain to a non-government-artist, they were taken out of prison and released by a special order from the *Mini-star* of Internal Affairs.

The truth was that the *wazee* in Government sympathized with the youth wingers. Not only because they were staunch, vigorous, enthusiastic and very vocal but fortunately ignorant Party members; but also because they, the people in power, too, felt that something had to be done about the growing lawlessness in the country and the moral degeneration in the capital. Only, they did not know how to set about it. How could they legislate or even use the existing laws against these plagues without incurring a dangerous amount of unpopularity? For, even in one-party states, popularity matters, as one inevitably discovers soon after outlawing the opposition.

Moreover, nearly all the policemen in Maalas, quite a large number of the M.P.s and several of the ministers frequented illegal drinking houses and prostitutes of one class or another, for example. How could you hope to launch a successful attack on these evils? This is the ruler's classic conflict of what you find is good for life and what you know is necessary for order.

Fortunately for the Tchwezan leaders, the youth wingers, in their enthusiasm, and owing to lack of anything constructive to spend their bubbling energies upon, had stepped in to resolve the conflict with their country-cleaning campaign. Their activities, however, had reached such a stage that they could not be left to continue without embarrassment to the President, to the Party and to the Government.

So, they had been ordered off the Maalas streets, and a squadron of the Special Security Police, designated the City Cleaning Squad, had been called in to keep an eye on rogues, pick-pockets and street- walkers. The C.C.S. were quite 'tough', and they had bundled quite a few people into their jeeps and off to the police cells. But, needless to say, they did not do anything with the same gusto and verve as the youth wingers had shown during the few months of their mission.

Hell, isn't she going to drop this ever? Lisa was thinking as

Immaculate mentioned her fear that she might have .been detained by the City Cleaning Squad. Lisa tried to lie as still as she could.

'Though even the C.C.S.,' Immaculate continued as she came and stood by Virgin Lisa's bed, looking down at her, 'would have eyes to see that such an innocent and sweet thing as you couldn't be a street-walker.'

A devil's agent, thought Lisa, *or perhaps God's? Whichever, she is positively torturing me now.* She closed her eyes and she thought about herself and about 'street-walkers', with that cover of Imma's euphemism peeled off. *What are harlots? Women who sleep with men... who are not their husbands.*

'Are you sleepy, Liz?'

'Yes, rather,' the Virgin said. She now felt wretched and vile, and she was painfully aware that she was lying as she went on, 'It's that woman; she kept me talking into the night.'

'Your uncle's wife?'

'Yes. You know how talkative she is.' The Virgin felt slightly better for stating this fact, and subconsciously suppressed the observation that even it was misplaced in the context.

'She was cross-examining you about the strike?' Immaculate's mind was drifting to Mutwe.

'Yes,' said the Virgin, inwardly cursing this bloody girl for keeping on at her like that, 'and her husband is still as angry with us as ever,'

'Mutwe was right,' said Immaculate almost jubilantly, stupidly; 'he feared you -'

'You saw him?' asked the Virgin, opening her eyes suddenly and then closing them again when Imma started to speak.

'Yes, at Mass. And he talked to me after Mass.'

'Did he ask -'

'Well, my dear Liz, better have a nap. I'll wake you up for lunch.'

Imma was at the door as she said the last word, and now she went out of the room.

The Virgin gazed at the closed door for some moments, then she shrugged, turned to the wall and closed her eyes again. She thought about Mutwe, for the first time in many hours. *A voice, a very individual voice. Eyes, peculiar eyes: they make you feel so self-conscious, all the time …*

Suddenly remembering, she jumped up and undressed. She took off everything and threw on her dressing gown. She rolled up all the clothes she had taken off, including the pink dress, and threw them into a pail at the foot of her bed. She would wash them after lunch. Not that they were dirty: only too full of 'memories'.

The Virgin lay back on the bed and looked at the ceiling. She felt much more at ease now that she had removed all those trappings of elegance, Physically she felt very well in fact. Perhaps sex was good for the body, as some manuals claimed. Even inwardly, she would be all right, she thought, provided Imma stopped talking, or did not keep saying the wrong things all the time at least …

*

It all seemed to be working. They did not meet Mutwe at lunch, but he came over to M.P, in the late afternoon and he sat on Lisa's bed, while Lisa sat on the chair at her desk. He shared their biscuits and orange squash with them and gravely cracked those jokes that only he could make. He swallowed whole the story of Lisa's visit to her uncle at the Ideological College. He left a few minutes after two women had 'hacked' loud and long laughs at the door of his friends' room.

Virgin Lisa 'was in fact mistaken to imagine that all was quiet and safe as far as the campus was concerned. At the Ghala Toplife, while Virgin Lisa had been thinking about her mother surrounded by her little ones, and John O'Goat recalling Lynne Horley, the Principal Secretary to the Ministry of Planning and Economic Development had come up, accompanied by a second-year female undergraduate in the Social Sciences. They had been looking for someone, and not finding him there, they had left immediately. But the girl did not fail to notice Virgin Lisa, and, seeing her in the company of O'Goat, she felt her socio-scientific curiosity keenly excited. She somehow managed to persuade the Principal Secretary to take her back to the campus that evening, and as soon as she got to Margaret Plantagenet, she told her room-mate about her 'new find'.

The two girls were not church-goers or, rather, one had been until she was dissuaded from it by the sweet peacefulness with which her room-mate snored on Sunday morning. So, about nine that fateful Sunday morning, waking up unusually early for them, they went for a walk along Hekima Road. It was in fact a disguised patrol in the vicinity of the block which contained Flat No. 5.

It was quite a long watch and, to the other girl, who was a mathematician, it looked like an eternity. But finally, as they leaned idly on the railing of a bridge over the dry valley between Residential Hill and a new staff housing estate, called the Annexe, they spotted Virgin Lisa, walking out of Flat No. 5. The 'discovery' had been established. They could start talking.

*

Mutwe sat huddled in the blue-cushioned arm-chair at the foot of his bed, sharply experiencing one of those moments of self-encounter that we call sorrow, or joy: joy when the self you meet is the self that you expected to meet, sorrow when it is not.

Rumours, nay, reliable news, that Lisa had been 'munched' by Senior Lecturer John O'Goat had begun to spread the very morning that Mutwe attended the Lisa-less Catholic Mass. The two 'detectives' waited at the bridge, still and quiet as statues, until Virgin Lisa had disappeared behind the palm bushes and the cashew trees. They cautiously stalked her into Margaret Plantagenet. First, they ran to their own room, just a floor above Lisa's, and they laughed, threw themselves on one of the beds, patted each other's thighs and hugged each other with such violent joy that an observer would have imagined that they had won a final victory over death.

'Wonder whether she's been at it before,' panted Stella, the mathematician, as soon as she could get enough breath back.

'I don't think so,' answered Diana, the one who had been to the Ghala Toplife with the Principal Secretary. 'Someone should've noticed. Moreover, there was Miriam.'

'Miriam never gave a damn who O'Goat fucked'; you had to have eavesdropped at the windows of Margaret Plantagenet to believe that ladies, or any woman, could be as verbally violent as Stella was now. 'And that Lisa is quite sly; behind all that show of softness and innocence!'

'Your good, holy, religious girls!' Through some form of vocal ingenuity Diana managed to make these words sound upside down. The two girls howled with laughter, so loudly in fact that one of their next-door neighbours came over and opened the door without knocking.

'What is it, Diana?' she asked, looking at the two girls' flushed faces.

'A discovery, Julie!' Stella announced, wiping away a tear from the corner of her left eye, 'a discovery!'

'A saint has been dethroned,' Diana clinched it.

This interested Julia - all the girls referred to one another by their European names, and for official records they all gave their fathers' names as their surnames - for Julia, a tall dark, thin girl with hair that always remained as short as a boy's, was Catholic; and, though one of the many who did not know what they believed or ever even bothered to check whether they believed at all, she liked hearing about saints.

'A saint?' Julia asked, coming into the room and closing the door behind her, for she was aware the other girls were talking inconsiderately loudly.

'Ye-es!' Diana copied a sound she had heard from, who was it?, on some film sound-track. 'A saint, your saint.'

With Stella filling in some details here and there, Diana told the story to Julia. Diana would have been what you might call a typical northern Muntu woman: light chocolate, of medium height, fleshy rather than fat, with shapely round legs, tiny fine wrists, generous lips, large dark-brown eyes and tough curls of glossy coal-black hair. But she had worked so hard at beautifying herself that it was now very difficult to talk intelligently about her identity.

Her hair was constantly struggling half-way between its original curl and the new blown-up, straightened tresses she 'roasted' it into. When she was not wearing stockings, her face, somewhere between the anaemic and the Afro-Asian half-caste, contrasted almost distressingly with her legs and thighs, which never seemed to receive or to respond to any cosmetics. Her ears too were much darker than her face, but those were normally covered by her hair or by gigantic, flowery ear-rings. In brief, she was the normal sort of thing that you would expect to find with any active Principal Secretary on a Saturday evening.

Julia supplied another link in the story, for she had been to the chapel, to 'realize' her Sunday, and she had observed that Imma had made the collection all by herself. Then Julia suddenly remembered something.

'But Lisa is going with the "Philosopher",' she said. (That was the nickname the girls had given to Mutwe.)

'All philosophers are either impotent or homosexual, my dear Julie,' Diana said in her defiantly nasal and barely feminine voice, which reminded one of some naughty and harlotish film actress.

'Go read your *Symposium*.'

Stella added, slightly shocking Julie, 'Even Christ has been declared a homosexual ...'

This then was the self that the Philosopher Mutwe was encountering as he simmered with awareness this Thursday evening, after John O'Goat's *sexual broomsticks* seminar. Social scientists, of a better brand than Diana-Principal-Secretary, have observed that the direst spiritual plight of the black man is that for so many ages he has looked at himself only through the un-understanding, jaundiced, hostile eyes of another race. Now Mutwe was trying to assemble the bits and pieces-pieces of himself as he had looked to the whole 'knowing' campus during those four days of his tragic ignorance. He remembered the hysterical laugh outside Lisa's door on Sunday evening, and many others like it every time the girls had seen him with the Virgin during that week.

He remembered Virgin Lisa's uneasy fidgeting when he sat beside her at John O'Goat's Monday morning lecture. He remembered how, very surprisingly then, the Virgin had practically thrown herself at him, to be kissed, when she came to his room to 'borrow his essay on Thomas Hardy' on Tuesday evening. They kissed unusually, absurdly, long, parting and starting again and again. But even when they had done, the Virgin lingered in Mutwe's arms, with an almost painful tenderness. Not understanding what she wanted to suggest, Mutwe felt embarrassed and even a little angry. For he did not get news of the 'munch' until Wednesday evening …

It was Peso who broke it to him. Mutwe was thinking that he was making an interesting discovery. It had been an unusually hot and heavy afternoon, and in the Lake Basin that is as good as saying it had been next-door to hell, and Mutwe had worked vigorously for four hours on end, in the library. When he got back to his room, he sat in his armchair and tried to read the *Tchwezan Mail*. But, what with his fatigue, the heaviness of the air and the soft comfort of the chair, he dropped asleep, the *Mail* agreeably falling over his face. He opened his eyes when the paper finally slipped away and fell at his feet. He consulted his watch. It was six-thirty-three. Winding the watch, he looked up at his desk and noticed, on the wall above the desk, a thin line of ants.

The Bishop had brought a cake to Mutwe's 'godown' on Tuesday afternoon. They had removed the wrapping paper and thrown it into the waste-paper basket. This the ants 'smelt' from no-one knew where, and now, from the waste-paper basket, they were trying to reach the piece of cake which Mutwe had shut up in his wardrobe. They had already established a track on the wall between the basket and the wardrobe, and they kept moving up and down this track.

Not very progressive, Mutwe thought, *moving endlessly between just those two points*. He also noticed that every two ants which met, going in opposite directions, touched each other with their short feelers. Were they exchanging bits of information about the path, or simply saying 'Hello'? They would even go out of their way to 'greet' a colleague who happened to stray a little off the track. *Primitive living*, Mutwe's mind recorded, *just like the country folk who stop and greet for three minutes on end. The more evolved species, like university students, do not have time to waste on such irrelevancies as 'hello', 'habari' or 'salaam'*. Then Mutwe suddenly realized that he was refreshed by his contemplation of the ants. *Does every idea have this power to -*

A knock at the door. Peso tapped very lightly and shyly, as he always did, and this time only twice.

'Hullo Peso!' Mutwe said, 'I'm making a very interesting discovery. Come and look at this.' Peso went over, as quietly and as soberly as a newly-qualified doctor goes to examine a critically sick person. Mutwe switched on the light, showed Peso the insects and let him watch them for several seconds. Then he asked, 'Give you any ideas?'

'No.' Peso lingered over the word.

It was by sheer luck that one got any ideas about ants on a wall. After all, they were such a common sight. All sorts of insects thrived excellently in the Lake Basin heat and humidity.

We mentioned the black socialist flies which shared the students' meals in the cafeteria. The more bourgeois-minded of their breed invaded the students' union canteen, which, incidentally, was the biggest beer-consuming centre in and around Maalas. One late afternoon, when Mutwe and the Virgin had gone there for ice-cream, the Virgin's favourite item on the bar provisions card, such a large squad of these flies tried to exploit the innocent student citizens that a brilliant young barmaid went round the place spraying the customers' *samosas*, roast chicken and beer with a Tchwezan pyrethrum insecticide.

But, even if ants had been as engaging as a honeymoon flight to the moon, Peso would not have been in the mood at that moment to get any ideas about them. The seconds of silence during which he was looking at the ants focused all his fears and his anxieties, and Mutwe's light-heartedness set him questioning the wisdom of his self-imposed mission.

'Have you seen Lisa today?' Peso started, fidgeting with a perforator on the desk, and Mutwe mistook the tremor in his voice for his usual diffidence.

From the moment when Mutwe started paying particular attention to her, Lisa's nickname had gradually fallen out of use among the members of the Academics Anonymous. Now Peso hardly ever referred to her as the Virgin, except when he was alone with Kale.

'Lisa?' Mutwe laughed. 'Lisa has nothing to do with

the ants. I asked you about the ants..'

'No. I'm serious, Mutwe..'

'Well?' Mutwe looked at Peso's face and noticed that Peso was eyeing him with a look full of worry, or pain, or sympathy, or a mixture of all these.

Then he remembered that Peso had never discussed the Virgin with him. It was only after their quarrel, Mutwe and Peso, that the former took to the Virgin; and Peso, in his delicate sensitiveness, felt a kind of guilty responsibility for the situation.

'Lisa was here yesterday evening, and I lunched with her today, and afterwards walked with her to M.P.,' Mutwe rattled off with the clarity of a co-operative patient answering a doctor's question. 'Why?' he added after a few seconds of awkward silence.

'Have you heard anything?'

'No,' Mutwe answered, getting quite concerned about his friend's apparent pain. 'What is it, Peso?'

'You won't tell?'

'Tell whom?' Mutwe asked.

'Anyone, Mutwe, anyone.'

'Well,' Mutwe said, hesitating, 'no, if you don't want me to.'

'There's a very disturbing rumour going round about Lisa, and I thought I should tell you about it, for old time's sake!' Peso attempted a faint cheerfulness in these last words. And, responding to a 'yes' from Mutwe, he narrated, in the softest terms that he could think of, the story of the Virgin - O'Goat night as he had received it from the 'Bitch'. This last character we shall hear about later.

'I'm sorry, Mutwe,' Peso said, after what seemed like aeons of vacuum-silence at the end of his story, 'I'm only hoping there's nothing in the rumours, but -'

'That's not the point,' Mutwe cut him short, his voice involuntarily hushed to a barely audible whisper.

The Philosopher's wife should be above suspicion, certainly above O'Goat, he would have thought and probably said under any reasonably normal circumstances. But now a journey seemed to have ended in a wilderness of clots in the blood-clots in the toes, in the legs, in the stomach; clots in the fingertips, in the arms; clots in the heart and clots in the brain-huge, rough clots that weighed as heavy as rocks and stung like a thousand red-hot needles. This was no region for thought... not until you were acclimatized to it.

'Let's go to supper, Mutwe,' Peso suggested. He suggested this triviality, as we all often do in such situations, in the hope that it might prove a glow-worm that would gradually direct the sufferer to the way out of the gloom.

Mutwe, glued to the straight-backed chair on which he had listened to Peso's story, shook his head slowly. 'I'll be coming later,' he finally managed to bring out the words, dismissing Peso. 'Thanks for telling me.'

'I'm sorry,' Peso said again, and he hurriedly went out and closed the door to escape from the pain of the thousand-and-one things he wanted to say but could not find the words for.

Mutwe's first urge as soon as feeling restarted in him – it took well over an hour – was to go and see the Virgin. But then, what would he tell her? Where would he start? Then he remembered that the Virgin had lied to him. It did not occur to him to even start questioning the truth of Peso's story. After another half-hour of reflection, he felt he should write to her. He pulled out an air-mail form and started, *'Dear Lisa. . .'Then what? What should I say? Absurd!* and he crumpled up the blue paper in his hand. Then he stretched it out again and tore it into a hundred bits, which he tossed into his tall, palm-leaf waste-paper basket. He finally rose from his desk, slightly revived by the violence with which he had torn up the *'Dear Lisa'* paper, and he made for the door.

Peso came in again just at that moment, carrying an egg and two large bananas'. 'I brought you these,' he said, making no further explanations.

'Thank you, Peso. Put them on the bookcase there. I was just going out.' They walked out into the corridor together.

'I'm going to try and re-read Forster,' Peso said as he parted from Mutwe. 'Would you like to drop in for some coffee at about ten?'

'O.K., thanks,' Mutwe said and walked down the steps.

It was only eight-thirty, but it would be dark already, for night falls faster in the Lake Basin than on the plateaux. But there were lights along the paths, and Mutwe felt as

153

if all these, as well as all the beams shooting out from the halls, were focused on him in one huge derisive glare. He would have put his fingers in his ears to keep out the radio noises if he had had the energy to raise his hands to his head. He walked as fast as his legs could carry him - and that was snail-slow that Wednesday evening - down the steps from Windsor Castle, across University Way, past the cafeteria, round the Students' Union Main Hall, across Hekima Road, and towards the swimming-pool.

There were lights round the pool, but they were only switched on on nights when there were functions and parties there. So now, as Mutwe approached the pool, the nearest lights to him were those along Hekima Road, now about two hundred metres behind him, and those in front of the Dispensary, just about the same distance on his left. He sighed dryly, feeling, more because it was his wish than the fact, that the air out here was cooler than that in the thick complex of buildings behind him, and grateful for the friendly impersonality of the dark.

He leant against the one-metre-thirty high concrete wall round the pool, and stood there for over forty minutes, gazing at the dark, dimly star-lit water, and not budging a centimetre from the spiritual pit into which he had fallen. The problem was that his thought was arrested. The clots were still there, in the heart and in the brain, and, for heaven or for hell, Mutwe could not act in the absence of thought.

Finally back in his room, he ate the egg and the bananas, more because of his love for the boy who had brought them than because he wanted to eat anything, though he had had nothing since lunch. However, he did not go for the coffee. Instead, he lay on his bed, face upwards, eyes fixed at the point where the Rwandese spear had emerged, and - felt blocked. Towards midnight, he tried the poetic morphia. But it did not work. For one thing, his hand fell on *Coups de Pilon*, and David Diop's virulent violence was entirely the wrong diet for a mind like Mutwe's that evening.

He came to that bit about *'my women grinding their reddened mouths against the thin and hard lips of the conqueror with eyes of steel'* and was stung to the quick by the picture. Yet he read on for some moments, in spite of himself. But when he caught himself at it, he was seized by such a violent fit of anger that he flung the slim volume tight across the room on to the top of his desk. Then he observed his 'wake' - over the corpse of fond ignorance.

But *'sleep knows not those mourning their mothers'*, as Mutwe's people say. He finally dropped off, and woke up so late and so hungry the next morning that he had to run to the cafeteria before he washed his face or brushed his teeth and went to O'Goat's seminar.

He had, however, had ample time to put bits and pieces together in his mind during the day. And his hour with both O'Goat and the Virgin, at the *broomsticks seminar*, somehow inspired a sort of hard courage in him. He did not, despite O'Goat's personal invitation, say a thing at that seminar. He utterly ignored and avoided the Virgin, who, poor girl, was writhing in her own safari-ant-infested pit.

But what do you do when a Senior Lecturer, *your* lecturer, sleeps with a girl whom you love and you have not slept with? and when the girl told you she had gone to visit her uncle the very night that she did it? and she has come and kissed you for minutes on end and pretended to be more fond of you than ever before her harlotish ways?

Now, as Mutwe rose from the blue-cushioned chair and walked out on to his balcony - Windsor Castle had been so luxuriously planned that every room had its private balcony - he knew, or at least he thought he knew, what he would do. He would get a revolver …

6 The hollow shots

Imagine a Frelimo fighter, grenade in hand, squatting in the thick, dark-green bush of Mozambique, ambushing a Portuguese army convoy; or a rifle-armed government artist in any other part of Africa, kneeling in a banana, cassava or rice garden some seven or eight kilometres outside the capital, rifle at the ready, eyes glued to the' road, waiting for the arrival of the presidential motorcade, having decided, as it often becomes necessary to decide on a continent where the ballot is bourgeois and reactionary, and does not project the African Image, that a too benevolent *Baba wa Taifa* should be eliminated.

This is heroism. Not the throwing of the grenade or the pulling of the trigger, but the physical inactivity of the waiting. And the examples of freedom fighters are perhaps unnecessary extremes. Any case of keeping still would do: from the second wife who sits listening to her husband making love to her co-wife in the next room, to the budding writer who checks his pen, despite a feeling of certainty that a new idea has blossomed in his mind, to the village shopkeeper who, outside the coffee and the cotton seasons, may not get a customer for six hours on end, to the young graduate who stands thirty minutes at an office reception desk before the standard-seven girl behind it even asks him what she can do for him. If any of these characters chooses to remain still, arrest all physical activity and concentrate on himself or herself, that character may be crowned a hero or heroine.

We could have chosen to tell a story of violent and swift physical action. And in the general stagnation of the Maalas campus, such stories, when they occurred, were marked by all the singularity and particularity that determines what is news and what is a story to tell. As for example when a member of that tribe which always fought its way into the cafeteria raped a girl.

Three Indian girls were walking home after the weekly Friday night film show at the Students' Union Main Hall when the maniac grabbed one of them by the hair and started dragging her to a nearby cashew tree whose branches almost touched the soft grass under them. The other two girls fled ahead in panic, and when they turned to look. they saw a knife being brandished at their companion. They ran on to the gates of Margaret Plantagenet, only two hundred metres away, and tried to tell the *askaris*. But by the time they switched from Gujarati to English and finally to horribly-garbled Kiswahili, the rape under the cashew boughs was finished, and the savage had disappeared. In any case, no one, not even an *askari*, would have been very keen on daring an armed barbarian for the sake of a *Mongol* woman.

'*Ana kisu?*' the two young men at the gate had exclaimed when the girls finally found the Swahili word for *knife*, '*Ha, taabu sana!*' Eventually, however, they went down the road, with the two girls trotting behind them. They found Fatma, the unfortunate girl, lying wretchedly under the cashew tree. When the men flashed their torches and she saw their black faces, she screamed, shot up and ran into the hall at the speed of a bullet. Her two friends picked up her handbag and they hurried into the hall, now genuinely afraid themselves - of the *askaris*.

The *askaris* did not report this incident to the authorities, and the three girls decided to hush it up, to avoid causing scandal in the (Asian) 'community'. In any case, it would not have helped if they had reported it themselves. The 'Wild Highlander', as the Scottish Dean of Students was known, would only have dismissed them with a *'we shall investigate'*. An Asian could not hope to win a case in Maalas, whichever way you looked at it. The African attitude, we know. The British expatriate experts told their African friends(!), 'I'm not a racist, you know, but, honestly, these Asians get on my nerves...' for very diplomatic nerves they were.

The story, however, spread, as such stories always did, all over the campus. For a full fortnight after the incident, everyone was discussing it, or, rather, gossiping about it. For you will by now know that discussion was not a popular activity in Maalas academic circles. Whether the story reached the High Jarnat Khana remained a matter of speculation among the black students. But what would have particularly intrigued a serious observer was that any male should have chosen to slake his sexual thirst on a girl from a race the myth, probably sour-grape-bred, of whose sexual 'uselessness' was everywhere held far dearer than most truths.

Perhaps the boy chose the Indian girl because she

had long hair by which he could grab her. Or perhaps he did not wish to subject a member of his own race to that wild violence when there was another race he could victimize. Or perhaps he was a genuinely objective scientist determined to get first-hand experience rather than depend on hearsay. Or, most probably, he simply followed the usual Maalas trend of either making no choice or making the wrong choice when one chose at all.

However. we only chose this episode to show that we could have chosen to tell such tales, full of swing and flare, signifying life.

But that is the easier life. Mutwe got the revolver much more easily than anyone would have imagined in a country where every civilian, except ministers and party organisers, was barred from possessing anything that even remotely resembled a gun. The sale of toy guns was illegal in Tchweza, and athletic races, where they were held, were started with a gong. But on the campus there was the Wild Highlander, the Dean of Students. He had revolvers, pistols, carbines and rifles of every description as well as, people said, enough ammunition to last several hours of concentrated shooting.

He had been an officer in the colonial service, you see. a commissioner of prisons in Montania (now Tchweza), but he had not gone home after the change of regimes and the after-effects of the Tchwezanization of the services. Instead, he successfully applied to the University for the post of Dean of Students, for which - since it entailed the duties of dealing with British and other English-speaking members of staff and students, and such things as locking up the campus gates at certain hours as well as disciplining offenders against the oath 'to live circumspectly' - he was particularly qualified by his Britishness, his degree in Social Psychology and, especially, his long experience in the prisons.

So, he had moved his headquarters, lock, stock and barrel, from the Central Prison on to the university campus. And, even long after the 'disappearance of the opposition', and the banning of firearms, no police or army officer dared search the Wild Highlander's house, though it was common knowledge that he possessed arms and ammunition. He was white, you see, and the colonial service had taught him all the techniques one might use to browbeat any black bastard. (It was rumoured that the Wild Highlander - Captain Mackee was his real name and title: he fought in the Second World War before coming to Africa - the Captain kept giving seminars and tutorials on these techniques to all new British arrivals at Maalas. He also gave them a "lot of useful tips on *how to be successful expatriates*.)

Moreover, the University was held in a sort of ignorant awe, or, as Mutwe put it to the A.A. once, 'excommunicatory isolation', by most members of the public. Very few of them, ministers and party leaders included, ever went there if they could help it. The people responsible for the control of firearms did not think it worth their while scaling the slippery steps of the 'Ivory Tower', (this, incidentally, is one of the Catholic litanies to the Virgin Mary), to confront a British army ex-captain whose mere look would probably have sent them hurtling down and scurrying back to their barracks without even as much as stating why they had come.

Mutwe and the Wild Highlander were good friends, though Mutwe could not bring himself to forget a dream he had had about him some six weeks before the strike. The boy's liberated mind carried him back some thousand years in time and more than six thousand kilometres away in space to mediaeval England, where he recognized himself as a noble condemned to death. He lay his head on the wooden block, and the executioner, the Wild Highlander, hacked it off with his axe. Mutwe felt a soft kind of relaxation in his breast as his head fell off his shoulders ...

*

They became friends at the beginning of Mutwe's second year in Maalas, when the Wild Highlander barked at Mutwe and called him a 'bloody absent-minded bastard', and Mutwe barked back, calling Captain Mackee a 'damned colonial hound'. At this, the Dean's Secretary, a delicate Goan girl, nearly fell off her chair, and the Wild Highlander's normally yellow-brown face turned as red as a flamboyant flower, and his thick, lousy - in Maalas anything dirty and disgusting was described as lousy - grey beard trembled as if it were going to fall off his face. But, cursing and stamping again, Mutwe had left the office.

Instead of leaving it to the Hall Wardens to receive old students back, which was their responsibility, Captain Mackee insisted on seeing each and every student at the beginning of every term. That particular time when he quarrelled with Mutwe he had sworn that he would not leave his desk until he had seen all the thousand or so students there were to see. He had been sitting six hours in the office, receiving student after student, giving them forms to sign, renewing their identity cards, handing them their room keys and wishing them a happy and prosperous new year, in July, for that is when the academic year began. Mutwe had forgotten to have his identity card renewed, and when he went back to the Dean's office just as another student took his place at the desk, the Captain burst out into his savage complaints, only to find that he had run against a rock this time.

Mutwe thought about the incident most of the afternoon, and, at about seven-thirty in the evening, he strolled to the Wild Highlander's house, only a few hundred metres away from Windsor Castle, on Carlyle Lane. Right up to the moment he was ushered into the animal-hide-littered living-room, however, he did not know whether he wanted to apologize, to protest or simply stage a confrontation.

'What can I do for you, young man?' the Wild Highlander asked him, breathing noisily through his moustache as he walked in from his study - where he kept the guns.

'I found your behaviour to me this afternoon most

revolting, Mr. Mackee.'

'Who are you?' the Captain could not remember the boy, but Mutwe thought that he was pretending.

'I'm the student who stamped in your office and called you a damned colonial hound.' Mutwe felt his muscles tense up, though he did not know whether it was for combat or for flight. His cheeks were suddenly inflamed and began to itch, and his heart pounded as strongly as a girl's pestle in a maize mortar. But his was a nature which could remain eternally calm even when he wanted to look excited. To the Wild Highlander, who did not notice the flap-flapping tip of his left shoe, he managed to give an impression of perfect composure and self-confidence.

'Ah well —' the soldier had been surprised from an entirely unguarded angle. Mutwe noticed this and offered battle.

'You called me a bloody absent-minded bastard,' he said in a very steady and even voice. The blow that makes an enemy surrender, if not a *coup de grâce*.

Well, I'm sorry,' hissed the Wild Highlander. Mrs. Mackee, a plump, thirty-five year old *white* South African with a touchingly missionary face, was in the kitchen. The Captain suspected that the boy's words had pierced her ears as aggressively as the smell of her cooking oil attacked their noses. He did not want her to hear the noise of the battle. If she had heard, she should hear no more. If not, the shorter he cut the whole business, the better. So, before Mutwe put in another word, the Wild Highlander had attached an explanation to his apology.

'You know, you tend to get a little snotty,' he said, 'when you've been sitting at your desk for six hours on end, and with such a noisy crowd milling at your door.'

Yes, a crowd there had been at the Dean's office when Mutwe called the Dean a damned *et cetera et cetera*, and a disorderly crowd it had been, to put it mildly. Many in that crowd, however, who had been fighting, literally, to be first into the office when Mutwe left it, had witnessed the outbursts, and Mutwe's courage was discussed, no, gossiped about, for more than three days on the campus.

The Captain's words immediately, and very surprisingly, assured Mutwe that he was going to call 'Pax'. The rarely personal and informal style - complete with slang and understatement - in which the Captain gave his excuse made the boy feel almost sorry for him. *Bullies bully for fear of being bullied*, he thought as he watched the Captain scratching his beard.

'Well, I'm sorry too, but-'

The Wild Highlander did not let Mutwe finish. 'Oh, well,' he said as he walked across the room to Mutwe, his hand stretched out to him, 'let's forget it.'

'Thank you,' Mutwe found himself saying as the Captain clasped his timidly-outstretched hand and squeezed it almost savagely. 'Like a drink?' the Captain asked the boy.

'Yes, please ... and they sipped Johnnie Walker 'on the rocks' together until about eight-thirty that evening. The Wild Highlander told Mutwe all sorts of thrilling stories. And, as he waxed more and more excited with drink and conversation, he imparted such confidential tips to Mutwe on how to deal with Africans that any observer would have wondered whether he was not mistaking the boy for a new expatriate arrival from Britain. For Mutwe had assumed his most 'British' attitude for this interview, so much so that even his subconscious sounded curiously unusual notes: like that intuition of his that the Captain was calling 'Pax'. He talked to the Wild Highlander in faultless colonial British.

The chief linguistic trouble with most Britishers at Maalas was that they imagined that, because one of the tribal languages in the country was called *Engleesh*, any African who spoke that language also spoke and understood colonial British. They did not realize that they had to learn our language, and most of them lived as many as five years in the country, barely making themselves understood and on most occasions understanding less than a quarter of what was said to them. Yet some Africans, Mutwe and his A.A. colleagues for example, learnt their British and even spoke it to perfection, occasionally, when they wanted to patronize the expatriates, or to protect themselves against them, as Mutwe did on his first visit to Captain Mackee.

And it was astonishing, the childish glee and ravished abandon with which a Britisher let himself, or especially herself, go when you spoke to them in British. It would have been utterly disgusting if it had not been British. They started making such stupid and vulgar jokes about your people that you could not help wondering whether either they simply despised you and did not care a rush what you thought or felt, which in all fairness is not very British, or, most probably, the sound of your voice had not made them forget the colour of your skin. Captain Mackee, for example, kept telling Mutwe about his plans to 'get tough with those black bastards', meaning the African students, adding that 'you've got to have been in this bloody country for some time before you get to understand *them*.'

'Nothing short of a kick in the arse will make a bloody African understand anything,' the Captain said as he refilled Mutwe's glass.

One battle an evening is enough. Although Mutwe was sharply aware of the Captain's colonial remarks, he chose not to hit back. At first it was out of a genuine sense of humour, just to see how far the Wild Highlander would go before he checked his stupidity. But as the Captain went on and on with less and less reserve and more and more sincerity, expounding the hopelessness of the African situation, nay, of *being an African*, Mutwe began to feel a grating sense of guilt.

I shouldn't have let him get away with even one silly phrase, Mutwe thought. After all, it was he who had chosen to Britannize the visit, for his own ends. He actually left the house because of his growing sense of sin: the misty awareness of treachery that swirls around you when you walk down a street with your white girl-friend ...

*

Mutwe and the Wild Highlander had remained

friends, however, and they used to nod to each other every time they met, and mumble 'hullo' when they passed each other close enough, in the best Britisb tradition. Mutwe was frequently invited to Captain Mackee's house and he got to like his four kids quite well, despite their endless asking him why he washed only the inside of his hands, and whether he would turn white one day. And now that he needed, or thought he needed, some murderous implement, after learning of the Lisa - O'Goat affair, Mutwe went to the Wild Highlander's house.

'It just occurred to me today,' the boy began, idly turning over the pages of a copy of *The Listener*, 'that I've never seen a revolver - or looked closely at any kind of gun for that matter.'

'You're lucky, my boy,' the Captain said; 'it seems some people have seen nothing else all their lives.'

'Do you have a revolver, Captain?' Mutwe had noticed that the Captain was in good mood, and the sooner he came to the point, the better.

'The possession of firearms is illegal in Mon-, in Tchweza, my dear.' the Wild Highlander said and roared with laughter.

'I'm serious, Mr. Mackee: I –'

'Serious? You can't be more serious than the law of the land,' and the Captain laughed uproariously again.

His wife had taken the children back 'home' to school after the Christmas break, and she was staying in Britain for some weeks. Yes, some lucky expatriates received allowances large enough for this sort of thing: travelling to Britain, for only British expatriates seemed to be lucky, and back two or three times a year, with their families. So, the Captain was making the most of these few days in that state to which every married man looks back with nostalgia: unwomaned, reckless, free to laugh, swear and curse without any bloody nonsensical *'Edward please's'* being clapped over your mouth. And Captain Mackee, like most bullies and belatedly-married men, was almost ridiculously afraid of his wife.

'I went to see this western they showed last Friday,' said Mutwe, trying to tame the Captain's humour by pretending to ignore it, 'but somehow I found the gun scenes unconvincing.'

Mutwe had not been to the western film at all. For the advertisements had said there were 'Injuns', and he had sworn, early in his first year at Maalas, never to go to those films, 'where the darker-skinned man always lost and died, for his land and gold, while everyone clapped their big dark-skinned hands and opened their big, blood-thirsty mouths to cheer.' But there are gun scenes in every western, surely?

'Those bloody actors are blockheads who can't use a gun for anything other than a film scene,' said the Captain indignantly. 'Bloody ignorant.'

'Like me?' asked Mutwe, not stopping to consider whether he would really own the 'bloodiness' along with his ignorance.

'At least you don't pretend,' said the Captain rising with his glass of whisky and soda in his hand. 'Well, swear mum, and I'll show you guns enough to glut your wildest desires.'

If only the Wild Highlander knew that Mutwe's only desire at that moment was to put a shot through ... Well, 'swear mum', that must be a quotation from one of those wild Scottish poets.

'Mum's the word!' Mutwe said as he followed the Captain to the door at the end of the living-room.

'Here, after you!' said the Captain, opening the door for Mutwe and hiccupping as he followed him. They walked down a short corridor, passing two cream doors on the right, a blue one on the left, and stopping at the second door, also cream, on the left. The Wild Highlander towered over Mutwe as he tried the handle.

'Blast, it's locked. Hold on here.' In four strides the Captain was at the farther door on the right, and he went in. It must have been his bedroom. Mutwe remained at the other door, burning with impatience to get - well, to see... what was inside.

It was rumoured all over the campus that, after the strike and the 'exile', the Government maintained a large number of secret agents in the student body. Some people even whispered that a promise to spy for the Government had, after consultations with the Vice-Chancellor, been put to several students as one of the conditions for their re-admission to the University. These rumours led to 'circumspect living' in many aspects; even the colonial insolence that several lecturers had previously displayed from the rostrum now became a little tempered. But the

Wild Highlander either thought Mutwe too good and too intelligent a boy to be caught in that bloody web - which would have been unrealistic - or he just didn't give a damn, as he would have put it, about spies.

He returned from the other room, holding a bunch of keys in his left hand, dangling his empty glass in his right and whistling *Scotland the Brave*. Mutwe backed against the narrow strip of wall at the end of the corridor to let him open the door.

'Ah!' Mutwe exclaimed with the gaping gesture he had been rehearsing since their arrival at the door. But there were no guns anywhere to be seen.

'This is my study,' said the Dean, banging his glass fiercely on the large desk in the middle of the room. The walls were littered with book-shelves, animal hides, bird plumes and African wood carvings.

'Now, let me get myself another drink. Would you like one too?' 'I'm all right, thanks,' Mutwe said, looking at the glass in his hand. It was still half full.

'O.K. One minute,' and the Wild Highlander went out, his whistle losing all traces of melody on the straining high notes of his patriotic tune.

Mutwe leaned against the desk, sipped at his glass, and looked listlessly round the room. He had noticed how stupid, more to himself than to the Captain, his mechanical exclamation had made him sound, and his excitement was beginning to ebb.

'*Now if you have tears,*' intoned the Captain as he walked to a huge wardrobe in one comer of his study, after he returned with his drink, '*prepare to shed them.*' He unlocked the doors of the wardrobe and threw them wide open. Mutwe did not budge from the edge of the desk. 'Well, come and look,' the Captain invited him.

The boy walked over to the wardrobe and looked at the line of rifles and carbines, about twenty in all, slung over the bar where one would have hung suits and shirts in an ordinary wardrobe. The French word for wardrobe gained a new dimension of significance in his mind: *armoire*. Suddenly, the Captain let go of the doors of the wardrobe which he was holding apart. Mutwe stepped back frantically. If his nose had been as long as a European's, it would have been caught between the wardrobe doors as they snapped shut.

The Wild Highlander did not notice Mutwe's narrow escape, for he was already hurrying to the windows of the study, closing them, pulling down the blinds over them and turning them in. 'We don't want any bloody intruder snooping around,' he said as he came back to the wardrobe. 'Now, let's wedge these doors.'

They used the room-door wedge on one of the doors and a rubber eraser from the desk on the other. Then the Captain proceeded to 'animate' the exhibition. He isolated each gun in turn, gave its origin, and its technical designation and explained all its details, calibre, magazine, range and a dozen or so *cetera* of which the boy did not have, and could not, at the pace at which the Captain was speaking, get the faintest idea. He also narrated very exciting, or at least excited, anecdotes of how he had acquired each gun and the service it had seen. There were rifles of every description, from .303 S.M.L.E. Mark Threes to German 7.92 Gewehrs Forty-threes to 9.5 Männlichers to 7.62 British FNs to the latest American M-Fifteens. *No pistols, no revolvers*; Mutwe's heart was sinking. 'But all those are quite heavy arms,' he said doubtfully.

'Oh no!' the Captain explained, 'on the contrary, all these are called *small* arms. And here are two shotguns.'

'I mean, in comparison with such things as pistols and revolvers,' Mutwe said, looking at the two dull 12-bore jobs on top of the chest of drawers in the left half of the *armoire*.

'Ah yes, you want to see the revolvers as well. Here!' The Captain pulled out the second drawer from the top, and there, lying in frozen murderousness, were a dozen or so black-headed and gleaming-barrelled pistols, revolvers and automatics.

'Aaa-ha!' exclaimed Mutwe enthusiastically, forgetting himself in his excitement and breaking into *Engleesh*. 'That's it, *bwana* - that's what I wanted to see.'

'Ah, you like revolvers, don't you?' The Captain, who was already boyishly excited, was warmly delighted to see Mutwe 'warming up to it' at last.

'Oh yes!' Mutwe answered and then, on a quieter note, added, 'Well, I really don't know anything about them.' A mysterious shadow, or an ultra-bright ray, was already stealing over his mind.

The Captain went through the same performance of locating, identifying, 'detailing' every gun and telling its life story as he had done with the rifles. But now he drew on all his dramatic resources to illustrate his 'lecture'. He would throw an automatic up into the air, catch it, point its muzzle at one wall after another in lightning-quick succession, striking wonderfully youthful and athletic poses, and all but shouting, 'Bang, bang, bang! And no bloody bastard would venture within four hundred yards of you.'

'How do you load them?' Mutwe asked him, taking advantage of a pause between the Captain's putting one gun back in the drawer and picking up another.

'Load? Oh, quite easy.' The Captain demonstrated with the shining American arm he had just picked up, a double-action revolver that must have been a remote derivation from the .38 Colt model. 'Push this to one side; here's the cylinder; you insert the cartridges into the chambers, click this back into position, and you're ready. This can fire six shots without reloading.'

'May I have a look, please?' Mutwe asked, stretching out his hand, for, in *Engleesh*, his question meant that he wanted to study the revolver with his hands. '*Our eyes are in our hands*,' they say among his people.

'Yes, of course,' the Dean said and handed the revolver to Mutwe and, as if with the gun, the last drop of energy seemed to go out of the ex-soldier's frame. He suddenly realized how vigorously he had been talking and moving for the last forty-or-so minutes. He moved to the desk as fast as his weary shuffle could carry him, took three draughts at his glass and squeezed his chest with both his

174

hands. Then with a grunt, he pulled a chair and sat down, facing the *armoire* and leaning against the desk.

For some three minutes his eyes lingered softly over the boy with the revolver in his hand: either in pity at his delicacy and inexperience or in envy at his quiet, self-reliant youth, or in a mixture of both and other emotions. For, now come to think of it. the Captain realized that, far from doing Mutwe a favour, it was he, the old man, who had been given the chance to renew old memories of daring and valiant deeds, and to display the skill and experience which he had so painfully and precariously acquired: and now his body was betraying him in the middle of the show...

Meanwhile, Mutwe was engrossed in the arm. He swung it lightly up and down to ascertain its weight, passed his right forefinger delicately over its elegantly-curved trigger, opened it as the Captain had shown him, looked at the grooves where one put the bullets, clicked it shut and held it as if ready for action.

'Ah, yes, those were the days, young man!' the Captain said with a sad touch of homesickness in his voice; one could not have told whether he was addressing his companion with the revolver or his own departed youthful self.

'Hm?' Mutwe looked up, suddenly remembering the presence of the Wild Highlander.

The Captain felt almost childishly glad at being noticed again. He jumped up, took a gulp of whisky and clapped the glass back on to the desk. 'Just wait one minute

175

here,' he said nasally and left the room.

Here, the revolver. Now the ammunition. Mutwe pulled out the first drawer of the chest. Only belts, gloves and bandoliers. He banged it shut and pulled out the third drawer. Yes, there, hundreds and hundreds of cartridges. But those were apparently for the rifles. He pushed back the drawer carefully; the first drawer had echoed hollowly throughout the house. Fourth drawer. That was it, *bwana!* One, two, three, four, five, six. He opened the gun, slid in the .38 cartridges, clicked it shut and - *Out of here now. at once. What if you meet the Wild Highlander in the corridor?* Mutwe thought that the Dean had gone to the toilet. *Well,* he started walking to the door, *if he makes any trouble.. Bang, bang! . . . . But no! I must save all my bullets for -*

For whom? Whom exactly did he want to shoot? John O'Goat. . .. was it really? Why? He had slept with his girl. His girl? Virgin Lisa. *Is she, was she ever, really my girl? She lied to me when she was going to deliver her goods to O'Goat.* And which is graver? munching a virgin-looking harlot when she throws herself into your arms, as she had thrown herself into Mutwe's arms the Tuesday after she had slept with O'Goat, and your blood warm up to her? Or fabricating a net of lies about uncles at ideological colleges and trying to throw it over the head of a person you know genuinely cares for you?

Shoot the Virgin. But what use would it be? Moreover, O'Goat must have planned it all. But why did she go all along with him? *Shoot both Lisa and O'Goat.* But what use would it be to him, Mutwe? Everyone was saying he was under-sexed and impotent, and he had starved the poor girl into throwing herself at O'Goat. Shooting them would make him only more loathsome to everyone. But they should not get away with it. *Shoot the Virgin, shoot O'Goat and then shoot yourself.* But why should he waste his time and energy chasing Senior Lecturer John O'Goat and Virgin Lisa Harlot when merely shooting himself would just as satisfactorily 'his quietus make'? *Shoot yourself* ... yes, yourself... your - NO!

Mutwe had halted at the desk with the first pang of questioning, and now he threw the revolver violently on to it. Then he picked it up quickly again, opened it, took out the cartridges, threw them into their drawer and he closed it. He had made a choice - chosen to do nothing, to remain still - he was a hero.

*

But if doing nothing in itself was the only measure for heroism, the whole university population in Maalas could have qualified, easily, as heroes. Or would they? Surely the typical *curriculum vitae* there seemed to be: *you came, you saw, you stagnated*. But what is stagnation? Might it not consist in over-activity - like the thousand-and-one ripples, and the million insignificant writhings of mosquito larvae that one notices in a stagnant pool? Nothing - heroism. Where is the missing link?

... It was raining in torrents. Peso stood on his balcony, looking at a young labourer on the brown-green lawn which stretched from under him down to the edge of Carlyle Lane. Holding a long green hose, the labourer was diligently irrigating the grass, his bare shoulders streaming with sweat, or with the rain water. Rain or no rain, he could not choose when to irrigate or even whether to irrigate or not. No tens of thousands of shillings had been spent on him to give him the power of choice. He was only a labourer. . .

'*Mzee, shikamoo!*' The old cleaner nearly fell back. His broom dropped from his hands. He gazed at Kale. He did not answer the greeting. The boy had broken a taboo. The *wazungu*, to whose ranks Kale belonged, never talked to the cleaners, except when they were giving them orders or scolding them when they did not do their work to the *wazungu*'s satisfaction. When you were talking to a friend in Anglo-Swahili, as was the general practice, and you saw a labourer approaching, you immediately switched to English or French. Not that you were backbiting him... just the way the world was, as Kale was to learn when he was no longer a fresher ...

... The President of the Students' Union had just finished his lunch. He was taking his tray of debris back to the counter. Someone stopped him suddenly. A soup spoon dropped from his tray. The student who had stopped the President mentioned something from the day's newspaper - about a call to students to prepare for an austerity campaign. This was before the strike.

Stepping on the neck of the spoon he had dropped, the President recited, in impressive, solemn tones, a passage from the works of the Father of the Nation, about Africa's future joy or misery depending on her youth. The members of the Academics Anonymous were coming behind the President. He had stopped between two tables and blocked the way. Mutwe nudged Peso and Kale, pointed with his mouth, as African gossips do, at the President's heavy boot on the neck of the poor spoon, and chanted:

> *'Les bourgeois:*
> *Ce son comme les cochons:*
> *Plus ça devient vieux,*
> *Plus ça devient bêtes.'*

He was quoting a Belgian singer, who claims that the bourgeois are like swine, and the older they grow, the more stupid they become. When the President finished his quotation, he walked over to the counter, threw his tray there, and marched out. Peso picked up the presidential spoon and put it on his own tray. It was bent.

The President's message had been too serious for him to stop to pick up that spoon before he delivered it, or to remember it afterwards. Well, nearly everyone in Maalas was dead serious, about everything. When a boy slept with a girl, it was made to sound like the fall of the British Commonwealth. When someone said a broomstick was highly sexed, everyone at the conference table took it down in his note-book, with a straight and solemn face. Everyone in that body academic seemed to be permanently frowning or 'slitting' his eyes so narrow with seriousness(!) that… We must find the link…

... The evening after Peso saw the labourer irrigating the lawn in the rain, he went to the Junior Common Room at the Students' Union. He had not bought the day's paper, and he wanted to look at the copy they put in the J.C.R. It was during the closing days of that lively exchange of press letters and press statements, between the Party and the Government on one side and the university students on the other, which preceded the strike.

Peso stood just inside the J.C.R. and wondered how he should go about the search for the paper, and whether it was worthwhile undertaking the search at all. The newspaper shelves were bare, except for two broken table-tennis bats. The newspapers and magazines formed a crazy, irregular carpet of torn, crumpled, mud-clogged pages from one end of the room to the other. Newspapers and magazines from all over the world, trodden by a thousand academic feet. For, although irrevocably committed to the ideals of black socialism, Tchweza was non-aligned, and accepted ideas, influences, and other things, from both East and West. Though several individual books were banned - for example, all the works of the former leader of the Opposition who was now in preventive detention - no body of literature as such was banned merely because of the country from which it came.

Peso eventually dived on to the carpet, and, after some ten minutes of concentrated search, came upon the day's issue of the *Tchwezan Mail*. The pages which were not plastered with mud were so ragged that all that Peso could read from the whole paper was a tiny report about a country where rats feasted on tons of sacred corn while the citizens round the temple starved to death. Peso threw the paper on to the broken ping-pong table under which he had found it. Feeling a kind of rising nausea, he turned to leave the room. He looked up at the large clock on the wall. It read a quarter to two. But it was just after supper. Then Peso remembered that that was the most constant clock he had ever seen. For the three years he had been in Maalas, and possibly longer, it had given the time as a quarter to two.

Under the clock, five men students sat in skeleton chairs round a wireless set. Those chairs, like many others, had once had beautiful blue, green and red cushions in them. Nobody knew or cared where the cushions had gone. The students in the ghost chairs were shouting, in a language which Peso could not identify, over the noise of the radio, which they kept tuning from station to station. Those garbled English, Kiswahili, Chinese, Arabic and German barks it emitted were probably its swan-song.

Peso was feeling quite sick now and there was a lump of pain in his stomach. Out in the corridor, he hurried to the toilet which served both the J.C.R. and the canteen. The walls, as well as the inside of the door, of the closet which he entered were full of messages, some in ink, red or blue, some in pencil and others scratched through the paint:

'*McAllister should be fucked by a baboon*' - Miss McAllister was a Tutorial Assistant in Law - '*Mongols wipe their bottoms with their bare hands*' - and below that, '*Savage*

Africans lick theirs' - 'Castrate O'Goat' - 'Savages, stop defiling our walls' - 'Comrades, the food is too lousy: let's strike' - 'Coward, can't you speak out?' - 'Barbarians, all of you, dirtier than the dung you throw here.' The author of the last-quoted message had drawn a huge circle over twenty-or-so other messages and written his own on its circumference. This was on the door. *Activity here*, thought Peso, *inactivity in the Junior Common Room...*

Where is the link?

... The cafeteria meals had struck again. Kale was staying in bed, after seeing Dr. Neurosis. He was itching with impatience and disappointment. That Wednesday morning Professor Hogg had, in his characteristic generous fashion, invited an African writer to address the English Literature finalists. The speaker was a poet, perhaps Africa's leading poet after the dissolution of Senghor's *tigritude*. Kale, though, did not like the poet. He hated him in fact. But he had been looking forward to meeting him. The boy wanted to ask the poet why he always wrote in what looked like incomprehensible telegraphic messages. That was Kale's own description. It was fairly accurate, for one of the achievements for which this muse-inspired son of Africa could claim distinction was that he had never written a complete sentence in his career. But American and British connoisseurs said he was very good.

Here, however, were Kale's chances of settling scores with him being foiled by the university cafeteria hygiene. Kale was lying in his bed, looking at the ceiling, thinking about what Peso and Mutwe would say to the poet, when a spasm of pain gripped his stomach. He dashed out of his room, ran down the corridor, past two doors, and he burst the third door open. Two bodies were writhing in agonized pleasure on the bed. The girl uttered a short scream as Kale rushed towards them. Then he stopped dead. He mumbled a a confused 'Sorry' and dashed out of the room, banging the door behind him. All the doors, you see, room doors, toilet doors, laundry doors and store doors, down that corridor were alike. And a man with the cafeteria 'special' experience in his stomach was liable to open the wrong door in his blind rush.

Those two whom Kale caught at the munch were well-known rebels. But they were also English Literature finalists. It was thirteen minutes before the end of the seminar at which the famed African poet spoke …

…'If I fail my preliminaries, I'm going to jump over this.' Mutwe said this to his tribesmen, when they had been only days in Maalas. It was a group of five, and they were standing on Mutwe's balcony, talking about their first impressions of the new 'school' and the new country. Mutwe said the words in English, and a Tchwezan boy, talking to his tribesmen on the terrace below, heard him. He looked up at Mutwe with coldly surprised eyes. *Poor boy!* he seemed to be thinking, *are preliminaries, or anything in this place, worth dying for?*

Yet before Mutwe's final departure from Maalas, the whole student body in the People's University of Maalas seemed to have found something worth dying for, a batch of goods for which they did risk a leap over the balconies of their ivory tower and land on the hard and merciless floor of politics and reality. That leap was the strike.

7 The strike

His Excellency the President of the Socialist Republic of Tchweza, *Mtumwamungu Baba wa Taifa*, Dr. Nge Kisusuli, one of the few African Doctor Presidents who had actually studied for their doctorates, had a wonderful flair for gestures.

One day, for example, he showed a member of the defunct opposition party a gesture of mercy unprecedented in the whole history of Tchweza. The man had been found guilty of treason and plotting to assassinate the President. He had been condemned to death by firing squad. The execution was to be held in Uhuru Square, opposite the capital's chief vegetable market, across Kisusuli Drive. It was to be the country's first public execution since independence, and spectators surged into the square, deserting the market and pushing and squeezing for the best possible view. Many of them had never seen a man die. Certainly not as violently and as dramatically as this promised to be. Although most of them, especially the men, assumed grave masks of concern and worry and kept shaking their heads, secretly they hoped this was going to be an entertaining experience.

The criminal was tied with strong linen cords to the stem of a coconut tree, the only tree in the square, which stood in the grey-brown sand about five metres away from the rear wall of a sturdy ancient building now blackened by weather and time. The structure had been erected as a fort by one of the many colonial powers that had tried to possess Lake Tudor and the heart of Africa during the glorious days of the 'scramble'. Since then, it had been many things in turn: barracks, prison, warehouse and now, very appropriately, the seat of the Department of Antiquities.

The firing party arrived in a land-rover and marched in formation from the Kisusuli Drive pavement to just a few metres away from their target, their heavy boots raising thick clouds of dust as they plodded their way through the loose sand. It was four minutes to ten, but the sun was already blazing fiercely, as if it too wanted to brand the criminal with its curse. The execution was scheduled for ten exactly... Three to ten. The man at the tree was absolutely still. He had been bound so fast that he could not possibly writhe or wriggle. The crowds were dying to look at his face, but he had been blindfolded.

As the last minute to the hour began, the commander of the squad started giving orders to his men, there were six of them, and they raised their guns and aimed for their bloody task. A brief document was to be read before the firing, but, as the law officer's trembling voice began, *Mlumwamungu Baba wa Taifa*, Dr. Nge Kisusuli strode out of the crowd, shouting, '*Ngoja, bwana. Ngoja, Mwananchi.*'

He stood between the squad and the condemned man, and, facing the squad, who had their backs to the majority of the spectators, he began: 'This man wanted to kill me . . ..' He talked for three hours. The members of the squad, who had not received any other order, had to stand with their rifles raised and at the ready through those three hours. One of the soldiers actually fainted and fell with a dull thud on the sand, making the criminal scream hysterically. Finally, the President commuted the man's sentence to life imprisonment. The criminal died in prison three days later - a natural death.

It was another such spectacular gesture that brought the 'Father of the Nation' into a head-on collision with the Maalas 'intellectuohs' as they called themselves, in which, however, Nge Kisusuli proved to be the locomotive engine, and the *intellectuohs* only a tiny scooter. The apple of discord, at least on the face of it, was the African Liberation Movement. At one of those routine summits within the framework of the OAU, Dr. Kisusuli, who had appointed himself Champion of the African Freedom Fighters, launched a scathing attack on those countries which had refused or failed to contribute to the Liberation Fund, and those which he thought had not contributed generously enough.

'I will put you to shame,' declared *Mtumwamungu* at the conference, waving his hands in a gesture that was amusingly reminiscent of Nikita Krushchev with his diplomatic shoe at the United Nations. 'My country is going to show Africa and all the world that we are determined to liberate our brothers now toiling under colonial and minority racist regimes - at all costs. And we are going to show the world that we are going to do this by ourselves. Africa must understand that only Africans can liberate Africa, and that everyone must co-operate. I solemnly promise before this august meeting that everyone, everyone, in the Socialist Republic of Tchweza is going to contribute, to the best of his abilities, to the Liberation Movement - even the babies at their mothers' breasts.'

There was a stir in the conference hall when this afterthought was translated into French, not because of its sensational implications, but because the interpreter put it as 'even the babies in their mothers' chests'. This set the Francophone brethren wondering whether there was a kind of biological abnormality about the Tchwezan reproductive system.

The summit conference was held in May, during the long vacation after the second academic year of Virgin Lisa and the Academics Anonymous's career at Maalas. In June, when the new national budget was presented to Parliament, it was accompanied by a special appeal from the President, for austerity. There were cuts in expense on several vital services, and the taxes had gone up by about two per cent on the average. It was explained in the 'Father of the Nation's' supplement to the budget that every effort and every sacrifice had to be made to ensure 'our promised contribution to the noble cause of African liberation'.

University students' bursaries were cut by a half.

*

'Let Kisusuli keep all his lousy money. We don't want it.' A voice.

'Well, he will be only too glad if you throw it back.'

Another voice.

'Gentlemen, gentlemen, er - ladies and gentlemen, this is a situation which calls for very careful and very well-weighed action ...' This was the President of the Students' Union cautioning those few voices at the *baraza* which were the first to advocate violent action. He had called an emergency *baraza* only a week after the new academic year began, to discuss the 'bursary crisis' and, if possible, take action before the halved grants were actually processed through the Ministry of Education and the university administration.

This was the first *baraza* that this President, Mr. Hannington George Kadala, had called since his election to office the previous November. Newcomers to Maalas used to hear stories of how lively and interesting *barazas* had been in the early days of the University, when it was only a college of an old British University. The *barazas* were general meetings where all the students of the University, as members of the Students' Union, came together to hear reports from their leaders, discuss general topics of interest and suggest broad outlines of policy to their executive.

But as time passed, the institution degenerated into a noisy arena where the students of Law and Government Arts went to display their 'legal and constitutional' gymnastics. They would, for example, discuss a point of order for three hours on end, then abandon that before it was closed and go off on a point of procedure for another four hours. If the Chairman (they called him 'Free Chairman', although he was the 'unfree-est' man alive as long as he sat in that Chair), if the Free Chairman suggested an adjournment, they would take some two hours questioning his legal right to do so, *et cetera, et cetera*.

Since the meetings normally started at eight-thirty in the evening, it was sometimes eight-thirty in the morning before they were adjourned, or rather broke up in chaos because the participants had to go to breakfast and find quiet comers in the lecture theatres, where they snored through the day's classes. But as fewer and fewer students attended the *barazas*, the lawyers and government artists eventually found themselves with no one to display their skill to. They too stopped going to the *barazas*, and the institution died a natural death.

The frightened haste in which Nge Kisusuli acted to crush student power when it tried to raise its head was perhaps partly due to the fact that to him it looked like encountering a ghost. As far as he was concerned, the students as a force did not exist. They had not said a thing as a body for over four years. Why should they begin now?

The 'bursary crisis' *baraza*, however, was the best-attended *baraza* ever in Maalas. Every student was there. The Main Hall was in fact so packed that a large number of students had to stand at the back and all along the walls throughout the meeting. The main door of the Hall was left open, so that a number of students could watch the proceedings from the terrace outside. For the Tchwezan students, you see, it was a matter of life and death. The Asian students, even those who did not receive government bursaries, saw it as an opportunity for answering, at the lowest possible cost, that constant African din about integration and identifying themselves with African aspirations.

Other students came, some because they looked forward to a chance of letting off all their pent-up aggressive tendencies - that cafeteria tribe, for example - others because, well, everyone was coming. The British and American Anglo-Saxons came because, as some people claimed, they wanted to report everything fresh to the CIA and other such organizations. (It should be noted that the British and American press reported the stages of the strike with a thoroughness and gusto that will remain a tribute to objective journalism for all time.) Mutwe and Peso attended partly in sympathy with their Tchwezan friend, Kale, partly out of an excited hope and belief that here at last was the day of salvation, something to arouse the sleeping giant, as Mutwe put it, and force him to look at himself and act with an aim.

The emergency *baraza* lasted six hours and twenty-one minutes. During it, many first reactions to the 'bursary crisis' were expressed. One was the feeling that Dr. Kisusuli should be castrated. Another *mzee*, as every member of the *baraza* was officially referred to during its session, came up with the suggestion that the students should burn down the University and go home, to look after cattle.

It was pointed out to him that some tribes did not have any cattle, or had had their cattle stolen by rustlers from across the border. Those should till the land then, the *mzee* suggested. When it was pointed out to him again that some tribes did not have any arable land, a refined way of saying *I have no strength or I am ashamed to dig*, the *mzee* supported the suggestion to castrate the 'Father of the Nation'. Yet another suggestion, which received wide and wild acclaim from the *wazee* at the *baraza*, was that the Student's Union should establish its own foreign aid programme and negotiate directly with American Universities, the Ford Foundation, Oxfam and other such institutions.

Finally, however, it was agreed that no extreme measures should be taken until and unless 'all peaceful and proper approaches' had been exhausted. The President of the Students' Union and his Secretaries would 'seek' a meeting with the University Vice-Chancellor - Nge Kisusuli was the Chancellor - and request him, if necessary, to meet the *Mini-star* of Education, and possibly the President of the Republic. In the meantime, it was agreed, all the students should stand together, avoid anything that might 'prejudice the negotiations', and use all peaceful means at their disposal to express their dissatisfaction with the Government's decision and to win public opinion(!) to their side.

A report of the proceedings of this *baraza* was sent to the *Voice of Tchweza*, which did not broadcast it, to the Party daily, which did not print it, and to the *Tchwezan* (formerly *Colonial*) *Mail*, which published it whole.

*

The meeting with the Vice-Chancellor, when it finally came, was a super-mini success, or, to put it bluntly, a dismal failure. The student leaders' application, you had to make a formal application, to meet the Vice-Chancellor had been delivered by hand at his office the day after the emergency *baraza* in July. They were, however, not granted an audience until mid-September, only a few days before the end of the first term. Whether the Vice-Chancellor had not considered their business all that urgent, or whether he had been consulting about it with the powers-that-be was his own secret.

Meanwhile the reduced bursaries had come, and the students, remembering that '*you should secure what you have under the arm while you demand more*', as their ancestors put the bird-in-the-hard philosophy had accepted the few coins given them after all the necessary deductions. You could not go on for six months without a booze or a visit to the 'people's goods' just because you were expecting an Nge Kisusuli to return the money which he had decided to rob from you. And, since employing students on vacation had long been scrapped, how could you get shoe-polish, tooth-paste and soap and, in the case of M.P. inmates, cosmetics, sex manuals and 'Tampax' tampons if you did not snatch the first coin Nge Kisusuli dangled before your nose?

And this perhaps was Nge's view of the students, when he thought of them at all: as beggars who depended on his charity at the best, or, at the worst, as pick-pockets who preyed on the tax-payer's money to keep themselves as snug as a bug in a rug in their skyscrapers.

But this time the beggars were refusing to be content with what they were given, and the pick-pockets were demanding rights. Since the day after the emergency *baraza*, students' letters were flooding the press, or, more precisely, the *Tchwezan Mail*. Scathing replies were written in the Party daily, and soon the 'bursary crisis' was turning into a Press dialogue between the two papers, or between their correspondents. But it was a rather confused dialogue. First, the students in their haste to get letters published did not check with one another what they sent in, and their arguments became inconsistent and sometimes downright self-contradictory.

Secondly, the students were not very well-informed - damn ignorant - of the facts relevant to their case. The per capita income in Tchweza, for example, was £20 per annum, which meant £20,000 or more per head on the average for Kisusuli, his ministers and a handful of Britishers and Indians, and £0 or less per head on the average for the twelve-or-so million *wananchi* in the bush. To claim, as some students claimed in their letters to the *Mail*, that you were demanding equality with your fellow citizens by seeking an extra £75 p.a. was not – good. Nor was it particularly intelligent in a black socialist state to use the leprous word *élite*, as many of those students who could not put an intelligible sentence on paper did in their letters to the *Tchwezan Mail*: '*a clear case of the victimization of the élites*' (sic). (To their mind, there were many intellectual *élites*, because every student was an *élite* in his own little

194

world.)

Thirdly, since the attacks and counter-attacks were written in different papers, neither side read or clearly understood the case of the other side. The students certainly never read the Party daily, first because it was edited by an African, secondly because they had enough material to read without desiring to ruin their eyes on illegible, and often indeed invisible print. So the polemics had gone on in ever- deepening mutual ignorance of the issues and arguments and sometimes of even the words used. A student who claimed that *'because we have no soap to wash our bodies and clothes, we are now littered with lice,'* was answered in the Party daily that there was nothing wrong with having plenty of rice to eat.

Two qualifications, however, should be made. First, as regards efforts to listen, the pro-Kisusuli, that is, anti-student side was slightly more energetic, thanks to the Research Bureau attached to the President's Office, whose main duty was to study all press reports and letters, and draft answers to those which were considered 'aggressive' enough to require them. Not that efficiency here was particularly high, since appointments were based more on Party loyalty than on any real qualifications for the job. That boy who wrote the bit on 'having plenty of rice to eat', for example, had left school after standard eight. and had only managed by some stroke of luck to get to an east European country, where he had studied politics, in the language of that country. And the Party daily editor had published his stuff on *rice*, probably because the editor was an African.

The second qualification is that there were some few strikingly intelligent and well-written letters in the depressing general welter of correspondence from the People's University. Take, for example, that student who compared the university student to a prisoner and, later, to a shop or a garden. '*We did not build these skyscrapers,*' the boy wrote, '*nor did we force our way into this place. We came here, nay, we were brought here, because of our qualifications, just as a convict is taken to prison owing to his criminal qualifications. If you decide to keep convicts in prison, you have got to pay for their upkeep. If this country decides to keep us at University, it must pay for our basic needs… Every university student is like a garden or a shop. If you want your garden to give you fruit, or your shop to bring you profit, you must invest thought, energy, and money, in it …*'

In a post-mortem of the strike, the Research Bureau attributed such letters to 'some anti-socialist foreign saboteurs' among the teaching staff. The boys of the Academics Anonymous roared with laughter when they discussed this assessment after the 'exile'. Such was the faith the leaders of the country had in the education which their youth were receiving at the People's University of Maalas. Kale had written the letter we have just quoted.

*

'I am ashamed of you, and the whole of Africa should be ashamed of you. Just imagine: our beloved President

196

decides to rationalize(!) your huge grants, for the noble purpose of helping our brothers and sisters suffering under colonial and racist regimes - and you start babbling out all that nonsense that you have been sending to the *Mail*. What Image of Africa do you think such things project to the people abroad?'

The Vice-Chancellor of the People's University of Maalas, Dr. Nyoka Kaniuma, belonged to that African Image-Creating, Image-Projecting generation of intellectuals who spoke loudest on this continent during the *pre-coup* years. In the year Seven of Uhuru he sounded, and looked, pathetically out-of-date. The tendency of the young people was to ignore him, like most of his agemates who were now forgotten in detention cells, 'self-exile' flats in London, Paris and New York, or in colonial State Houses. Also, like most of them, he had studied at Harvard and Cambridge, and, still in keeping with the conventions of his age-group, he had married a hideous English woman, undoubtedly the ugliest woman on the university campus. As Kale said once, citing a proverb from our Moslem-oriented lingua franca, '*if you are to eat pork, you might as well eat it fat*.' But one could not help wondering why those who chose to search for the African Image in the eyes of white women almost invariably chose the ugliest creatures there were of the whole white brood.

Now the President of the Students' Union and his Cabinet had been forced by circumstances into the presence of the Vice-Chancellor, and he was mincing no words with them. Another student leader had ventured, alone, into this spacious office about a year before. He had gone to request the Vice-Chancellor to take some action against an expatriate member of staff who had struck a student with a bottle and called him a 'black baboon' in the Students' Canteen. The expatriate was a Tutorial Fellow in Linguistics and he was collecting material for a dissertation on the *Vestigial Initial Vowel in Swahili*.

It was alleged that the 'black baboon' caught the linguist caressing his girl, a barmaid, at the counter. The girl started so violently out of the expatriate's arms that she knocked down his glass. The 'black baboon' exchanged a few quick words with the girl. The linguist, who did not know a word of spoken Kiswahili, and was gravely upset about his spilt booze, thought that the boy was reprimanding the girl. He struck the boy on the head with a bottle of 'Lake Basin' beer, using the magic phrase 'black baboon' to spur him on to action.

Deportation was the normal punishment for an Albino or Mongol who used such words to a citizen of the land anywhere in Tchweza, except on the campus of the People's University. Dr. Nyoka Kaniuma had replaced his expatriate predecessor at the personal recommendation of his old friend, Dr. Nge Kisusuli, whom he obeyed to the minutest detail. But he was also keenly aware that without the co-operation of his brothers- and sisters-in-law, the expatriates, he could not rule the campus. In the 'black baboon' case, for example, the Vice-Chancellor accepted the linguist's explanation that he had only been using the girl as a Swahili informant, and he kicked the students'

President out of his office with a severe reprimand to him for spreading unfounded rumours which damage 'our African IMAGE'. After all, the students were only noisy tots. The Vice-Chancellor had been a school-master before going to Harvard.

'But, Mr. Vice-Chancellor-' Hannington George Kadala was trying to explain the 'bursary crisis'. But Dr. Nyoka Kaniuma was already floating out of his office, to look for his Image in the fresh air outside. He needed it, because of his horribly-tailored *agbada*.

But things were moving faster than he suspected. The students went home on their short vacation, explained that they were unable to help with their younger brothers' and sisters' school fees, and returned to Maalas early in October. A week after their return, the *Tchwezan Mail*, reacting to a stiff warning from the Minister of Information, announced that 'correspondence on this subject' meaning the bursary crisis 'was closed'.

*

CASTRATE KISUSULI

WAR ON ACADEMIC PERSECUTION

NGE KISUSULI: WORSE THAN
A BLOODY COLONIALIST

DICTATOR, DEATH

199

WE DEMAND OUR RIGHTS

RELEASE DETAINEES

REDUCE YOUR SALARIES

WE ARE THE FIRST FREEDOM FIGHTERS

LIBERATE US

NGE : AUTOCRAT

ACT NOW: 'DOUGH' OR BLOOD

ARMY SAVE US: TAKE OVER

STUDENTS OF THE WORLD UNITE

It was like a festive procession. Vehicles stopped and hawkers and market women abandoned their wares on tables and mats and came to watch as the thick column of nearly two thousand university students streamed down Kisusuli Drive. All of them had come to demonstrate, except three who were in the sick bay: a girl who had plucked a child out of her womb, with rather unpleasant consequences, a boy, one of the very few who did any sports, who had broken his leg at a football match, and another boy who had simply gone 'neurotic' - after 'boozing' too much local *pombe* some people suggested, since he could not afford *Engleesh* beer in his 'reduced circumstances.'

The sun inflamed the demonstrators' deep-blue academic gowns which streamed in the beautiful breeze on which the deep-blue Lake Tudor seemed to be blowing kisses to them. The students marched with youthful elegance, led by their President, Mr. Hannington George Kadala, waving high their red-sloganed placards - they had attached them to tall, sexual broomsticks - and chanting *We Shall Overcome,* and *Oh, Freedom.*

The evening before, another emergency *baraza* had been held, the third since the beginning of the crisis. The second had been held only days before the September vacation, to receive Kadala's report of his interview with the Vice-Chancellor. The Vice-Chancellor had refused to present the students' case to the Minister of Education, let alone to the President of the Republic. He had also refused to arrange for the students themselves to meet Dr. Nge Kisusuli, even in his capacity as Chancellor of the People's University.

At the *baraza* on the eve of the demonstration some instinct told the students that what was now required was not arguments, but some magic formula to set them aflame, ready for action. So, all the speakers at the *baraza*, except Peso, concentrated on curses and attacks, more or less founded, on Dr. Nge Kisusuli and 'henchmen'. Or perhaps it was because of this approach that the students finally decided to demonstrate.

. . . 'Some dowdy old dogs imagine,' said one of

the *wazee*, a History Honours finalist, 'that because the accidents of history happened to place them at a turning point in our fight against colonialism, we should always take them for god-sent liberators, and keep singing: *yes, bwana, yes mzee, ndio, baba wa taifa*, even to their most depraved whims.' The *baraza* yelled out cheers. Not everyone had heard, or understood, but that did not matter. Moreover, the *mzee* had very successfully dramatized the subservient attitude that Kisusuli and his brood expected of the African people.

... 'Do you want to know a secret?' asked Paul Pundadume, a *mzee* from Kisusuli's tribe.

'Yeeeaahl' roared the *baraza*.

'This is a real secret: Nge Kisusuli keeps a huge harem on our location. In it, he has collected women from all over Tchweza, and from all over the world. There are Arabs, Indians, Englishwomen, Chinese and Americans. Kisusuli and his henchmen go there every time they want a large-scale munch. To us in the neighbourhood, their orgies are as common as the rising and setting of the sun. But recently there was trouble at the harem. The American women started it. They said they wanted the harem to be provided with every modern amenity, and that if that was not done within six months, they would go on strike, and tell all their fellow party-harem women to strike. Now listen,' and here the *mzee* dramatically raised his voice, 'all that talk about liberation movements is sheer rubbish. Kisusuli wants our money to furnish his giant harem. If anyone doubts what I say, let him come, and I will lead him straight to that harem.' Thunderous applause and exclamations of contemptuous surprise.

That story, however, was a lie. But then, the *mzee* who told it spoke as if he was the administrative secretary to the harem. And he knew that no student was prepared to leave the *baraza* at nine-thirty in the evening and travel six hundred kilometres out of Maalas to go and verify the existence or otherwise of Nge Kisusuli's harem. In any case, anything that blasted Kisusuli was just right for the occasion.

Peso's testimony was less sensational, and it sought to justify immediate action on the grounds of the intellectual impoverishment, degradation and 'eventual total recolonization' of Tchweza's youth that he, and his A.A. friends who had helped him prepare his address, felt was the 'most malicious crime perpetrated against our generation'. Peso had become more and more deeply involved in the 'bursary crisis' as it gathered speed and momentum. This was perhaps because of his academic pursuits. You remember he was taking combined Honours in English Literature and Government Arts. Peso attacked the Tchwezan leaders' habit of using 'endless isms' to justify every stupid action they did, and to silence every independent voice in the country:

'Patriotism, nationalism, humanism, Panafricanism, black socialism - Kisusulism,' applause. 'Where do we end? Since all isms are made by men, and belong to men, and men do make mistakes, any ism can go wrong. You cannot rule a nation by merely fabricating isms. We want more imaginative leadership.' Applause. Quoting the 'black baboon' case, Peso pointed out that the University was a pool of undisturbed colonialism and white supremacy in a country that was fighting hand and foot to be free.

'We are the most desperate freedom fighters,' Peso said; 'Nge Kisusuli should liberate us first. We know that there are Tchwezans and other Africans qualified to teach at this University, better qualified than any of these pale-faced Britishers; and we know that these Africans have been trying to get into this institution. But they have failed, owing to the efforts of a determined clique of racists at this University, supported and abetted by Nge Kisusuli and Nyoka Kaniuma, the two lousiest colonialists on this continent.'

'Hear, hear!!!' A thousand and twenty-one hand-salute, and a legion of feet tapping the floor. Peso's speech was to inspire some of the most inflammatory slogans and placards carried during the demonstration.

Another student came up with the story that Nge Kisusuli was a big imperialist. It was true that he supported the Liberation Movements. But these, the *mzee* disclosed, included clubs in independent African states, whose sworn aim was to overthrow African leaders who did not support the idea of a 'United States of Africa' - with Kisusuli as their President. The hushed silence in which the *baraza* received this story was perhaps an indication of how frightening it was in its probability.

'Student Power!'

'Eeeh!' Two thousand voices.

'Student Power!'

'Yeah!'

'Student Power!'

'Yeeeeaaah!' The windows rattled as they do during a thundery storm. Nyoka Kaniuma heard the shout from his study in the Vice-Chancellor's palace half a kilometre away, on Madaraka Hill. He thought some students were drunk.

Meanwhile, a very sober and very embittered Hannington George Kadala, who had just raised the 'student power' rallying cry was exhorting his forces for the last time before battle: 'Let us not be afraid of action. Students everywhere in the world are fighting for their rights and for the liberation of the world. In Indonesia they have toppled a government; in America, student power is dreaded; in Italy, in South Africa - even in Britain.' Applause. 'Try and be peaceful and orderly. But we have no choice but uncompromising action. Either we make this University a reasonable place to live and work in, or we destroy it. Student Power!...'

So, it had been decided to hold a demonstration through Maalas the next day, present a statement to the Minister of Education, outlining the students' arguments against the bursary reduction, and giving the Government three days in which to act or... Meantime all lectures, seminars and tutorials as well as the library should be boycotted.

A committee was elected to put final touches to the arrangements for the demonstration, and to draft the formal statement to hand to the Minister. Peso was on the committee and his Academics Anonymous friends kept vigil in Mutwe's 'godown' until four-thirty in the morning, when he came up. Mutwe had bought a bottle of Tuscany wine and three small packets of cashew nuts, and he and Kale talked over these as they waited for Peso, Peso was boyishly excited when he finally arrived. He downed in one gulp the first glass of wine Mutwe poured out for him, Then he recited: '*If I should die, think only this of me...*' But he picked up three nuts and started munching them before he had said what should be thought of him.

'The only remaining snag's the police,' Peso told Mutwe and Kale as he began to sip at his second glass of wine.

Yes, you had to have written permission from the Inspector General of Police if you were going to hold a demonstration. And you could be sure of being refused permission unless your demonstration was in support of the 'three-in-one' that made up the state of Tchweza: the Government, the Party, Kisusuli - in ascending order. You could not get permission to demonstrate in support of anything else, not even in support of God: church processions were banned in Tchweza. The demonstration working committee had decided that there was nothing that could be done about this. The students would have to take a risk and demonstrate without police permission.

A law finalist on the committee came up with the ingenious suggestion that they should telephone the police first thing in the morning and inform them that they were going to see the Minister of Education, to discuss some academic problems with him, adding an inquiry whether that fell under the legal description of demonstration. And this is what they did. Since their message was originally received by a poor semi-literate constable at the Police Headquarters' reception desk, a boy who could hardly make out what an 'academic problem' was, by the time it was communicated to his superiors and eventually to the Minister of Education, who said he knew nothing about the appointment and referred the matter to the Minister of Internal Affairs, who was not in his office when the message got there... and finally to the President of the Republic, the demonstration had already begun.

*

'And before I be a slave,
I'll be buried in my grave
And go home to my Lord
And be free ...'
down Kisusuli Drive.

Here student power had broken down every barrier that Maalas Campus had ever known. Peso was rubbing shoulders with Virgin Lisa. She loved singing, and her soprano on the high notes of *Oh, Freedom*, and especially of *We Shall Overcome*, was enough to melt a fossil heart. Kale and a tall, dark boy from the 'cafeteria' tribe flanked the social scientist, Diana. Mutwe marched in step with Fatma, the Asian girl who had been raped. He tried his best to ignore the nauseating scent of her perfume, or of something she had chewed.

A squad of riot police, the Special Security Police, were lined up in the court of Ujuzi House, the seat of the Ministry of Education. With their helmets, complete with visors, their thick, protective jackets and their shields and tear-gas guns - or were they only tear-gas? - they looked like figures from renaissance Europe. The students in the vanguard of the procession fell quiet abruptly. The squad commander spoke to the President of the Students' Union.

'But we want to see the Minister of Education,' insisted Mr. Kadala. Rank by rank the songs were dying out down the column of demonstrators.

A huge crowd of observers had now gathered, and they trotted behind the students and on their right and left, but not mixing with them, nor forgetting to keep at a respectful distance from the gowned *wazungu*. The townspeople always kept a respectful distance between themselves and the university students. When a student sat on a public bus seat, most *wananchi* preferred to stand rather than join the *mzungu* on that seat.

Well, there had been no universities in Tchweza since the beginning of time. In four years a university shot up, turned into a gigantic city, inhabited by white men and black men who spoke a language which no one but themselves understood, and who did not build houses, did not construct roads, did not repair cars, did not buy cotton or sell clothes, did not treat patients or preach religion, were not ministers or district commissioners, but were paid, one heard, for reading books. There must be something suspicious about them: probably a sort of contagious madness. Or perhaps the workers feared they might soil the *mzungu*'s starched shirt, or offend his nostrils with the smell of their sweat.

'I have been instructed to advise you,' said the squad commander to Mr. Kadala, 'to go to State House.'

'But we want to hand our statement to the Minister of Education.'

'The Minister is at State House.'

Hannington George Kadala turned to the students. Everyone was now streaming with sweat. The girls' faces looked terrifying with the gullies of sweat through the make-up. 'This gentleman tells me,' - the commander would have preferred to be called officer - 'that the Minister has gone to State House.'

'Coward! He fled! To State House then! Student Power!!' The shouts rose gradually along the column, as the songs had died.

'Therefore,' Mr. Kadala shouted, 'we will go to State House.'

'Yeah! Student Power!...' and the phalanx curled out of the Ujuzi House court, back on to the road, and headed for State House. But the songs did not resume. The students were now escorted by Special Security Policemen. This was Nge Kisusuli's plan. In the thirty-or-so minutes he had between the news and the beginning of the demonstration, he instructed the SSP to be at the ready but not to molest the students, and to direct them to State House, where he had gathered all his ministers. Knowing what the telephone services were like, Kisusuli had had all his messages delivered by runners.

The happenings at State House were brief and quiet. At the entrance, the students met more police, who directed them to the park which rolled from the back verandah of State House down to the beach. The students entered the park. They were now very quiet and a little - no, not worried - more serious than when they started their march. The sweat was beginning to dry on their faces, and not only because of the cool breeze in the park. Hannington George Kadala wished, as he was ushered into Kisusuli's presence, that he had resigned student leadership the evening before.

Mtumwamungu Baba wa Taifa, Dr. Nge Kisusuli and all his Cabinet were sitting on tall, hard-backed chairs on the back verandah of State House. 'Well, what is it, my children?' *Mtumwamungu* asked the students as they lined up in a thick crescent behind their President. They had now lowered their placards. But Kisusuli had already read several of them.

'We came to discuss our problems with the Minister of Education, *Mtumwamungu*.' Mr. Kadala's voice was trembling. The students were now surrounded by Special Security Policemen, as many as the grains of sand that surround the Lake, as a Lake Basin *mwananchi* would have put it. The students were not aware before that the country was so well-policed.

'They did not make an appoint-' the Minister of Education, a huge, bulky man with a lousy grey beard, rose to protest. But Kisusuli, who had remained seated, silenced him with a gesture of the hand.

'The Minister is here, my child,' Kisusuli said. His voice was chillingly suave. 'Tell him your problems.'

'We had prepared a statement, Your Excellency,' said Kadala, tearing open an envelope and taking out the statement to which he, Peso and other colleagues had put final touches in the small hours of the morning.

'You can say what you wrote,' said Dr. Kisusuli a little impatiently.

'We are old men, and our eyes should not be tortured with what you youngsters write. Tell us.'

'Read the statement,' Peso whispered behind Kadala. Kadala turned to the students, and ten other whispers repeated Peso's suggestion. He hated all this gang of students, but most of all, he hated himself. He wished he could drop dead at that very moment.

However, it was too late to withdraw or to die. Casting a quick glance at Mtumwamungu and clearing his throat noisily, Kadala began to read. His voice was trembling embarrassingly when he began. But he had gained confidence by the time he was half-way through:-

'...We must sound a very clear and serious warning to Tchweza's leaders: we have often been regarded as children. We are not children. Our suggestions have always been disregarded or brusquely ignored and contemptuously turned down without being given a thought! (The students had never made a suggestion to the Government, on anything, before the 'bursary crisis'.) *'We are the country's best brains, and its future depends on us. If we are not given the opportunities and the respect we need to develop into respectable and responsible leaders, this country is heading for chaos.'*

And he was the same old aggressive Kadala, who had campaigned for the students' Presidency the November before by the time he concluded: *'This is an ultimatum. We give the Tchwezan Government three days, three days, we repeat, to show whether or not it can keep us decently at the People's University of Maalas. If not, we will take drastic action, and the leaders of this nation shall be held responsible for the consequences. Finally, we resolve to abstain from all academic activities at the University until the Government answers us!*

Mr. Kadala wiped his brow, and he signalled his fellow students to sit down. He needed it, and he guessed that his followers, especially the girls, must be feeling the same. The students sat down on the green-brown grass. Round them, the policemen, in their clay-coloured uniforms, looked like an old bamboo fence.

There was an embarrassing silence after Kadala had read the statement. It began while he was still reading. The students, who, like Kisusuli and his 'henchmen' were hearing it for the first time in its final form, were at first greatly excited by its sharp wording and its chiselled logic. At certain points they had felt like clapping or cheering, but it was not easy cheering or clapping with an Nge Kisusuli before you and a forest of SSP men behind you and on your left and right. So there was no clapping, even after the reading of the statement. The students waited gloomily for a reply. But it seemed none was forthcoming.

A gentle breeze rustled through the old jacaranda and eucalyptus trees. The sun, peeping through gaps in the branches above the students' heads, played a thousand variations of blue on their gowns.

His Excellency the President of the Republic, now more of a mere Dr. Nge Kisusuli than of a *Baba wa Taifa Mtumwamungu*, sat absolutely still, gazing thoughtfully at the branches of the old trees and puffing slowly at his pipe. He might have been simply recalling his past years. Twenty years before today, a dashing, talkative undergraduate at a South African university... a chum and colleague of many of those guys who had now long since been legally murdered, or were rotting in endless ninety-day detention cells and penal colonies, or were hiding in caves under some thick bush, planning sabotage strategies in Mozambique, South Africa or Namibia ... Then Oxford. St. Giles, the spiked gates, the domes, St. Mary's, the 'Eights' on the River ... Defending a doctoral thesis written without any research, on the customs of his people ... A Ph.D. in Anthropology ... The independence of India ... Return to Montania (now Tchweza) ... Assistant Secretary in the colonial Department of African Development. Working under a man without a degree ... Quarrel with boss, sacked ... The Montania African Organization (MAO) ...

Finally, *Mtumwamungu* spoke. He did not rise. His voice was deep, quiet and strikingly elderish. He had not been thinking about his life story. For if he had, he would

213

have told it to the students there and then, and they might have understood. Why did no one ever explain things to them?

'My children,' said Dr. Kisusuli, 'we have heard your demands. We have noted your ultimatum. But, as our forefathers said, *a case is best decided overnight*. Leave us a day to deliberate and we shall come and answer you - before the three days are out.' The students clapped soberly. *Mtumwamungu* turned suddenly personal. 'Only, I am requesting you to do me a few things. First, do not throng the streets again, to obstruct the traffic and distract workers from their jobs. Secondly, give me that statement which you have just read to me, and all the other statements you brought me on the placards. Collect them, *askaris*.' Many students wished they had destroyed their red-sloganed placards during the reading of the statement or during the subsequent silence. Some actually managed to tear a few and stuff them under their gowns before the SSP men got to them. But quite a large pile of 'declarations' was collected.

'Thank you for these messages,' Dr. Kisusuli said as the pile of placards was placed on the low balustrade before him, and the neatly-typed statement handed to him. 'Now you may go. Remember to give a thought to the African Liberation Movement.'

Yes, the students supported the Liberation Movement. They had organized(!) dances and rag-days in aid of the Liberation Movement. But here was a higher principle at stake, a principle inherent in the very concept of a university. You went there to have a good time. To be bribed by the colonial government, or whichever government happened to inhabit that colonial State House, so that you would not use your enlightenment to denounce their corrupt activities or wish to overthrow them. To get a gentleman's pass and work as an assistant to a colonial officer or an expatriate volunteer in the colonial or national civil service. But if the bloody government refused to bribe you, an unprecedented refusal, then you had to denounce them, go on strike, demonstrate, and give the President an ultimatum.

*

The immediate results of the demonstration were simple and vivid: mass rustication, batons, boots, bullets, blood.

But before these there was a day and a half of intoxicated celebrations on the campus of the People's University of Maalas. On getting back to the University, Hannington George Kadala was cheered and carried shoulder-high by his fellow students. He remained in the cafeteria throughout the lunch hours, congratulating every group which came in and thanking them for their co-operation. 'The first bout has been won,' he said; 'now we move to the next stage. At three o'clock this afternoon, we shall go to Academic Hill and make sure that everyone, and I mean everyone, observes the strike.'

'Hear, hear! Kill Nyoka Kaniumal Kadala is our man!

Student Power! …'

At three o'clock, 'Student Power' marched on the Library. They just marched in, hundreds and hundreds of them, thronged the first floor, round the index-card boxes, chanting, clapping and stamping so vigorously and insistently that the building trembled. After a few minutes, Kadala raised his hand for silence.

'Listen, everyone in this Library, we give you five minutes to get out of here, or face us.' He announced this in English and Kiswahili, and each announcement was underlined with wild cheers from his followers. The Chief Librarian, a huge Northern Irishman with bloated cheeks and a pock-marked face, was clambering down the steps to face the students when Kadala repeated, 'Five minutes: and do not come back until we call you,' and led the students out of the Library. The Chief Librarian went back to his office and tried to call the Operator …

Then the students headed for the Faculties and Departments. For these they split, and each group of students were left to deal with their own Faculty. Here victory was easy. The trembling secretaries ran out as soon as they got the warning, and most of the professors, readers, senior lecturers, lecturers, assistant lecturers, tutorial assistants and others were not in their offices. They did not normally come to the offices unless they had to, and, since they had discovered quite early in the morning that there would be no lectures that day, most of them were now out on the beaches.

The Administrative Block next. The Vice-Chancellor

was not there. He was conferring with the President at State House. The Registrar, a tall, yellow-brown Rhodesian-born Britisher called Smith, tried to call the Operator … Meanwhile, high-heeled secretaries, khaki-clad messengers, ragged-tied clerks and dirty-sandalled sweepers were stamping out of the Block. The Bursar, a Canadian, Sir Francis Calder, ordered the cashiers to lock up the safes at once, and he tried to call the Operator … The Dean of Students, the Wild Highlander, who wished sincerely that he had brought a gun to his office this blasted afternoon, tried to call the Operator …

The Chief Librarian hung up with an obscene oath and a bang after holding the receiver to his ear for nearly ten minutes. He rushed down to talk to his staff. There was not a soul. And the chanting students were coming back. He locked the Library hurriedly, ran up to the top floor, the Fourth, collected his briefcase and fled to safety by the fire-escape. The students knew some cranks would be trying that 999 business. The girl who worked at the university telephone exchange was Hannington George Kadala's 'territory', and she had been the first person to be sent on holiday.

At tea, Kadala, 'the hero', announced that there would be celebrations at the Swimming Pool after supper. And grand celebrations they were. Booze was provided out of public funds, that is, students' union money, and everyone drank his or her fill. Someone brought down a huge old radiogram and it barked out Congolese tunes for the first part of the evening. But later, as people got more and more merry, some boys brought three drums and the *ngoma* dances began.

Ngoma iko wapi?

Ngoma iko huku?

... and the girls wagged their bottoms and set their hips gyrating while the boys leapt wildly round them. Miriam, Senior Lecturer John O'Goat's girl, was the first to throw off her blouse and bra' and defy the electric lights with the dark nipples of her banana-flower, firm breasts. The boys roared and the *ngoma* thundered as other girls followed suit, and things got very hot, *bwana*. The party did not break up until about four in the morning.

The next day, most students seemed to have boycotted breakfast. They stayed in bed until lunch time. Some Britishers had finally managed to get the Police on to Academic Hill, but it was completely deserted. The students had succeeded even better than they had hoped in 'closing it down'. Kadala tried to suggest a *baraza* after supper, but the students said 'no'. The hangover still remained. They did, however, hold the *ngoma* again, and they made a bonfire of the leaflets which Dr. Nyoka Kaniuma had sent to the cafeteria on that and the previous day.

One of the notes read:-

'It has been brought to my notice that some students are planning to hold a demonstration in town. I should like to warn you that such a demonstration would be illegal, and to advise you to go and attend your classes as usual, since your purpose here is to study.

Nyoka Kaniuma,
Vice-Chancellor.'

This note had come out of the Vice-Chancellor's Office just as the students' procession arrived at the Ministry of Education at Ujuzi House.

Another note, issued on that day after the demonstration, was more concise:-

'Strong disciplinary measures will be taken against any student who does not return to lectures today, or tries to interfere with the smooth running of the University.

Nyoka Kaniuma,
Vice-Chancellor.'

The *ngoma* ended at about eleven that evening, immediately after the burning of Dr. Kaniuma's messages.

*

Dr. Nge Kisusuli was clad in a leopard skin. His head was wreathed with a creeper used during funeral rites among some tribes. He had marched all the way from town to the campus, at the head of his Cabinet, the Party Elders, the Youth Wing, the Women's League, the Workers' Solidarity, and a huge, dirty mob of town idlers. This was the second day after the demonstration. It was a Thursday. A third note from the Vice-Chancellor had informed the students, at breakfast, that the 'Father of the Nation' was coming to address them that morning. The students had a row of chairs arranged on the verandah of their Main Hall, got a technician to fix speakers, put on their academic gowns and waited in the car park in front of the Main Hall.

A handful of security men arrived at nine and they scanned every nook and cranny of the students' union premises, and then they planted themselves at strategic points, with their shotguns. Then almost immediately, truck loads and truck loads, and truck loads - and still more truck loads - of Special Security Policemen began to pour on to the campus. They surrounded the students, who remained absolutely still and quiet. The SSP men were fully armed and dressed for action, and they looked as ugly as Zinjanthropuses.

Mtumwamungu Baba wa Taifa, Dr. Nge Kisusuli, arrived at seven minutes to ten, with the Vice-Chancellor. The Vice-Chancellor welcomed the President and the *wananchi* to the campus. (Everyone spoke in Kiswahili at this rally.) Dr. Kaniuma said that he regretted that the occasion should be such a sad one. He outlined the situation, and said that the students had decided, without ever consulting him. to go and 'be insolent' to the 'Father of the Nation'. 'I, as director of this institution, felt obliged to apologize for this incident to our beloved President, and to report it to you, *wananchi*, so that we may decide what to do.' The Vice-Chancellor bowed, put on his mortar-board, he was in full academic dress, and sat down.

Then the leader of each organization which had accompanied *Mtumwamungu*, starting with the Doyen of the Party Elders, made a speech, each speech more vitriolic than its predecessor, cursing and condemning the students, and advocating the harshest measures against them. The mob of town idlers was not represented by any particular speaker, but they kept cheering at every dagger that shot out of the speakers' mouths into the students' breasts. The students grew tired of standing, and they squatted or sat on the hard tarmac of the car park, leaving the bamboo fence of the SSP men, now three rows thick, towering over their heads. Some of the girls sat in the boys' blue-gowned laps and others leaned against their shoulders.

Bibi Chanze, the lady M.P., represented the Women's League, and we may quote a line or two from her speech as a general illustration of the sense that was uttered on this occasion. 'You girls', she said, 'you paraded arrogantly down the streets of Maalas in your smart dresses and your *kitungu* gowns. But through all these, the country could see your shameful nakedness: a nakedness eaten by gonorrhoea and syphilis: the gonorrhoea of neo-colonialism, and the syphilis of the spirit of exploitation ...' Bibi Chanze received the wildest cheers at that rally. Even the Special Security Policemen cheered her.

'We have come here for a funeral.' The voice of His Excellency the President of the Socialist Republic of Tchweza, Founder of the Party, *Mtumwamungu*, 'Father of the Nation', Dr. Nge Kisusuli, sounded deep, steady and sad over the loudspeakers. He had stood silent for three minutes, waiting for the *Voice of Tchweza* men, who arrived just before he began to speak, to fix their machines. Other pressmen had arrived just before the security squad.

Kisusuli had dabbed red ochre on both his cheeks and on his forehead. His clean- shaven face looked like a wooden mask.

'These, once your children, and mine, elders and citizens, are now corpses.' He did not have much to say. He spoke for only two hours. He read passages from the students' statement and translated them into Kiswahili, creating an impression of fascinating erudition. Then he commented on them. He also concentrated on some of the students' placards which he had brought with him. 'These youths said that I should be castrated.' The word sounded terribly embarrassing in Kiswahili: '*Hawa vijana wakasema kwamba nihasiwe...* that I should be gelded like a goat fattened for slaughter. And this is exactly what they want. They want to hand you and me and all our fellow Africans to Vorster, Smith and Salazar for slaughter.'

'Burn them ! ! ! !'

A cry that pierced the sky. 'They want me castrated. They want me deprived of my manhood. Now, am I not old enough to be father to them all?'

'*Baba wa Taifa!*' A yell that shook the earth.

'If your child insults an elder or any visitor in your presence, what do you do? These boys and girls insulted me... Wait, citizens, wait until I have told you the whole story.' The citizens, the whole mob at the rally, had fallen upon the innocent cashew and flamboyant trees and broken off twigs to beat the students. In spite of the fence of Special Security Policemen round them, some students felt like 'going piss for trouser (or knicker)', as a Nigerian

222

(or a Biafran) might have put it, when they heard the cashew branches snap.

'These students also said that I was worse than a colonialist. I cannot fully translate what they said: worse than a bloody colonialist. But think of it, elders and citizens. Me a colonialist ('The new Swahili word for colonialist originally means he-goat, and, as a sequel to the castration episode, it would have been amusingly striking. But no one was in the mood to be amused. *Mtumwamungu* briefly outlined the story of the liberation of Tchweza and the role he had played. Then he asked: 'Which of us is worse than a colonialist? I, Nge Kisusuli, or these students, these exploiters who feast sumptuously every day and wallow in feather-beds, at your expense? Who would rather sell us to colonial and racist regimes than part with a coin for the liberation of our black brothers?'

'They!'

Finally, Kisusuli stamped and said, 'You gave me an ultimatum. Now I am answering you. I can't keep you at this University. Therefore, go where you will: to Vorster, to Smith or to Salazar, or to Gehenna. You marched on me, now *I* am marching on you, and we shall see which of us two is the better marcher. You insolently violated the sanctity of my enclosure. Now *I* am respectfully returning your visit. We shall see which of us will oust the other from his enclosure. I give you only one hour to leave this campus.'

It was about two-thirty, and the students were rather hungry. 'Guardians of law and order,' Kisusuli said to the

SSP men, 'remove these corpses from our midst.' The word he used would actually mean *carcasses*. 'And I, like the bereaved father I am, will go and weep.

It was said that Kisusuli had a girl - in the sense of mistress as well - with a B. Litt. (Oxon), who prepared all his speeches. It would have been interesting to ascertain how far this woman ruled the Socialist Republic of Tchweza.

*

Mutwe *was not happy*, as the *Engleesh* saying goes. He and the Bishop had decided to leave all their books and boxes behind and try to catch the three-thirty plane to their eastern country. Luckily, they had bought return tickets on their flight to Maalas after the September vacation.

(The whole story of all the students' departure from Maalas is too 'lousy' for any ears to hear in detail. Many of them, especially the Tchwezan students, did not have a coin in their pockets when Kisusuli rusticated them. Some had to sell their suits and cocktail dresses for as little as thirty shillings, to town second-hand clothing merchants, who called them colonialists and exploiters and spat on them, to get money to travel home. Some desperate girls had to spend a 'working night' at the Hotel Ghala, earning their fares home.)

Mutwe and the Bishop rang up the national airline who said they had some vacant seats and would make emergency arrangements to put them on the three-thirty flight. They sent them a van immediately. Only, Mutwe and the Bishop nearly failed to get seats on the van. It was crowded by all their countrymen, as well as other students, who intended to travel by plane, or only wanted to get away from the campus as quickly as possible.

'May I, on behalf of Captain Blishen and the crew, welcome you all aboard... Fasten your seat belts please.' Mutwe did not fasten his belt. He wanted to slap the air hostess. Why was she in such a hurry? Peso was not on the plane. Mutwe had run to his room when the van came. Peso was not there. Mutwe had nearly missed the van, looking for Peso. Mutwe had to squeeze past the two armed SSP men guarding the back door of the airline's van to get in. The SSP men stood on the doorstep of the van all the way to the airport. Mutwe had tried to whistle *We Shall Overcome* as the van tore through Maalas and entered the countryside. One of the guards had barked at him: '*Nyamaza wewe!*' Mutwe had felt an urge to spit, but the self-preservation instinct... Mutwe still hoped that Peso might arrive at the last moment. There were still some vacant seats... The jet-engines started. Peso had missed the plane.

Mutwe had, fortunately, missed something too. On the campus. Even as he got into the airline's van at the University, a group of town thugs, still holding their cashew twig whips, and thoroughly incited to murder by Nge Kisusuli's speech, came upon a party of blue-gowned students and fell upon them. A battle ensued. By the time the SSP men intervened the students were throwing stones. The stones hit some of the SSP men, and they retaliated with batons, boots and bullets. The whole campus exploded. Hundreds of students were caught in the explosion, some fatally.

Peso fled from the thick fighting at the Students' Union Main Hall towards the Swimming Pool. As he crossed Hekima Road, he saw thighs sticking out of a spreading blue gown and a light-yellow *plus-que-nue* Parisian mini-skirt. The girl had fallen unconscious. Peso picked her up from the road, grateful that she was not a 'king-size'. But already a mob of bleeding and screaming people was rushing towards him. Peso ran a few steps, went down into the gutter along Hekima Road and disappeared into a drain, with the – 'Bitch'.

8 A thousand and four love affairs

The 'Bitch,' that is what they called her. And this was not a nickname like the 'Virgin', used by only a few individuals. Everyone knew it. And everyone knew her story, everyone, from the Vice-Chancellor to the humblest *askari*. The Bitch had slept with the last colonial Governor of Montania (now Tchweza), had in fact been his mistress from the age of fourteen. Her father had been a cook at Government House (now State House) during the days of Sir Nathaniel Barry, the Governor. You know the English used to send the tough wild Scots to the colonies.

The Bitch was in primary school, and just beginning to blossom, when Sir Nathaniel saw her. There was a large old incense tree in that park where Kadala read the ultimatum to Nge Kisusuli. The Bitch was collecting incense fruit under it when the Governor, on his usual evening walk, saw her. She was running here and there, singing to herself. Kisusuli and the MAO (the Montania African Organization), were making a lot of noise at the time, and the Colonial Office had just written to say Sir Nathaniel might as well let some natives go to London and negotiate with the Colonial Secretary. Sir Nathaniel took this as a negative comment on his ability to keep the situation under control. The Colonial Secretary was English, and Sir Nathaniel sensed some tribal undertones in his decision. He was not happy.

The Governor saw the girl before she saw him. Actually, he had been looking at her for some minutes when she noticed him. The Bitch, well, she was only a delicate young thing then, just over the threshold into womanhood, was petrified with terror when she saw the Governor. First, she was trespassing, gravely, for no one was allowed in the park during the hour of the Governor's walk. He had once had a boy whipped for deciding to water the roses during this hour. Secondly, Sir Nathaniel Barry was so hairy that he would have been frightening to any young woman.

'Kuja happer!' the Governor called the girl in *Kisettlah*. The girl had been six years at school and she spoke English much better than the Governor spoke Kiswahili.

She came and knelt before the Governor, muttering 'I'm sorry, Sir.' She did not know his official title. Her *kanga*, the only thing she had on, was knotted just above her cotton-boll breasts. They were just beginning 'to smile', as Mutwe's people would have put it. The girl's shoulders were bare, and as smooth and red-brown as a chief's gourd. Her hair was done in six neat plaits, and there was a faint smell of 'Palmolive' about her. She had just finished her bath. Yes, her womanhood was there, but it was the kind of 'half-ripe goods' that would normally make you feel sorry rather than sexually excited. But Sir Nathaniel was not happy.

'*Unafani-ah nini happer?*' he asked. The Bitch did not answer. However, she was relieved to note from the tone of the Governor's voice that he was not angry. '*Haya, kuja,*' said the Governor, raising the girl by the wrist. Then he noticed the tiny black incense fruit in her hand 'What's this?' he asked in English.

'It is fruit, Sir,' the girl said.

'Oh, you speak English?'

'Yes, Sir. Just a little, Sir.' The girl's teacher would have been thrilled to bits to hear her pupil speak to the Governor in *Engleesh!*

'Oh, good!' The usual, unenthusiastic British grunt. The Governor led the girl to a dark-green bench behind a hibiscus bush. and they sat down. It was about a quarter to seven and darkness was slowly descending upon the park. Sir Nathaniel took one of the incense fruit from the girl's hand and bit through it. It was very bitter. The Governor spat vehemently and frowned at the girl. Did he not know that you have to keep the incense fruit in body-temperature water or in the mouth for at least ten minutes before you can eat it? He threw the mangled fruit some metres away on the grass before him. Then he turned back to the girl.

'You're very pretty,' he said as the bitterness in his mouth began to subside.

The girl laughed, partly because she did not know that people say 'thank you' for such compliments, partly because she thought the Governor very greedy when he bit through the fresh incense fruit. Dimples formed on the girl's cheeks when she laughed. Then the Governor ravished the girl. It was easy. The girl had no panties under her *kanga*, and the Governor had on only a thin shirt and tiny shorts. You know they only wore those tight black things and plumed hats on public appearances, to impress the natives; and they felt terribly uncomfortable in them. The girl tried to scream, but the Governor ordered her not to. He also instructed her, after the munch, not to mention the incident to anyone.

But the girl was not feeling very well when she got back to the servants' quarters and there were drops of blood on her *kanga*. So, she had to explain to her mother, who told the girl's father, the Governor's cook. The Governor's cook *was not happy*. You see, you risk public shame and the loss of a special present from your son-in-law if your daughter is not a maid on her wedding night. The Governor's cook was in fact so angry with his master that, without giving a thought to the possible repercussions, he went and confronted His Excellency in person.

Sir Nathaniel did not make any trouble. There were too many issues at stake: his personal reputation, his wife and children, that devil Nge Kisusuli and the MAO shouting about *Uhuru* all over the country; then the dispatch from the Colonial Office. So he agreed to 'marry' the girl, under customary law. He was made to pay a huge bride-price, and, since he had no cows, it was even bigger than it might have been. And he had to pay an extra few thousand shillings to make sure that the whole story, including the 'marriage', did not spread beyond him and the girl's family.

But when the cook and his family moved into new quarters, where the Governor frequently visited his second 'wife' in her private suite of rooms, rumours began to spread. They even reached the ears of Lady Barry, the Governor's elderly, white, first wife, who ignored them.

The Bitch's father bought a vast tea plantation on the Southern Plateau, from a European who wanted to go home before *Uhuru*. He also bought a string of Indian *dukas* round Tchweza's big towns, and he had a fleet of taxis in Maalas. He lived on the tea plantation, after his retirement from Sir Nathaniel's service, and he was certainly one of the richest Africans in Tchweza.

His daughter, the Bitch, had missed a year of school, because she was pregnant when Sir Nathaniel left, in the year One of Our Lord Nge Kisusuli, and *Uhuru*. She had, however, resumed school after having her child, a blithe, good and bonny, unacknowledged, Miss Barry, and she had eventually made it to the People's University of Maalas, where she was entirely self-supporting.

That was the Bitch's story, as Peso got it from her, and from a few other reliable sources. But it had now become a legend, and its many narrators played several variations on its theme. The university students, for example, told it with such gusto and exaggeration that the Wild Highlander, who had served under Sir Nat Barry, at one time threatened to rusticate some of them for slander. The students said that the Bitch had bribed the Dean with her goods, which was possible. For one thing that the girl's early experience with Sir Nathaniel had taught her was a cool, shameless sexual cynicism, or liberalism.

In the boys' halls, for example, before she met Peso, she could sleep with a boy in one room one day, sleep with his next-door neighbour the following day, and have herself munched at the third door only six hours later. And you hesitated to call her a prostitute, because she did not do it for money. And perhaps she did not do it for pleasure either, for some people said she was as frigid as the inside of a fridge.

*

'Bon jour.'
'Mm. . . Bonjour, mademoiselle.'

Mutwe did not normally talk to the Bitch, but his apparent hesitation in returning her greeting was more due to his usual self- concentration than to any surprise or displeasure at being hailed by her. Any student could talk to any other student now, freely. Memories of the strike and of the 'exile' were still fresh in everyone's mind, and they formed a chain of intimacy among all the students who had returned to the University. This was the first day they were attending lectures after the exile.

Two days earlier, at an impressive ceremony, they had been formally received back into the University. The Vice-Chancellor, Dr. Nyoka Kaniuma, and all the academic and senior administrative members of staff gathered on the verandah of the Main Hall, where *Mtumwamungu* had pronounced sentence on the students two months before. Everybody was in academic dress, except the *Mini-star* of Education, who did not have any academic dress, or any academic standing. He was representing the Party, the

Government and the People of Tchweza at the ceremony.

The students, in their deep-blue academic gowns, now loathed throughout Tchweza as symbols of exploitation, reaction and neo- colonialism, stood in the car park, where the SSP men had surrounded them on the day of wrath. And, one by one, as they were called, they went up and took the 'second oath', administered by the Wild Highlander in his capacity as Dean of Students. Every student held the new Tchweza Socialist Union manifesto in his right hand, raised it and recited:

'I, (Moses Kale), do solemnly swear and promise to aspire to the ideals of black socialism and African Liberation, to be inspired in word and deed by the thoughts of our great Leader, Mtumwamungu Baba wa Taifa, Nge Kisumli, and to refrain from any acts, suggestions or intentions that the leaders of this Republic and the authorities of this University may deem contrary to these.'

Those who framed the oath refrained from any mention of God because of the difficulty of deciding on who came before whom: God or Nge Kisusuli.

After taking the oath, the student signed a copy of it, witnessed by the Dean of his Faculty or the Director of his Institute, and he deposited this with the Registrar, Mr. Smith, for safe custody. Then the student knelt before Dr. Nyoka Kaniuma and, placing his right hand on the student's shoulder, the Vice-Chancellor recited: 'By the powers invested in the Chancellor, and now delegated to me, I re-admit you to the People's University of Maalas.' It was like a mammoth graduation ceremony, with fewer caps and black gowns, and without Kisusuli.

Perhaps, more than any black cap-and-gowned or Kisusulied ritual, this was real graduation, from the contented self-ignorance that had bred all the students' tragedies. Or at least it should have been. For ignorance is no defence; but no one ever learnt anything by being punished for ignorance. Why did no one ever explain things to them?

Their return was as abrupt as their dismissal. After their rustication in October, the whole of Tchweza burst aflame with praises for Dr. Kisusuli and curses against the students. The *Voice of Tchweza* broadcast Kisusuli's dismissal speech after every two hours, for fifteen days on end. It became the fashion for anyone who opened his mouth anywhere in Tchweza to attack the students. Then, as November wore on, and people became filled with end-of-year cares and Christmas preparations, the students were forgotten. No one talked about them in fashionable (Party) society. The Party daily, which had published sensational reports of parents disowning their student children and refusing to feed or lodge them after they had rebelled against 'our beloved President', now published no more student reports.

It was unfortunate, because if it had kept its columns open a little longer, it would have received even more exciting reports: of parents who wailed and wreathed their temples with funeral herbs when they learnt that Nge Kisusuli was bringing their children's careers to an abrupt and meaningless end; of village *barazas* at which the elders asked their dismissed sons why they did not throw Kisusuli out and declare themselves Presidents, since they were as well-read as Kisusuli himself; of expert *waganga* and famed *wachawi* who, when consulted by anxious parents, promised to get rid of Kisusuli in two months, or to make him change his mind. It might have been their charms which effected the students' return to Maalas.

Or it might have been the few voices, all foreign, which remained talking after the Tchwezans had forgotten. Some foreign papers and magazines reported the strike, the demonstration and the 'exile' in minute (and sometimes exaggerated) detail. Their reports sent a current of indignation and shock through academic communities all over the world. Hundreds of students' organizations sent pleas and protests to Kisusuli. And, owing to the time it took some post office wretches to decide what to do with a letter addressed to Tchweza when all they had on their mailing lists was Montania, pleas and protests were still arriving in Maalas four months after the event, and some two months after the students had been reinstated.

Economic attaches to the embassies in Maalas, whose duty it was to see how the aid given by their countries was used in the Republic, reported to their countries. These in turn protested to (i.e. threatened to withdraw aid from) Tchweza. The Tchwezan Government's own (expatriate) economic advisers pointed out that it was not very economical sending to the bush two thousand students after you have been paying 23,000/- p.a. for each of them for a year or two, or three: especially when you were still rather short of high-skilled manpower.

Then there was Professor Hogg, Head of the English Literature Department and Dean of the Faculty of Arts and Social Chaos. He was one of the very few members of the academic staff who took sides in the quarrel at all, and he came out strongly in defence of the students. Professor Hogg pointed out that, although he did not support the grounds on which the students had called the strike, and he regretted some of the unfortunate things they had said, he felt that the measures taken against them were 'hasty, emotional and unrealistic'. Those at the Academic Board meeting at which the Professor and Dean revealed this, only a few days after the day of wrath, were stunned by his courage. No one had imagined that the old hog had such lots of guts in him. And he all but blasted the Vice-Chancellor for what he called his 'intellectual cowardice and political blinkers'. (The Party Youth Wingers howled for Hogg's blood when they learnt of his stand.)

Or, possibly, like a little boy who has sulked his fill, Nge Kisusuli simply decided to start smiling again. He called off the 'exile' during his Christmas message to the nation, without giving any details. No one commented. No one cheered. Hatred had been too spectacularly released for it to be tamed by such a casual gesture of reconciliation. The Party daily printed the news in the right-hand bottom corner of its back page, in only four lines, two of which were illegible …

'Your friend saved me,' said the Bitch. Her French would have made Charles de Gaulle rub his hands in satisfaction at the French achievement abroad. It was so *sans accent*.

The few French volunteers whom the French Government sent to Maalas to propagate their 'language and civilization' found themselves exiles in that wilderness of British influence, and, suspending their social life for a while, they poured all their energies into their work. In three years they turned out more accomplished linguistic and cultural *assimilés* than the English did in seventeen years.

'*Quel ami?*' Mutwe asked the Bitch as she sat on a concrete bench sticking out of a low stone wall outside the Arts Lower Lecture Theatre. He did not particularly care for being pinned down to a long conversation with the Bitch. But he did not want to be impolite.

'Why, Peso,' said the Bitch, and Mutwe started visibly.

'Ohl' he almost shouted, and he fixed the Bitch with an excited gaze. 'You know where he is?'

'*Mais oui!*' The Bitch laughed quietly, and Mutwe felt a little stupid. 'He is on my father's plantation.'

Mutwe sat beside the Bitch. 'I haven't heard from him since we were sent down,' he said in a near-whisper.

'He kept talking about you and Kale all the time I was there …' And, in clear, brisk French, the girl told Mutwe her story, and Peso's, from the day they were sent down.

She had fled, pursued by a Special Security Policeman, from the fighting which broke out immediately after Kisusuli's dismissal speech. She must have been heading for the Dispensary. Then she fell, and the SSP man planted one of his six-kilo boots on her right knee. It was very badly sprained but, fortunately or unfortunately, the SSP man did not stop. Perhaps he was chasing another student. The Bitch fainted.

She came round in Peso's arms, in the coolness of the large concrete drums under Hekima Road, where they had taken shelter from the explosion. Peso wanted to rush her to the Dispensary at once, to have her knee attended to, but the SSP men were still roaming like safari ants all over the campus, and sporadic shooting and screams could still be heard. So, they remained in hiding until sunset, Peso helplessly trying to nurse the girl's ever-worsening knee. It became as swollen as a hippo's neck.

When the sun set, Peso stuck his head out of the drain to check whether the coast was clear. Then he decided to rush the Bitch to the Dispensary. The pain in her knee was agonizing, but Peso beseeched her not to scream as he lifted her, for the campus was most probably patrolled by Police. Even approaching the Dispensary, which was only a few hundred metres away, was just one of those risks which necessity forces on one from time to time.

The Bitch was almost fainting again when they reached the door of the Dispensary, and the nurse on duty ran to help Peso. But she stopped short, a few paces away from him and his human load, saying, 'But we can't keep you here.' Then Peso suddenly realized with a pang of shock that he was still wearing the deep-blue academic gown; so was the Bitch.

'I'll call you an ambulance,' the nurse said.

This pulled the Bitch a few centimetres out of her abyss of pain. 'No, call a taxi,' she said and spelt the telephone number with dry, trembling lips. She was very feverish now, and her body burnt like a tea-kettle against Peso's breast.

Peso put her down on the dispensary door-step. It cost twenty-five shillings to travel by taxi from the University to town. Peso had only three shillings in his pocket. He had left the other shs. 120/- he had in his room. But the Bitch insisted on a taxi, and the nurse was already dialling the number. Peso stood scratching his head for some minutes. Then he asked the nurse whether she could not do anything for them while they were waiting for the taxi. The nurse brought some warm water, bandages and a liniment. The Bitch screamed as the nurse rubbed her knee. The taxi which came belonged to the Bitch's father, and she ordered the driver to head for a private hospital …

'And Peso insisted on staying around till I had completely recovered,'

'Where was he staying?' Mutwe asked,

'At the Hotel Ghala..'

'At the *Hotel Ghala*!' exclaimed Mutwe. 'Where did he get the money?'

The Bitch laughed a guttural laugh. 'Money is no problem,' she said, 'and when I left hospital, Peso said he must see me safely home.

Just like Peso, thought Mutwe, *he can't leave a bit of kindness undone*. He was feeling either puzzled or downright jealous at the devoted admiration with which the Bitch talked about Peso.

'So, we travelled together to the plantation.. There was a pause, then the Bitch added, as a kind of explanation or excuse for her talk with Mutwe, 'He told me to say hullo to you and Kale,'

'Thank you. Was this when you were coming up?'
'Well,' the Bitch said, 'I heard from him yesterday. He wrote to ask how I was, and to say he's fine,'

Mutwe remained quiet. *Peso never wrote letters*, Mutwe had always thought, *except business letters* ...

*

'Life has never been romantically happy or romantically sad to me; it has always been realistic, and I would be cheating life if I tried to be anything else.' That is how Kale of the Academics Anonymous explained to Mutwe of the same fraternity his decision to get married at once.

To several students life became romantically different after the strike. One issue of a popular American weekly was banned in Tchweza. It had reported that one student died on the spot during the shooting incidents on the campus, and that two others died later in hospital. These reports were never confirmed in Maalas. But no one knew why Paul Pundadume, the second-year biologist who told the story of Kisusuli's harem, and Osuk, a historian who came from Tchweza's northern neighbour, had not come back after the exile and had actually remained unaccounted for.

Hannington George Kadala, former President of the now-outlawed Students' Union, it was known, was in preventive detention; and he was awaiting trial on charges of holding an unlawful assembly, attempting to bring the person of the President into disaffection, behaving in a manner likely to cause a breach of the peace, contravening section 23 (b) of the Traffic Ordinance (1922) by blocking the streets with his unlawful assembly, and a dozen or so other charges. Law experts said that, if he was convicted on all of them, he would get fines up to £20,000,000 or eighty-seven years in prison, or both.

Those who had played any significant role in the strike and the demonstration, including Peso, were kept out, whether on permanent expulsion or on extended suspension no one could tell immediately. The American and British students were refused re-entry permits to Tchweza, luckily, for they would have had a difficult time pronouncing all Kisusuli's titles and names in the second oath. (Mutwe took the oath in English and he consequently and deliberately mispronounced all those titles and names.) Several students were left with life souvenirs of the strike. The Bitch's knee was never quite whole again.

'*La, bwana*! I'll never forget that.' That is how Mzee Chayo, a fifty-year old mature-age student concluded his story of the strike, in which he had been 'slightly injured' as the *Voice of Tchweza* announcers put it. Mzee Chayo eventually failed all his preliminaries, and he was sent down without a degree, and with a huge scar on the forehead.

But … does a big scar on the face, or being put in prison, or even dying, really constitute *change*? Two or three weeks after the exile, and life on Maalas Campus had returned to normal, and that means the Maalas, pre-strike normal, except for a very few individuals. The students had known persecution, and they had learnt one important thing: they were hated. But beyond that… why did no one ever explain?

For Kale's wedding, Mutwe and Kale borrowed money from everyone they knew, including Kale's fiancée, Professor Hogg and Senior Lecturer John O'Goat. The preparations were frantic and almost killingly tiring for the two boys. They had, for example, to find a house in town where they could put their bride. Students could not keep wives, or husbands, on the campus. There was no corner of Maalas, except perhaps the Ideological College, which the two boys did not visit in the search. Every reasonably clean house they found was madly 'high-rented'. And, after the strike, the boys did not know whether it would be to their advantage to say that they were students. And if you did not tell a landlord or a landlady your job, they would take you for a thief. So, Mutwe and Kale went inventing themselves jobs from house to house.

Finally, they found a one-room apartment in a 'middle-brow' suburb only six kilometres away from the campus. The rent was shs. 200/- a month, and they were told by the landlady that they had to pay four months' rent in advance. They paid the shs. 800/- immediately and left, quietly searching their near-empty pockets for the *pesa* to furnish the room, buy utensils and so on.

They often argued and disagreed so violently between themselves during these arrangements that one would have wondered whether they would ever complete them at all. In furnishing the house, for example, Kale kept saying that the bed could wait, that they should first get a table, chairs and a carpet. Mutwe called this thinking backwards. Then they both concluded with their now-favourite refrain: '*If Peso were here!*'

Mutwe was to be best man, but he withdrew the evening before the wedding. Kale and the Bishop, who was finally the best man, thought that, being Catholic, Mutwe did not wish to play a prominent role in a protestant church service. This was not the case. The heat and rush of the preparations had left Mutwe no time to think about the significance of Kale's wedding. It was on the eve of the wedding that a ray of awareness suddenly shot through his mind.

For a man with a wife is a divided man. This now assumed very concrete meaning for Mutwe, and it was not very pleasant meaning. *Times change and we with them are transformed*, ran a sentence in his literal school translation of Cicero. But, by some unfortunate *refusal* of his emotions to establish any connection with the intellect, Mutwe found it impossible to accept the 'change'.

If he stood by Kale at the altar, he would have either to shut off his mind altogether, so that it registered nothing throughout that ritual plucking away of Kale from him and from the Academics Anonymous, or else run crazy at the realization. He actually left the big old cathedral in town where the wedding took place just as Kale was saying, '*With my body I thee honour...*' Mutwe went and took a walk along the beach. He was feeling very faint, and he missed the reception at Professor Hogg's.

Ruth, now Mrs. Kale, was a childhood friend of Kale's. She had gone home after her School Certificate finals in Maalas and met Kale there, in exile. Throughout December, she was his only link with the 'well-read' world from which he had been violently ejected by Nge Kisusuli. Nature took advantage of the situation, and, a few weeks after Ruth got a secretarial job with a Maalas car firm, she noticed that things were not 'normal'. Since her parents did not raise any objections and, like the staunch Christians they were, proved very reasonable about that old business of bride-price, Kale decided to make an honest woman of Ruth.

*

'I can't let you descend so low,' said Mutwe of the Academics Anonymous.

'Thank you,' answered Peso of the same fraternity, 'but I think I can quite well do without your protection.'

'No – yes, but – this is a girl whose scandalous story is known to everyone.' !

'I did not expect you to be so narrow-minded,

Mutwe,' Peso said.

Yes, the story was known, very well known, better known to Peso than to any other students, for she had told it to him herself, in an attempt, whose sincerity no one could estimate, to make him drop her, 'for his own good'.

The two Academics were talking about the Bitch. *Peso was at last there*. He and a few other students with similar offences were given only three more weeks of 'exile', and they were re-admltted to the People's University of Maalas without any ceremony. No one had pleaded for them, no one had complained or protested about their treatment. Peso had taken to frequenting Margaret Plantagenet Hall, and the Bitch.

At first people thought that Peso was just another fly in the spider's web. But as he and the Bitch went steadier and steadier, and she showed every sign of determination to cut out all her former 'munchers' discussion of - gossip about - their affair intensified and became quite serious. Kale was hardly ever on the campus now, except during lecture hours. He stayed in town with Ruth. So, all inquiries, suggestions and comments about Peso and the Bitch were directed to Mutwe.

Mutwe looked quietly at Peso when he called him narrow- minded. Peso looked fatter and lighter-brown than ever before. Mutwe remembered how he had missed him on that three-thirty plane; how after reading of the fighting and the deaths on the campus, he had worried about Peso; how he had written to his home, although, as he had always believed, Peso never wrote letters, except business letters. He remembered how, more recently, he and Kale had time and again held their chins, shaken their heads and sighed, '*If Peso were here!*' How warmly he had hugged Peso when he came upon him, accidentally, in the cafeteria, sitting beside the Bitch.

When a boy and a girl have spent five hours together in a gutter, and when they have lived two months together in a farm house, they may fall in love. If the girl considers the boy her hero and saviour, and the boy is an innocent, sensitive young man who has just shared a shattering experience with the girl, they will probably fall in love, even if the boy is a Peso and the girl a Bitch. But once again, Mutwe's heart had refused to receive this communication from the head.

'You're confused about the issues, my dear Mutwe,' Peso had told him when they began this frank talk, which ended as a quarrel, about the Bitch, 'as you perhaps have never been confused before.'

Man dreads loneliness, and few of us, when confronted with the icy silence which is all that we can give ourselves, can help being confused. They had talked for over an hour, and discussed every 'aspect' of the Bitch. At one time, Mutwe raised the objection, from hearsay, that she was frigid. Peso swore that she achieved an orgasm the first time he munched her. Perhaps she had finally found the man to cure her of the sexual paralysis inflicted on her by Sir Nat Barry when she was fourteen. Mutwe asked how acceptable Peso was to the Bitch's father, in view of the fact that he was from another tribe, and another country. Peso answered that he was not concerned about marriage at all for the time being; that even if it meant his romancing with the Bitch, simply romancing, until they parted at the end of their course, he would go on.

But beneath all Mutwe's attempts to be reasonable and fair, there was only one force which dominated his whole approach, perhaps without his even realizing it: the hope that he would persuade Peso to change his mind, leave the Bitch and remain a companion to him.

'Well, I may be narrow-minded,' he said, 'but we've got to draw a line somewhere. I don't think you'd be doing yourself justice by associating with such a girl.'

'I don't think I would be doing myself any justice by letting my personal relationships be controlled by one smug, self-satisfied critic in Windsor Castle.'

'I don't – '

Peso cut Mutwe short: 'Yes, that's what you are, you're too sure of yourself. And, if you care to know what I think, it's rather stupid to be so utterly convinced of your being right.' And he banged Mutwe's door behind him as he left the 'godown'...

I am lonely, so lonely that I envy the corpses in their graves ... Where had he heard that? It was in French... But, hating a vacuum, Nature was already sucking Virgin Lisa into Mutwe's life.

*

247

A rubber condom, still retaining the shape of the organ over which it had been worn, floated in the closet basin. Mutwe, who had just returned from a short vacation, looked at it and, perhaps for the first time since his coming to Maalas, he felt seriously sorry for an *intellectuoh*. Here was a young man dying to express his feelings to his girl, and to safeguard her career. The lover(!) understood enough science to know that a rubber sheath could prevent conception, but not enough to realize that it could not be flushed down the toilet in its inflated state! Mutwe felt sorry also for Love.

For Love was an unfortunate god. He had very few true worshippers in Maalas. The workers simply did not have the leisure for him. To them love was indeed a bourgeois and reactionary practice. The *intellectuohs* did not have the time, or the application or, especially, the faith necessary for Love's cult.

'The trouble with schoolgirls is that they believe in love.' The biologist Paul Pundadume had said this to a friend, before he 'disappeared' during the strike. Conformity was a plague in Maalas. And in this matter of Love and his earthly sister, Sex, the principle to which most students conformed was to pretend that you had nothing between your legs, until Saturday night. Then you went out with a *Mini-star* or principal secretary or a doctor or a senior lecturer if you were a girl, or to the brothel if you were a boy.

Stories from the brothel were often sad music, and they threw a sort of lurid light on the emotional predicament of the average (male) *intellectuoh* in Maalas. For a sip at the 'people's goods' often proved to be a more demanding experience than many *non-intellectuohs* imagine. For the five, ten or fifteen shillings which you paid, it all depended on the quality of the goods and the shops to which you went, you had to suspend your disbelief for a while and tell yourself that you were deeply in love with that dull object of pleasure (!) which had passed through thirty men's hands, and legs, that one same day. And, if you wished to add to your meagre enjoyment, you had to convince yourself that she was an intact virgin whom you were launching on a happy, fruitful, lifelong bedfellowship with you. Etiquette also demanded that before you 'cleared the room' for the next lover, you had to bestow upon her that intimate kiss and broken, agonized 'darling' that is the swan-song of a really satisfied gentleman.

This effort of the imagination was one reason why, apart from financial considerations and such minor fears as that of V.D. (treatment was free), quite a handful of students did not frequent 'people's goods'. Instead, they slaked their thirst at quieter springs, like masturbation. It must be said in all fairness to the People's University of Maalas, though, that no confirmed case of homosexuality was ever reported there (except among the staff), and only two *Mongol* girls were rumoured to be Lesbians.

Among members of staff faith in Love was even thinner. They were white, you see, generally older than the students, and, normally, married. But Maalas weather was far more predictable than any Maalas marriage. A Mrs.

O'Cock today might have become a Mrs. O'Duck, only next door, the following month, a Mrs. Pigson a week later and, seventy-two hours after that, a mere Miss McBitch, And in the meantime, a whole bevy of whorish academic doctors, wire-haired research fellows, thick-breasted undergraduates and cushion-bottomed barmaids would be successively filling the temporary marital posts she had quit. This state of affairs sometimes caused a little confusion about some women's names, but, on the whole, it was a happy manifestation of the broad-mindedness and liberalism that one expected of such accomplished *intellectuals*.

However, it hit quite hard when you ran into it personally. Take the case of Vivienne O'Goat. It was somewhere during the second term of Mutwe's second year. Mutwe wanted to ask John O'Goat something about T .S. Eliot, and he telephoned from Windsor Castle.

'Mr. O'Goat is not here,' Vivienne said icily over the phone and banged down the receiver.

Puzzled, Mutwe went back to his room. Vivienne was always very sweet. A quarter of an hour later, Peso joined Mutwe, and the two boys decided to walk up to John O'Goat's house. (He was only a lecturer then; not yet a senior lecturer.) John and Vivienne, and their two daughters, lived in the Annexe Estate, in a cream low bungalow, up a sandy path, on top of a hill which overlooked the Lake.

'Mr. O'Goat is not here,' Vivienne told the boys as she held the door half-open and stood in the entrance. She looked pale, and her eyes were swollen. 'He and I have split. He's in Flat 5, Hekima Road,'

'Oh, I see.' Mutwe had not seen anything; and he had hardly finished telling that lie when Vivienne banged the door shut in his face. She still looked very lovely.

Five days later, Lecturer John O'Goat drove with Mutwe up that sandy path to the cream low bungalow where loveliness dwelt still, but whence beauty had forever eloped with love. Mutwe and O'Goat put Vivienne's boxes in the boot of the car. They put the children's pram on the passenger's front seat. Finally, John O'Goat carried his elder daughter out of the house. She kept hugging him and mumbling, 'Daddy, daddy.' Vivienne carried the younger baby.

'Would you like to drive – please?' John O'Goat asked Vivienne O'Goat as they reached the car. They had said nothing to each other all this while. And Mutwe dared not break the solemn silence.

'All right.' Vivienne gave the child to Mutwe.

John O'Goat and Mutwe sat on the rear seat of the car and anxiously held the little girls against their breasts while Vivienne O'Goat raced into and through Maalas, sometimes at over 130 k.p.h., to the airport. In the airport building, Mutwe and O'Goat supervised the porters as they put Vivienne's luggage on the scales. Vivienne put her younger daughter in the pram and pushed it before her as she led the other child by the hand. She 'checked in' and entered the departing passengers' lounge without as much as turning once to wave or smile at John O'Goat.

Mutwe and O'Goat left immediately. And, as they re-entered Maalas - *sscrrreeeeech* ... their brakes; a violent jolt which made them almost hit the windscreen; and, out of the cabin window of a petrol tanker, a bearded face that screamed at them the most 'conc' Swahili obscenities either of them had ever heard.

'Would you like to drive, please?' O'Goat asked Mutwe quietly. It was only a week after Mutwe had passed his driving test.

'I didn't bring my driving permit,' he said.

'That will be all right.'

Mutwe piloted O'Goat's ramshackle Volkswagen clumsily through Maalas on to the campus. O'Goat sat beside him holding his head between his hands.

'Shall I take you to the house?' Mutwe asked as they turned into Hekima Road.

'No, Flat 5, please.' Bachelors were not entitled to houses; and, in any case, that house on the top of the hill was still too full of memories.

Two days later, John O'Goat gave a grand party and hired a jazz band from town. Meanwhile, people were making up all sorts of theories to explain his tragedy(!). Some mentioned Miriam and a score of other girls. Some imaginative mind came up with the story that Vivienne and Mutwe had formed a very dangerous liaison, and that O'Goat had kicked Vivienne out: after he caught her in bed with Mutwe. One story, however, emerged more credibly from all this welter of gossip.

About a week after Vivienne left Maalas, a Dr. Bleary,

M.A. (Harvard), Ph.D. (Oxon.), was giving a lecture on
- *the collocability of language elements in English*, or something
like that. The hum of a jet was heard in the skies outside.

'My woman must be on that plane,' said Dr. Bleary,
and he and all his class of fifty, including Mutwe, Kale and
the Virgin, abandoned *collocability* and went out to gaze at
the plane that was taking away ex-Mrs. Bleary, now a mere
Miss Hore or Slud. When the bits and pieces of the story
were assembled, it appeared that Mrs. Bleary had proved
childless. Dr. Bleary, for even academic doctors have such
feelings, was dying to get a child, and he was getting on
in years. He tried his luck with Vivienne O' Goat. But
without much luck, for their affair was soon discovered,
and the situation blew up. Dr. Bleary was a very good
lecturer.

Perhaps it was such broken lecturers and precociously
initiated students, like Miriam and the Bitch, and a few
other bored characters, who formed that small but
colourfully active group of sexual cynics who munched
any goods when they could get them, or gave their goods
when anyone was willing to take them. How can you
blame a man, even a senior lecturer, whose bedfellow
for over six years leaves him without even a 'bye', when
he says that love is dead? Or if a girl, whose introduction
to love's gesture was a rape by a Governor old enough to
be her grandfather, says that Love does not exist, can you
answer her?

Mutwe had one such *special* in his bed once. It was
an American Anglo-Saxon girl working on a dissertation

on three black writers. You know, whether it is on *vestigial initial vowels in Swahili*, or *antigenes in amphibians*, or *similarities and differences between Achebe and Baldwin*, the rule in the academic world is always the same: *Publish or perish*. This particular scholar came to discuss (to encounter for the first time probably the name of) Achebe with Mutwe. The 'Academic' gave her all the tips he considered relevant, but the girl came again, this time with sandwiches and Coca-Cola. It was a Sunday afternoon in the August before the strike, and the Academics Anonymous were assembled in Mutwe's 'godown.' When Carol entered, however, Peso and Kale took the earliest opportunity to withdraw, though Mutwe had told them that Carol wanted suggestions on Achebe. For the three boys were, in many respects, very ordinary young men, and they enjoyed a joke. Carol and Mutwe munched sandwiches and sipped Coca-Cola as Mutwe tried to dig up every detail he could remember or imagine about the great African novelist. And, since Carol made no secret of her desire, they ended up in bed. That would perhaps give her a deeper insight into black psychology.

'This a sort of payment in kind?' Mutwe asked as he stroked Carol's downy arms. They had been *siestering*, as the *Engleesh* expression goes, for over two hours.

'Don't be silly,' Carol said, laughing. 'What do you do on a Sunday afternoon in a place like this?' and she snuggled closer to her man-of-the-moment …

But Nature could not let her thread be broken by cynicism or by that normless norm to which one felt called to conform in Maalas - stagnation: Nature chose her own agents: girls and boys from every tribe, colour and creed, who, ignoring all gossip, censure and ostracism, and daring all other obstacles, like the Margaret Plantagenet fence and its guards, 'visiting rules' and the threat of rustication, loved as men and women love everywhere else in the world. Or was it really like anywhere else in the world?

Man cannot live in a vacuum; and. however radically you rebel against your society, the student lovers were called 'rebels', that society will necessarily impose some patterns of behaviour, however faint, on you. Is it the practice anywhere in the world, as it was in Maalas, that if you are to keep your lover, the first thing you have to do is to munch her or get him to munch you?

This was the eternal problem bedevilling love affairs between students. Affairs cropped up like mushrooms on the campus, especially at the beginning of the academic year, but they disappeared just as fast. A few affairs survived, where the sex snag was overcome, with rubber sheaths or pills or, in a few rare cases, personal or religious restraint. But most exploded. After an abortion, or after a boy's overbold advance, thrust off by the girl like an attempted rape, or a girl's overgenerous offer declined by an overcautious boy, an affair stood no chance.

This then was the thunder, lightning and rain, in which Mutwe the Philosopher 'presented his credentials' to Lisa the Virgin.

*

He felt a sort of intense congratulatory self-hatred that must be the dominant feeling in the hearts of those who have carried out a successful planned murder. It was that same old struggle in a man's heart between freedom and slavery, a struggle in which freedom is bound to lose, as the owner of the heart well knows, with alarm, but without regret. In short, Mutwe was falling in love.

He had just parted from Virgin Lisa, at the gates of Margaret Plantagenet Hall, after a party at Dr. Bleary's, at which he had 'discovered' her. It was the day after his quarrel with Peso, and Peso and the Bitch were also at the party. In his attempts to avoid them, Mutwe found himself engaged in a concentrated conversation with the Virgin. The Virgin talked about her experiences during the 'exile', and Mutwe, reclining beside her on the big green cushion on which she sat with her legs stretched out in front of her, listened, and fell. Was it the high-class perfume she had used, was it her light-brown thighs, was it the lisp in her speech, or was it her story, of how every big man she asked for a job in her small home town wanted goods from her, that made Mutwe fall?

He had been seeing this girl for over two years, at the English Literature and at the Language lectures and seminars, and in the chapel, and he knew that she was very good-looking. But that particular evening she had suddenly become attractive, that is, personal, to him. It was like finding yourself one day on a street down which you have been walking ever since you can remember, but on a pavement, whether left or right, on which it has never occurred to you to step before.

When the Virgin rose to leave the party, Mutwe asked her if she would like him to accompany her home, and she said 'please'. On the way he quietly took her hand, and the Virgin let him. The next morning Mutwe invited Lisa to join him at breakfast in the cafeteria, and everyone kept 'clear 'of their table. At lunch, a few rebels joined them, and after lunch, Mutwe walked down to Margaret Plantagenet with Lisa. He passed the gates and actually went into Lisa's room. Imma, her room-mate, was at first embarrassingly confused, but her natural charm eventually made Mutwe feel quite at home after a while.

At first it meant quite a brave effort for both Mutwe and Lisa to show any gesture of – friendship to each other. A sort of shyness or arrogance made one feel very nervous. But that gradually passed. In any case, everyone was already discussing, gossiping about, their affair: Mutwe, the Philosopher as he was known to the girls, had 'presented his credentials' to Lisa, and she had accepted them. The two had become *rebels*.

But their rebellion, as we have seen, was quite short-lived. For, perhaps without their even giving a thought to it, they pushed their rebellion a step further than the normal. They rebelled against the rebels. They did not have a munch. And this was not due to any religious sentiment or ambitions of personal 'restraint'. They just did not come to feel like it, *both at the same time*.

Perhaps they were entering that experience, coming

only once in a man's life, if it comes at all, where they felt that their feelings should be left to build up their own pressure, until that pressure automatically drew them into a sexual expression of their emotions. Idealists would call this a spiritual experience. Amateurs (i.e. love-worshippers) would call it a 'true falling in love'.

We who know the story, know Virgin Lisa and Mutwe, might attribute it to a thousand and one little details: Mutwe's academic 'overconcentration', his eyes and voice, as the Virgin remembered after she returned from O'Goat's flat that Sunday morning, symbols of his heavy-weighing inability to forget himself, or to make others forget themselves; the nastiness of Virgin Lisa's first sexual experience, in that school frolic four years earlier ... But all these put together pointed at one fact: both Mutwe and Virgin Lisa had one vital thing in common. They had not yet decided what to do with their sex; neither had decided; or rather, nothing had happened to force them into a decision. But something was soon going to happen, to Virgin Lisa at least.

For, despite what we said, the Virgin was in one crucial aspect still a virgin when Senior Lecturer John O'Goat first munched her. There are people who believe that once a girl's maidenhead is gone, she has been sexually launched. Very often this is not the case. Physically, yes: sex may start with that sprinkle of blood. But no thinking person can escape the realization that there is a super-physical, and even super-freudian side to sex. (*Spiritual*, I understand, is what the religious say, but it is rather archaic and unscientific.) It is only in very rare cases that the realization of this, to use the shorter word, *spiritual* aspect of sex happens to come at the same time with the physical knowledge. A boy, or a girl may be, physically speaking, as sexually well-versed as a Dr. Kinsey and yet be a virgin where his or her heart is concerned.

Even when you sleep with the most promiscuous prostitute, you may still be launching a virgin. And such a launching may, as in the physical case, be a rape: that is, it may be negative. When a sensitive woman discovers after her first spiritual sex experience that she was cheated of her right of choice, that she was hypnotized, compromised, wine-bemused and the like, she will rave with bitterness and chagrin, and will not rest until she gets the man who did it, or any other representative of his sex, to make up for that insult.

That painful lingering of the Virgin in Mutwe's arms after their kiss - their last - on the Tuesday following her munch at Flat 5, Hekima Road, was both a sacrifice and a prayer: I know now that you have some feeling/or me. Take me now, make love to me: fill this emptiness that has followed my polite rape by John O'Goat. But Mutwe did not answer that prayer - because he did not hear it. Can men really communicate? on anything that matters?

9 And sex shall have no dominion

As Mutwe closed the drawerful of revolvers and pistols, Captain Mackee, the Wild Highlander, called from outside the room, 'Open, please!'

Mutwe jumped up and hurried towards the door. He thought the Captain was carrying something heavy. When Mutwe opened the door, the Captain marched in, resplendent in a captain's army uniform, complete with gloves, ribbons and other decorations. He was whistling the British Grenadiers. He strutted about the room for some minutes and then halted. He saluted smartly, pulled his sword out of the scabbard and made a series of ingenious gestures with it. Then he thrust it back and roared with laughter. *'Exhibitionism' is only used in the analysis of sexual behaviour these days*, thought Mutwe. But he had just seized that divine desire to sit still and think, and he was anxious to get back to his room ...

For a week after the *sexual broomsticks* seminar, Virgin Lisa did not attend classes. She had gone neurotic. Diana Principal Secretary, Stella, and everyone, talked about her affair with O'Goat until it boomeranged against the poor girl. It was after lunch on that Thursday of the seminar, and of Mutwe's visit to the Captain. Imma had heard the shocking story from Julia. and she could not see how life could go on without her discussing it with Lisa, her room-mate. As cautiously and as painfully as Peso had told the story to Mutwe. Imma broached the subject.

At first, the Virgin sat absolutely still and listened. Then she burst out sobbing. She went over to Imma's bed, buried her head in her friend's lap and wept and wept. Eventually, Imma started weeping too; and they cried and cried for nearly forty-five minutes on end. 'I didn't want you not to know what they were saying,' Imma said at last, and the two girls remained there. Imma sitting on the bed and bending her head over Virgin Lisa's in her lap. The Virgin was kneeling on the mat beside Imma's bed. They were now absolutely quiet and still …

Mutwe went to a tourist company in town and booked a seat on one of their week-end coaches to Shika. This was the Tuesday a week after Virgin Lisa had kissed him, for the last time. Shika is a town on the shores of Lake Tudor, some sixty kilometres notth of Maalas. It is quite an old town. In the last century it was an important trading centre where the Arabs bought and penned their black slaves before ferrying them across the Lake and beating them to the coast or to death. Tourists and some Maalas residents went to Shika to spend the weekend in special thatched family cottages, or in isolated one-man tents for those who had accepted themselves as sufficient unto themselves.

The Virgin stayed in bed. She refused to be taken to the Dispensary. and she instructed Imma to let no one come to see her. On the Sunday following her breakfast with O'Goat. after Imma had left for chapel. Lisa painfully wished that she too could go to church. Mutwe did not try to visit Virgin Lisa. For. after his moment of awareness in Captain Mackee's study. and what passed through his mind during the six-or-so hours after he came back to his room. he felt there was simply no way of going on. In fact, he discovered that he did not know, and he had never stopped to ask, where he was going with Lisa.

He went on attending lectures, seminars and tutorials, and going to the cafeteria. And Peso, Kale when he was around. and even the Bitch were very kind and gentle to him. But he could not help feeling that the gossip about him was still too slimy. He felt that if he 'removed' his figure for a few days. as the Virgin had done with hers. things might improve for him, for the Virgin, and for the poor boys and girls who were gossiping themselves to death.

Mutwe was to leave on Saturday morning. Very early on the morning before, that is Friday, Virgin Lisa got up, took a warm bath and put on a rather 'ageing' light-green dress. She was not suffering from anything in particular, and she was not feeling weak. The week's isolation had only slightly dulled her light-brown complexion.

She walked briskly, past Windsor Castle, past the cafeteria and on to Academic Hill. Those hurrying to have an early breakfast barely noticed her before she crossed the valley between Residential Hill and her destination. She entered the Faculty of Arts and Social Chaos, went up a flight of steps to the Department of English Literature, and waited at the office of Senior Lecturer John O'Goat, B.A. (Cantab.), M.A. (London.), Ph. D. (Inferno etc...).

'Hullo, Lisa! How are you?'

'Fine thanks, Professor Hogg,' the Virgin said coldly.

This seemed to remind Professor Hogg. 'You've been down with a fever, haven't you?'

'Yes.'

'Oh dear!' The Professor frowned painfully. 'How are you feeling now, dear?'

'Much better, thank you, Professor Hogg.' The Virgin dimly felt that she was being unreasonable. The old hog was not guilty of anything. But John O'Goat was already arriving.

'You've been waiting for me, Miss Kabachi?' asked the Senior Lecturer as Professor Hogg entered his office.

'Yes.' The Virgin nearly choked, though she did not know with what.

'I'm sorry, my car broke down just as I was coming up the hill. Come in, please.' John O'Goat closed the door carefully after the Virgin had entered.

'Well, what can I do for you?' he asked in a business-like tone as he planted himself at his desk.

The Virgin tried to glare at O'Goat with those eyes that had refused to grow up. 'Why did you -' she began. Then she burst into tears. She did not know any more what she had come to say, if she had known it at all.

'What is it?' John's voice was very soft as he asked this; and when he repeated, 'What is it, dear?' it was a barely-audible whisper.

The Virgin did not answer. She just stood there,

holding her handkerchief over her face and heaving with sobs. John O'Goat had a lecture with some first-year students at eight-thirty, and it was now eight-twenty-five. *What a tough job teaching young people*, he thought as he rose from his chair and went round to Virgin Lisa. He held her close to himself and he threw a quick glance over his shoulder at the windows of the Faculty of Science. Then he looked at Virgin Lisa's hair, and at her temples. Then he felt his manhood rising. The warmth of Lisa's body was running through him.

'Look, Lisa dear,' he said slowly, 'why don't you come back later and tell me what has happened? I've got a class now, and you're in no mood to explain.'

O'Goat was five minutes late for his lecture. Virgin Lisa hurried out of the Faculty and towards the Administrative Block. She passed through its main gate, beside the Wild Highlander's office, and she reached the road from town. She got on to the eight-forty-five bus from town, which dropped her only a few metres away from M.P. and roared on to the Annexe Estate, where it turned.

Back in his office, Senior Lecturer John O'Goat pulled a memo pad and a Biro pen and wrote in an unusually neat handwriting:

'Dear Lisa,

I'm very sorry if anything unpleasant has happened. Would you like to come to my flat tomorrow evening and tell me about it, please?

As ever,

John O'Goat.'

He typed a neat envelope address at his portable 'Olivetti', and he sealed his note and gave it to the department messenger. He told the messenger to take the note straight to Margaret Plantagenet Hall.

It was about half a kilometre's distance, and the Lake Basin sun was already getting angry.

Virgin Lisa responded immediately to John O'Goat's note. To Flat 5 Hekima Road she went on Saturday evening, carrying a towel in her bag this time, and introduced John O'Goat to a new experience of sexual devotion which he perhaps – deserved.

Meanwhile, on the moon-silvered sands of a beach sixty kilometres north of Maalas, a young man paced up and down the ruins of the Arab slave-market, taking in deep breaths of the mud-fish scented air, gazing now and then at the dim yellow lights of Shika town, about three kilometres away, and feeling sweetly happy and vicariously triumphant that slavery had disappeared from the face of the earth. Or had it? Wasn't he still a slave to those threatening B.A. final examinations?

*

Quarrel or no quarrel, rejecting or rejected, it is *jinis* living in a small place with a woman that you once loved and no longer love.

'*God is dead, there's no God.*' That was the announcement with which John O'Goat always started his lectures. No one took him seriously, except the girls he had slept with. Only these were sometimes such a large fraction of the class. The last time that Mutwe came reasonably close to Virgin Lisa before the examinations was at a cocktail party at Miss McAllister's flat. Mutwe was standing on the balcony, looking at the lights in the windows of Margaret Plantagenet Hall, when behind him, he heard the Virgin vigorously trying to convince Dr. Bleary that God was dead.

The examinations finally came, and only one unfortunate thing happened as far as the characters we have met were concerned. The first paper that the three Academics, Peso, Mutwe and Kale, as well as the Virgin were to write was a paper on the *English Novel*. In the examination hall, the students were seated according to their subjects, and in alphabetical order. In the English Literature row, the Virgin, officially known as Miss Kabachi, was two desks ahead of Kale; Mutwe was four desks behind Kale, while Peso was three desks farther down the row.

The chief invigilator had just announced that the students could start writing, and his black-capped, black-gowned assistants, including John O'Goat, were beginning to pace up and down the aisles. Suddenly there was a thud, and everyone turned towards Virgin Lisa's desk. She had fallen on the floor, and apparently fainted. In a flash, all the eyes were taken off Virgin Lisa and turned towards Mutwe. But no student was allowed to budge from his or her desk once the examination had started. John O'Goat and two other invigilators carried Virgin Lisa out of the hall and eventually got her to the Dispensary.

Story-tellers would give you the impression that life and time move forwards, or backwards, linearly. Perhaps they do in some cases, but in many others they do not. At best, they only wave-like hit the shores of misery or joy, only to roll back to the centre and start flowing out again. If we have recorded some of the ripples that formed on the apparently stagnant pool that was the campus of the People's University of Maalas, it was only to show that, even there, life existed. But how do you prove the existence of that life that has nothing to do with biology or even with Freud? It is as difficult as defining the meaning of nothing.

*

'You've made it, Mutwe!'

'What?'

'You've made it, man!' Kale was literally shouting with excitement, despite Mutwe's ice-cold response. 'You got a *First*'

'That ends this stupid *eventless* histah-ree.'

Mutwe was thinking about Peso when Kale came to announce the examination results. Peso and the Bitch left the campus a week before the results were out. Immediately after the examinations, they had flown down to the Southern Plateau and gone to the plantation. The Bitch's father was so angry at learning that his daughter wanted to get married, and that to an absolute foreigner, that he quarrelled violently with her. With the courage and violence that only love can lend, the girl did not leave a bitter thing unsaid to her father. She even told him all his riches flowed directly from her sex. Then she and Peso left, returned to the campus and then set out again, a few days later, for Peso's, and Mutwe's, eastern country.

'How did Peso do?' Mutwe asked, looking up from the open old volume of *War and Peace* which he was looking at without reading.

'He got Lower Honours,' said Kale, now considerably sobered by Mutwe's quietness, 'and his girl passed.'

'They've scored First-Class Honours in other fields,' Mutwe said. 'And you?'

'I got an Upper Second!' Kale was very satisfied with his performance, and Mutwe's heart went out to him. He jumped up from his desk and came to him where he was standing in the middle of the room.

'Congratulations, old man!' Mutwe said as he hugged Kale. Below, they heard voices already turning Mutwe into a racial symbol: *That boy is tough*, bwana. *The bloody whites tried to say an African couldn't get a First. I thought O'Goat would fail him because of that butterlike girl...*

'Lisa has been awarded an *aegrotat*,' said Kale, still in Mutwe's arms. He said this in a low voice, and with an amount of hesitation. He was not quite sure whether Mutwe wanted to be reminded of that episode. An *aegrotat* is a kind of compliment you get paid for falling sick during examinations. After her misfortune in the examination hall on the very first day, the Virgin missed all the papers. Mutwe sighed lightly when Kale mentioned Lisa's name, and he let go of Kale.

Glossary

Agbada a West African gown
askari warder, policeman
baba father
baraza meeting
bwana sir or master
kisu knife
makaa charcoal
mtumwa mungu servant of God
mvule tree with beautiful wood for furniture
mwananchi ordinary man
mzee elder
mzungu European
ngoja wait
ngoma dance
nyamaza shut up
samosa Indian savoury
taifa nation
uhuru freedom
wananchi ordinary men
wazee elders
wazungu Europeans